DARK CAPITAL

TALES FROM THE DARK PAST BOOK 3

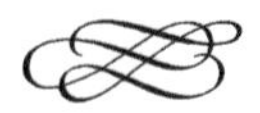

HELEN SUSAN SWIFT

Published 2021 by Next Chapter

Edited by Terry Hughes

Cover art by Cover Mint

"The whole city leads a double existence."
Robert Louis Stevenson

"It is quite lovely – bits of it."
Oscar Wilde

PRELUDE

I sit here in the dim candlelight, with the remainder of my life steadily ticking away.

Tick, tock, tick, tock.

As I sit, I ponder. A clock is a very sinister machine as it slowly marks the passage of one's life, with every tick a second less to live, every trembling movement of the hand informing the watcher that he has used up more of his allotted span.

Tick, tock, tick, tock.

My clock sits in the corner of the room. Tall as a man, it has the maker's name, *Thomas Reid of Edinburgh*, scrolled behind the hands, as if in mockery of the buyer, laughing at me for having purchased the object that counts down what remains of my life. I watch it through narrowed eyes, aware of the exact second it will stop, aware of the implications and now aware of the reasons.

Tick, tock, tick, tock.

Shadows flit outside this room, moving around in this cursed house, silent as the ghosts of the long-dead and the recently departed. I know the shadows are gathering for me. I was responsible for some, while others existed many years before my time, although in a different place in this dark city. I must wait, aching my life away, knowing how long I have.

Tick, tock, tick, tock.

There it is again, that sonorous whirr of machinery, that inexorable mechanical hum that does not care about the frail man who sits in the room, fearful of every sound, jumping at every soft scuff of feet in the street outside, every voice raised in drunken debauchery. I am numb to every sensation except fear, and cannot welcome death as a relief, for I know what must come next.

Tick, tock, tick, tock.

The candle is burning low now, pooling a gradually decreasing circle of yellow light across the table. I should start another before I have to sit in the dark with my thoughts and memories. At one time, I had servants to perform such tasks for me. Now I am alone as my candle comes to an end. See? The flame gutters, flicking this way and that in this draughty room. The sounds outside are fading as the city retires to sleep. Only the night-prowlers are out, those half-human denizens of the dark closes, these predatory creatures who thrive on the weaknesses of their fellow beings, who prey on the vacillating, the foolish and the uncontrolled. I pity them, for they are without pity, as was I, God help me.

Tick, tock, tick, tock.

The candle is about gone, the flame little more than a memory, the smell of melted tallow thick in the room. The dying flame is shining red through the dregs of my claret, reflecting from the cut-crystal in a hundred different patterns, throwing a scarlet glow across the document on which I write. It is like spreading blood, that light, a suitable colour for the paper on which I will inscribe an account of what brought me to this pass.

Tick, tock, tick, tock.

I need more light. I cannot see to guide my pen, my old-fashioned, inexpensive goose-wing quill, across the page. I have to put flame to another candle, a dozen candles, although no amount of light can chase away the darkness that crouches at the periphery of this room and in all the rooms of this house. No flame can clear the shadows from my memory, and light will reflect from that hideous white object that grins and rattles at me always from its position opposite my desk. I have brought myself to this state, and only I can atone for my actions.

Tick, tock, tick.

I must have light. I scramble feverishly to apply a flame to all the candles I can find, gather my papers and place them on the desk to my left, fill my inkwell and sharpen the tip of my pen before leaving the penknife at my side. To some, a penknife may be a potential weapon, but no weapon can defend me now. The candlelight grows, fever-bright, expelling all external darkness without easing my torment in the slightest.

Tick, tock, tick.

I begin to write, in the hope that somebody, anybody, will read this and perhaps understand what I have done. Maybe somebody will forgive me. Perhaps.

Tick, tock.

Oh, dear God in heaven help me.

CHAPTER 1

Edinburgh April 1825

"Your name, sir?" Mrs MacHardy frowned at me from outside the closed door of the house. A big, busty woman, she stood with her arms akimbo, as if daring me to give a name that was not my own.

"Martin Elliot," I said.

"Are you Irish?" Mrs MacHardy was immediately suspicious. "I want none of your wild Irish ways here, bringing pigs into houses and drinking all night long."

For some reason, Mrs MacHardy's words set the gathered crowd screeching with laughter.

"I am as Scottish as you are," I said, lifting my chin. "From Roxburghshire."

Mrs MacHardy grunted, do doubt wondering where Roxburghshire might be.

"Elliot, you say."

"Martin Elliot," I repeated, adding, "Doctor Martin Elliot," in the hope of gaining the woman's respect.

'Doctor?" The woman ran her jaundiced gaze up and down the length of my body. I felt she was showing her contempt of people who claimed a medical degree yet who could not afford accommodation in a more respectable part of the city. "Are you one of these wild students that kick up a rumpus every night?"

"I am no student," I hastened to convince her. "I am a fully qualified doctor of medicine."

"Are you indeed?" Mrs MacHardy was about 50, by my reckoning, with her nose displaying the broken blood vessels of too-frequent imbibing, while the rest of her was sufficiently large for her weight to strain her heart. I gave her 10 years to live, and that was a generous estimate. "Well, *Doctor*." She emphasised the word as if my standing left a foul taste in her mouth. "You sound eminently suitable." Charitable people might have construed Mrs MacHardy's grimace as a smile. "If you are sure you want the lease."

"Thank you." I tried to hide my relief as I gave a small bow for, in truth, finding affordable accommodation in Edinburgh had been troublesome.

I was in the West Bow, that curious, Z-shaped street that angles down from the Lawnmarket to the Grassmarket, beset with ancient, crumbling houses, secret courts and half-hidden passageways, known as closes. It was not the most salubrious of neighbourhoods, but a purse-pinched doctor must seek accommodation wherever he can. The house outside which I stood was in a dirty little private courtyard, with a small close leading to it, affording a little seclusion without spoiling my access. Quite apart from its affordability, it was within easy reach of the High Street, Old Edinburgh's main thoroughfare.

A group of people had gathered as we spoke, ragged-looking men and women who watched me suspiciously while bare-footed children made a hideous din that echoed around the courtyard. Above me, the ubiquitous tall tenements of Scotland's capital city rose to a dull, grey sky, with women leaning out of most windows to observe whatever the world offered in the way of entertainment.

Mrs MacHardy remained on the doorstep, studying me with the strangest of expressions on her broad face.

"That man's going to live there," one gaunt-faced woman in the crowd screeched, pointing a long-taloned finger at me.

"He doesn't know." Another woman, all dolled up and with a painted face, shook her head, so the profusion of ribbons around her neck shivered in a multi-coloured display of tawdriness. "He surely doesn't know."

"He'll find out soon enough," a third woman said, pulling a threadbare shawl close over her head.

"Don't be a fool, man!" a gaunt-faced fellow tried to shout above the hubbub of the crowd.

I attempted to ignore the noise as I watched Mrs MacHardy hold the massive, old-fashioned key as if reluctant to hand it over.

"Do you know anything about Edinburgh?" Mrs MacHardy remained in the doorway, inadvertently blocking my entrance.

"No," I admitted foolishly. "I gained my degree in Glasgow."

For some reason, my answer seemed to please the woman. "This house is not a bad place." The old besom seemed inclined to be garrulous now she was convinced I was neither Irish nor a student. "A major of the City Guard used to live here in the old days. A most respectable gentleman." She patted the door as if to convince me to come to a decision.

"I'll take it," I said, for in truth I was desperate for any sort of accommodation so I could set up my practice. "I'll soon have this house set to rights."

The old besom grunted in a most unladylike fashion. "Will

you be bringing your patients here? I don't want a lot of sick people spreading their diseases around. I have my reputation to consider."

I tried to raise a smile. "I will not," I said. "I will have my practice in quite another part of the city. I don't wish to mix business with my home life."

"Three shillings a week." Mrs MacHardy held out a grimy hand. "One week in advance."

I paid her, counting out the silver from my slender resources and watched her secret it away in some recess in her voluminous clothing. Even then, I wondered at the low rent for a fairly sizeable residence, but one must be grateful for small mercies. I could feel the tension from the crowd behind me as if they had never seen a man part with money before.

"Here's the key." Mrs MacHardy handed over the iron key that looked as if it might open the gates to Edinburgh Castle, let alone a private house in the West Bow.

The metal felt cold and worn as I grasped it.

"I'll be back next week," Mrs MacHardy said. And with that, she was gone, leaving me alone outside that dark doorway, with my single case of belongings, my medical bag and my hopes for the future.

"He's took it!" the garrulous woman shrieked to her companions. "He's moving in!"

I was not sure if it was amusement or astonishment that caused the uproar in the ever-increasing crowd. Three men began to argue, pushing at each other until one, a medium-sized fellow with a broken nose and a pockmarked face, smashed his fist into the mouth of his nearest neighbour and elbowed the other in the throat.

"Enough of that," the gaunt-faced fellow said, pulling the fighting men apart.

As the battlers finished the business with growls and vague

threats, I fitted the key in the lock and opened the door. I was not here to pacify drunken brawlers but to attend the capital's sick, be they poor or wealthy, old or young. Leaving the pugilists to sort out their dispute, I stepped inside.

I did not know when anybody had last occupied the house, but whoever the tenant had been, he had left the place in some confusion. The advertisement had claimed the house to be fully furnished, which was accurate, although the furniture lay around the floor in the wildest disorder, and a man might lose himself in the thick dust that lay on top. Augmenting the grime were the cobwebs, great silver-grey constructions that harboured arachnids half the size of my hand. The creatures scuttled away from me, presumably having never seen a human being before. The house was stuffy, if surprisingly dry, with an atmosphere such as I cannot describe, never having experienced the like before.

"Well now," I said to myself. "You have made your bed here, Doctor Martin Elliot, and now you must lie in it."

I am not one of these people who likes to sit and wait for events. Instead, I prefer to make them bend to my will, so, removing my coat, I folded it neatly on top of my baggage and set to work. My first job was to throw back the internal shutters and force open the windows, for I believe that fresh air is a wonderful restorative and cleanser. Unfortunately, opening the window allowed in a profusion of foul scents and raucous voices. I quickly learned that there is little fresh air in an Edinburgh close, so densely packed are the people.

I spent the remainder of that day attempting to clean and scrub the house. I was fortunate that there was a brush-maker in the West Bow, so I spent more of my meagre store of money purchasing a variety of brushes and parted with more copper in buying two wooden buckets.

I locked the door most carefully on each occasion I left the house, although none of the gathered crowd of idlers seemed interested in entering.

"You're wasting your time," the gaunt-faced man told me.

"I'll get the house clean," I told him, sternly.

"No." His blue bonnet nearly fell off when he shook his head. "I mean you're wasting your time locking the door. Nobody will go into that house."

"I'll make sure of that," I said.

The man shrugged and said no more, watching me from the corner of narrow eyes.

Naturally, in a house so old, there was no access to water, so I took many trips to the pump, filling up buckets and bringing them inside to remove what seemed to be the dirt of ages. The people watched me, none offering to help, and most drawing back to create a corridor of humanity on my journey between house and pump. Despite the words of the gaunt-faced man, I had feared that leaving the door open would be an invitation for the petty thieves of the area. However, the crowd seemed content only to look inside, with strange comments in a mixture of Highland, Irish and gutter Edinburgh accents.

"You're a fool man, a fool," an elderly man told me as he sucked on an empty pipe.

"In what way?" I asked him pleasantly.

"You're a fool to take on that house." He pointed the stem of his pipe towards me. "I'm telling you, no good will come of it."

"Thank you for the warning," I said, cutting half an inch off a plug of tobacco and passing it to him.

"Aye," he said, looking at the tobacco as if it was a block of gold. "You may be a fool, but you're a gentleman."

The gaunt-faced man was still watching. He gave a single nod, which might have meant approval, and retained his place against the wall, a position that allowed him the best view inside my house. I marked him down as a possible thief.

Given the apparent reluctance of anybody to cross my threshold, I was surprised when one woman had the temerity, or the bad manners, to step inside my door. She stood there like a statue, watching me without lifting a finger to help or hinder. I bade her a cheerful good morning as I passed, to which she responded with a somewhat brighter smile than any of her compatriots.

My visitor was slightly better dressed than most of the crowd, a woman of about 30, with a bold eye and a fine figure. She stood proudly, eyeing everything as if sizing the house up. Allowing her to remain where she was, I continued with my work.

The bed was sound, but the mattress was crawling with vermin, so out it went, along with the bedclothes. Although I thought these articles might tempt a thief, not one person touched them, forcing me to pay a couple of Irish vagrants to dispose of them, I don't know where. The gaunt-faced man watched everything, pulling on his pipe and with his bonnet low over his forehead.

By the time I finished my cleansing, the house reeked of strong soap, and the crowd of interested spectators had increased. I allowed them to watch, as I studied them, wondering how such a diverse mix of people could squeeze into such a small area. Among the small tradespeople were the expected ladybirds, the hawkers and pimps, the scavengers and petty thieves, an honest woman or two, a thimble-rigger, a clutch of unemployed navigators, and a minister of the cloth.

"What are you doing with these?" the pockmarked brawler asked when I dragged out the final parcel of unwanted material from the house.

"Getting rid of them," I said, pleasantly.

"I'll take them off your hands for five shillings." Pockmarked held out his hand hopefully.

"Take them if you want them," I said, "but you'll not get a penny from me."

Pockmarked dropped his hand and any interest until I tossed him a silver threepence and watched him disappear with my unwanted rags.

"You'll be the doctor," the woman within my door said, staring directly at my face.

"That news travelled fast," I said.

"Oh." She stepped further into my house and looked around. "We've no secrets in the West Bow, Dr Elliot. I'm Ruth Anderson, as you'll find out."

"Good morning, Mrs Anderson." My bow was more in mockery than sincerity, although the woman returned it with a surprisingly elegant curtsey.

"Miss Anderson."

"Miss Anderson," I corrected.

Miss Anderson nodded. "You've made a change here already," she said.

"It needed a good clean."

"The house has lain empty for a while," Miss Anderson said.

The crowd were peering in as if I was some sort of exhibit at a show although only Miss Anderson had crossed the threshold. Even the pockmarked man balked at the prospect of facing me inside my house, it seemed, yet all seemed surprised when I firmly closed the door on them.

"Why has the house lain empty for a while?" I asked.

"One of the previous residents was not the best of men," Miss Anderson said.

I nodded. In that area, I was not surprised. "You don't seem to mind coming inside."

"Not at all." Miss Anderson was examining my house. "I'm not from Edinburgh." She gave a small smile that revealed surprisingly well-cared-for teeth. "I'm not scared of devils or men."

I thought that was rather a strange statement, but let it pass. "You're a Highlander, to judge by your accent."

"Inverness way," she said at once. "You'll be needing a woman."

"What do you mean?" I admit I was startled by her words. Although medical students and young doctors had a reputation as loose-living, women did not habitually proposition themselves.

Miss Anderson walked through the house, examining every room. "You'll need a woman to clean and cook."

I smiled with relief. "I'll think about that later," I said.

Miss Anderson laughed. "Don't think too long, doctor. You won't find many people willing to work in here. Not in this house."

"Why is that? Surely one unpleasant tenant won't frighten everybody off."

Miss Anderson put a finger along the side of her nose and gave a conspiratorial wink. "This house can have a bad effect on people, doctor, and that's all I am saying."

With that, Miss Anderson opened the door and stepped past the few who remained of the crowd and walked away with more dignity than I had expected. The pile of bedding and other materials had entirely disappeared.

I closed the door, for I was tired.

Medical students are not the most prosperous of men, so I was used to living a comfortless existence. Resolving to deplete further the contents of my wallet by purchasing bed covers on the following day, I sat on one of the hard chairs, laid my head on the table and slept. It was not difficult after such a busy day.

I do not know what woke me. It was not the occasional drunken roar from outside the house; I was used to such things from my student days. It may have been the strange light that danced at the periphery of my vision the second I opened my eyes. That was some optical illusion, no doubt. Whatever it was, I jerked awake right away and looked around at the unfamiliar surroundings before I recollected where I was.

When I cleaned the room, I had dusted down the long-case clock in the corner, without winding it up, yet I could swear that it was ticking. Scratching a spark, I lit a candle and allowed the flame to grow a little before lifting the brass candlestick and walking to the clock. I knew my ears were deceiving me, yet I had to make sure.

There was no ticking. The clock was silent, with the hands pointing to six minutes past six. On a whim, I moved the hands to midnight. It seemed neater that way, although according to my watch, it was one in the morning. My candle sent long shadows flickering around the room, showing furniture that was years, if not centuries, out of date. Old, heavy, cumbersome pieces that somebody should have condemned to the fireplace generations ago. I resolved to replace them, provided Mrs MacHardy had no objections. I wanted a home with the most fashionable pieces my pocketbook could afford.

I heard the rattle of wheels on cobblestones and shook my head. Who the devil was driving a coach at this time of night? Unable to resist the temptation, I drew back the shutters and peered outside. The courtyard was empty of course, but by craning my neck, I could see over the rooftops to the West Bow. That too was empty. There was nobody, not even a stray drunkard and certainly not a coach, yet I could swear I heard the rumble of iron-shod wheels on the cobbles and the drumbeat of hooves. Many hooves, too, not just four.

Shaking my head, I closed the shutters again, convinced

that either my imagination was taking over, or my hearing was at fault. No, I told myself, I had merely been dreaming, a dream caused by exhaustion and the experience of sleeping in an unfamiliar house.

The candlelight cast strange shadows, highlighting areas of the room I had not previously noticed and created shapes from the furniture, so that I imagined a tall man standing beside the clock, a man with a pronounced stoop and a prominent nose. The shadows darkened a small depression above the fireplace and revealed intricate carvings in the wainscotting. By now, I was wide awake and eager to investigate my new house. I knelt by the wainscotting, tracing the pattern with my fingers. At first, I thought the carvings were merely abstract designs, and then I realised they were animals and people, and such beautifully carved animals as I had never seen before. There were cats and rabbits and horses, all in intricate detail, combined with what looked like human figures, men and women in a state of perfect nudity.

Whoever carved these had an accurate knowledge of the human anatomy, I told myself. I wondered if he had been a student of Greek art, or perhaps had an occupation as a figurehead carver or some such.

I followed the carvings to the furthest corner of the room, placed my candle on a small table and allowed the light to play on the workmanship. The design was different here, vertical rather than horizontal, and abstract, yet still felt as if carved by a master, rather than an apprentice. When I touched the carvings, they moved, and I realised the entire corner piece detached.

"What have we here?" I pulled the corner piece away. It was a walking stick, or rather an old-fashioned staff of dark, heavy blackthorn, surmounted by the image of a man's head. When I held the candle closer, I realised that the head was only an outline without features or form, while the abstract designs covered the entire shaft of the stick. I held the staff closer, finding it curiously warm and, to my nighttime imagination, it seemed to be pulsating as if it were alive. I smiled at the fancy even as I noted that, although the wood was scorched, the carvings were intact. Overall, it was an imposing piece of craftsmanship.

Holding the staff in my right hand, I walked around the room, smiling. I rather liked the feel of that stick. It seemed to enhance my position, somehow, as if it belonged with me. Perhaps it was because of the high quality of its artistry, but I gained a new sense of power.

I shook my head, smiling at the strange fancies that flooded through my mind. Indeed I laughed out loud, telling myself that I had only found a walking stick, and there was no reason for such foolish excitement. Checking my watch, I saw it was now nearer two o'clock than one, and the day had been busy. Removing my clothes, I lay on the bed frame and was asleep in minutes, with the glow from the unlit fire permeating the room and my staff propped against the wall.

CHAPTER 2

"THIS IS GRANTON BEACH," Charles said.

I looked along the coast. With the picturesque old port of Newhaven to the east and the humped, green island of Cramond to the west, it was an idyllic spot, yet within easy walking distance of Edinburgh. The waves of the Firth of Forth broke gently on the curving shore, with the spring sun kissing the coast of Fife opposite and a two-masted collier brig nosing through a fleet of a score of local fishing boats half a mile offshore.

"I should be working," I said. "I should be in my surgery, trying to convince sick and wealthy patients to come to me."

"You need some relaxation." Charles was quite persuasive when he tried. "Nothing beats a good swim. Come on!"

The temptation was too much. Pushing my financial and professional worries to one side, I succumbed to the lure of the sea. Hiding behind a group of whins, I dropped my staff on to the turf, and we stripped off and ran into the water. Though it was spring, the water was cold enough to elicit a yelp from me.

"Never mind the chill. You'll get used to it!" Charles was

10 paces ahead of me, laughing as he splashed through the water.

"You Hebrideans should have gills and fins," I said, as Charles leapt up and dived under the water, to power forward as gracefully as any fish.

I had always fancied myself as a good waterman, for I grew up beside the River Teviot and spent much of my childhood in the various swimming holes there, yet compared to Charles I was a mere tyro. I laboured in his wake, joying in the exercise and the fresh air, so much more healthy than sitting in my surgery.

"To the island!" Charles shouted over his shoulder and headed for Cramond Island, which was much further than I had intended swimming that day. However, no Borderer can resist a challenge, and I followed, splashing furiously in my attempt to catch him. I did not succeed and was gasping like a grampus long before I came to Cramond, where Charles was sitting on a bank of grass above the beach, grinning at me.

"Welcome to Crusoe's island," Charles greeted me, not even out of breath.

"Blasted MacNeils." I dragged myself on to the grass at his side and lay there, face down and chest heaving.

"We had our own boat in the Flood," Charles said. "But we men from Barra had to learn how to swim as well." He grinned. "Here we are, Martin, both of us finally qualified doctors and free of all commitments, loose in the capital city. Imagine!"

I grinned at him. "Aye, imagine, Charles! Imagine what good we can do here, what cures we can affect among the sick and needy." I watched two kittiwakes wheeling above the water, breathed deeply of the fresh sea air and lay back down. "We can maybe clean up some of the diseases in this city. God knows it needs cleansing in my area. I live in the heart of the Old Town, the Auld Toun, where the good and the great once lived, and now it is a veritable sink of disease, begging for a doctor."

"And you are the very man to do it," Charles flattered me. "Top man in your class in nearly all subjects. You are too idealistic though, Martin. You need to make money as well."

"As long as I have enough to live," I said, "I don't need more."

Charles and I had met on our first day in the Glasgow School of Medicine, and immediately became fast friends, despite our geographical differences. We roomed together in various less-than-salubrious parts of Glasgow, and both decided to further our careers in Edinburgh, rather than returning to our respective homes. Now we were meeting for the first time in weeks, but without any of the awkwardness that occasionally blights such reunions.

We lay for a while, enjoying each other's company without saying a word as the waves surged and broke a few feet away until Charles broke the silence. "I've told you your only weakness, Martin. Now you must tell me mine."

"Women," I said solemnly. "Women like you and you like women. You will have to find a *good* woman and settle down rather than spreading yourself among many women who are anything but good."

Charles laughed. "I was doing good, Martin, keeping the flashtails in work."

I shook my head, for Charles's reputation among the Glasgow prostitutes was legendary.

Charles glanced at the mainland. "The tide will be ebbing soon, and people will be able to walk out to this island. It's tidal, you see."

"We'd best leave before then," I said.

"An hour yet," Charles said. "Are you going to set up your practice from the house?"

"No." I shook my head. "I want somewhere separate, if I can."

"I have a practice in the New Town," Charles said. "In Thistle Street." He turned to face me. "I found a sponsor, an elderly doctor and another University of Glasgow man, who wishes to pass on his patients to me."

I could only hide my jealousy behind a smile, although, in truth, I wished nothing but success for Charles. "I am sure that will prove very popular," I said. "The New Town is the heart of respectable Edinburgh. You could not find a better place to work, and you'll soon build up your reputation."

"I hope so," Charles said. "As will you, once your patients learn about you."

"I hope so, too." I lay back, luxuriating in the sunlight. "Lack of finances may delay that day."

Charles rolled over on to his face and chewed on a stalk of grass. "There are methods to alleviate that problem," he spoke around his grass. "You know that I was not born into money."

I did know that. Charles was one of these rarities, a man who had raised himself from a Hebridean cottage to above respectability. "However did you manage?"

"By skirting the edges of fate," Charles said. "One cannot rise in this world solely by hard work. One needs an influential patron, which I was fortunate enough to find. But even then, one must step outside the normal bounds of society and take to chance."

"Chance?" I asked carelessly, watching a pair of black-headed gulls circle overhead.

"Games of chance." Charles looked at me sideways. From behind a screen of grass, he looked young, with his freckled face, devil-may-care grin and bright blue eyes.

"Gambling," I said.

"Exactly so." Charles winked at me. "If one hits a winning streak, one can pocket a small fortune."

My Presbyterian soul rebelled against such things. "My father called playing cards the Devil's Bible," I said.

"Your father was a good man," Charles said. "How much did he leave you when he died?"

"Not a farthing to scratch myself with," I said. "Father was a tenant farmer at the foot of the Cheviot Hills and laboured every day of his life just to survive."

"Pious poverty does not help one make one's way in this world." Charles wriggled himself into a more comfortable position.

"The MacNeils were ayeways pirates," I said, trying to prick his smug bubble.

"We were," Charles agreed, unperturbed. "I am a member of a certain club in Edinburgh if you ever wish to join."

"I won't," I said, searching my brain for something to alter the subject, for I did not care to think of Charles indulging in the devil's playground. My thought must have transferred to him, for he shifted position, affording me a splendid view of his back, tattooed buttocks and legs. I had never examined Charles's tattoo before, although we shared a room when we were students in Glasgow, but now I found myself staring at his right hip. "Where did you get your tattoo, Charles?"

"In a whaling ship off Greenland," Charles said. "Last year. You'll recall that I signed articles on a Leith whaling ship to raise finances and gain experience."

"I remember," I said.

Charles laughed, looking over his shoulder at his right hip and buttock, where the tattoo stood out against his pale skin. "My crewmates thought it would be fun to have an initiation for the Greenman surgeon."

"It's an interesting design," I said. "Interlocking lines, like somebody wove a pattern on your body."

Charles laughed again. He had a very distinctive laugh that started with a low gurgle and rose in pitch. "I can't say that I've ever studied it! An Orcadian drew the design and somebody else marked it in."

I left it at that, for even a doctor does not wish to examine that part of a man's anatomy. However, the design remained in my mind.

"Are you ready to swim back?" Charles had been studying the tide with all the acumen of a Hebridean. "If we stay here much longer, somebody might walk out and catch us in nature's garb."

I sat up, somewhat reluctant to return to reality after our relaxing time on the island. "Come on then, Charles."

We swam to the mainland with more decorum than we had shown on our outward excursion, to find the ebbing tide forced us to walk 100 yards from the edge of the sea to the whins. I was laughing at some sally of Charles's when I saw the group of three people. They were about 200 yards from us but walking briskly in our direction.

"People," I warned.

"I see them," Charles said.

"They're approaching our clothes." I began to hurry, moving in a half-crouch to conceal as much of my person as possible. We were right in the open when I heard the unmistakable light tones of a female. "And there's a woman among them."

"Two women, I say." Charles did not sound concerned. "This beach is well known as a place where men bathe," he said. "Women should keep their distance or be prepared to see naked men. Or perhaps that's why they are here!"

I was not as blasé as Charles, so increased my speed, yet I

had hardly reached the shelter of the whins when one of the approaching party pointed to us.

"I say," she said, with a tone that may have been either wonder or delight. "Would you look at that?"

As I hurriedly hauled on my clothes, the deeper voice of a man broke in.

"Turn your back at once, Evelyn, and you too, Mrs Swinton."

I hurried, even more, covering as much of myself as I could before the party came any closer. When I looked sideways, Charles was casually dressing without any pretence at concealment. I must admit a moment of envy, for surely he had nothing of which to be ashamed.

There were three people in the party, one middle-aged man, a middle-aged woman whom I took to be the man's wife and the most attractive young woman I had ever seen. I instinctively knew the younger woman was the daughter. The man was looking at me with a surprisingly benevolent smile on his face, his wife was pointedly looking in the opposite direction and the girl, the one who interested me the most, was staring at Charles's Apollo-like physique.

I lifted my staff and stepped sideways to shield Charles's still imperfectly clad person. "I do apologise," I said. "We did not intend to cause any offence."

"The fault is ours, if anything," the lady said, still staring at Cramond Island as if she had never seen such a thing before. "I had heard that gentlemen used this beach for bathing but had not expected to find it occupied." She gave a brief laugh. "I hope we have not caused you any embarrassment, although I do assure you that we did not see anything untoward."

As I tapped my staff on the ground, the daughter looked at me for the first time. I saw her eyes widen as she smiled. "I am

Evelyn Swinton," she said with a sweeping curtsey. "This is my father, Mr James Swinton and my mother, Mrs Eliza Swinton."

"I am Martin Elliot." I met her curtsey with a bow. "And my ill-clad companion is Charles MacNeil." She had the most marvellous grey eyes and I swear they were laughing at me, although they did flick sideways towards Charles for a second, no doubt to check his progress in dressing.

There was a few seconds of mutual bowing and curtseying, with a curious seagull watching from the shelter of the whins before Mrs Swinton spoke.

"Well, gentlemen, we are sorry to disturb you." She glanced at her husband. "We will leave you in peace."

"Oh, no, mother." Evelyn touched her mother's arm, with her gaze still fixed on me. "We must apologise properly by inviting these gentlemen to visit."

Mr Swinton's expression altered. His eyebrows rose, he glanced from Evelyn to me, then to Charles, and his lips twitched in a smile. He nodded. "Shall we say next Tuesday at five?"

"That would be admirable, sir," I said.

Mr Swinton nodded. "Queen Street," he said. "The house with the green door."

"Nothing formal," Mrs Swinton said, looking at us at last. "Pray, don't dress up."

"But do come dressed," Evelyn said, for her mother to award her a sharp elbow and a hissed rebuke.

I smiled, for I do like a girl with a sense of humour, and bowed again, unwilling to admit that I possessed no formal clothes. As the Swintons walked away, I watched Evelyn. I knew she would turn around when she reached the wind-gnarled elder tree and was waiting with my smile and a raised hand. I gave another little bow, to which she had no time to respond before her mother pulled her away, rather sharply, I thought.

"Well, Martin," Charles said. "You made an impact there. I thought you were always shy with girls."

"I am," I said, tapping my staff on the sand. "But perhaps not with that one."

"Perhaps not," Charles said, looking at me thoughtfully. "I might have to challenge you for the fair Miss Swinton."

"You would not win," I said, for already I felt affection for that lady. "I want her for myself." I did not mention her side-long glance at Charles.

I remember that afternoon on the beach as one of the happiest days I spent in Edinburgh, yet even then I was aware that the seeds planted were not all of the healthiest variety.

CHAPTER 3

NOW THAT I had a home address, it was easier to find rooms for a surgery. I was very fortunate, for an elderly doctor had died, leaving his premises unoccupied and I saw the advertisement in the *Caledonian Mercury*.

It was a strange sequence of events, for I had flicked through the paper without noticing anything of interest, and laid it down on the floor beside my chair. I prepared to go for a walk and lifted my staff, but the thing seemed to have a life of its own. It slipped from my hand and rolled until the carved head rested on top of the newspaper. Only then did I notice the advertisement, as if the rounded head had indicated the place.

To Lease

A prime set of rooms in the historic Grassmarket. This establishment was the surgery of the late Doctor Walter Ogilvie and is complete in every way for a doctor's surgery. It can also be easily adapted for use as living accommodation or any other commercial or business purpose.

For further details, apply to Messrs Mackay and Malvern, Lawnmarket.

"Good God," I said. "How ever did I miss that?"

Lifting the staff, I left my house immediately to find Messrs Mackay and Malvern. I exchanged the echoes of the courtyard for the noises of the street, with the clatter of horseshoes on granite cobblestones, the clamour of blacksmiths working with red-hot iron and the chatter of a thousand people. I breathed deeply, inhaling the various scents of Edinburgh, not all of them pleasant. There was the scent of smouldering hoof-horn as a farrier fitted a horseshoe, the sharply ammoniac stink of human and animal urine, the constant smell of human sweat and the sweet invitations of whisky from the publics and spirit palaces that sat on every corner. I savoured each sight, smell and sound like a new experience and wondered why I had not noticed them before, or rather why I had taken them for granted. Life was scintillating, with so many adventures beckoning at every close-mouth and new friendships waiting with every smiling woman.

Tapping my staff on the ground, I strolled up the street, nodding amiably to anybody who caught my eye. Most returned my greetings, although one very respectably dressed gentleman gave me a glower in return. My surge of anger was unexpected, and I had to fight my desire to swing the staff at him and stride away. I seemed to be in the grip of new passions now, veering from extreme benevolence to sudden, nearly uncontrollable rage.

The solicitors dealing with the property in the Lawnmarket were only a 10-minute walk away, and the fellow who answered my rather peremptory rap on his door looked somewhat surprised.

"I was just opening up," he said.

"The early bird catches the worm," I told him, folding the *Mercury* to show him the advertisement. "I am interested in leasing this property."

A young man with a prematurely balding head, he ushered me to a chair and cleared a space in the files on his desk. "Why," he said, "that advertisement was not meant to be in until after the funeral. The newspaper must have made a mistake."

"It may be an extremely fortunate mistake for us both," I said lightly. "For it could secure me suitable premises and furnish you with an immediate client."

The solicitor burrowed in the pile of documents on his desk before emerging with a piece of folded parchment, tied with ribbon and sealed with red wax. "Here we are, sir," he said, as he untied the ribbon and broke the seal. "Doctor Ogilvie died only two nights ago, and we were notified yesterday evening." He looked up at me. "I am surprised, amazed that we should advertise the vacancy with such alacrity."

"It is proof of a very efficient office," I said, tapping the desk with my staff. "What is on offer?"

"The entire premises, including a desk, surgery and a back room with a surgical table, a small garden and easy access to a well."

I nodded, still tapping my staff, an action that seemed to accelerate events. "How much is the rent?"

The solicitor consulted his documents, with his forehead creasing into a frown. "I cannot see a figure," he said.

"Try the third page," I suggested, although for the life of me I did not know what made me say that.

The solicitor turned the pages of the parchment as the lantern on the wall swayed in a slight draught. "You are right!" He said. "Doctor Ogilvy died shortly after six in the morning and his widow asked that we lease the premises to a medical man at a nominal rent."

"How much of a nominal rent?" I asked and could have smiled at the figure the solicitor quoted. "I will take it."

"This is most irregular," the solicitor said. "I have never known a property change hands so quickly."

That is how I came to be the tenant of a house in the West Bow and a surgery in the Grassmarket, all within three busy days. I walked away from the solicitor's office in high good humour, swinging the staff that had pointed me in the right direction.

Life was good, I decided and winked at a shy-faced young woman before stepping inside a whisky shop to treat us both to a warming dram.

Us both? From where did that idea come?

"Are you ready?" Charles looked slightly nervous as we stood outside the green door in Queen Street.

I was ready. I leaned on my staff, waiting for Charles to use the gleaming brass knocker.

"You look very relaxed," Charles said. "All the years I have known you, you've avoided social gatherings, and now you're almost eager to visit the Swintons after the briefest of introductions." He shook his head. "I don't understand."

"Neither do I," I admitted, smiling. "Perhaps I have merely conquered my fear."

The contrast between the Swintons' house in the New Town and my Old Town close could not have been more extreme. Queen Street was broad and airy and the houses were large and well designed, with tall windows, spacious rooms and every convenience possible for modern living. On one side, splendid houses paraded classical architecture that could match any street in the world, while on the other were private pleasure gardens behind a formidable iron railing. The sound of birds in the trees was pleasant after the raucous noises of the West Bow.

I prepared my smile as the door opened.

All three Swintons greeted us with beams of welcome, with Mr Swinton shaking our hands as if we were long-lost relatives and Mrs Swinton curtseying low to the ground. However, it was Evelyn Swinton who seemed most pleased to see us, with her eyes sparkling as she approached and her speech so rapid that her mother rebuked her gently.

"Evelyn, dear, you will scare the poor gentlemen away with your prattle!"

I laughed at that. "Nothing could be further from the truth, Mrs Swinton. It is a delight to meet such a friendly family," I said, which seemed to please everybody.

"Mr Elliot! Mr MacNeil! I am so pleased to see you again!" Evelyn refused to be subdued as she spoke to us both simultaneously, under the benevolent, if watchful, gaze of her father.

"Come in, come away in," Mrs Swinton ushered us into the parlour as a calm-faced maid took our hats and coats.

After that welcome, we all got along famously. In most social situations, I sit quietly in the corner, speaking only when necessary but, with the Swintons, I seemed to blossom. I found conversation came easily to me, with witty remarks sliding from my tongue as I charmed them with a personality I had not known I possessed. From time to time, Charles glanced at me, no doubt wondering who this stranger was.

Mr Swinton was a gentleman, a dabbler in the stock-market and a solicitor, as I learned, with a small but stable practice in Rose Street in the New Town. Mrs Swinton ran the house, and they had two daughters, of whom Evelyn was the younger.

"Our older daughter, Elaine, has left the family home," Mrs Swinton said, and then closed her mouth, leading me to surmise that there was some family dispute there. Without being told, I knew that the Swintons were eyeing Charles and me up as possible marriage material for their remaining daughter. I allowed them to probe as I watched the light play across Evelyn's face, showing her delicate cheekbones and those marvellous grey eyes.

"Have you been in practice long?" Mrs Swinton asked as we sat around the table, quite relaxed.

"Only a few weeks," Charles said honestly.

"And how long is your patient list?" Mr Swinton drove straight to the heart of the matter.

"Very short at present," Charles said, an admission which immediately passed the marriage-ball from his side to mine.

"I don't yet know about my patients," I temporised. "I have hopes of maintaining a successful practice." When the two elder Swintons exchanged glances, I knew I had said the correct thing. The Swintons wanted a son-in-law who could keep their daughter in financial security.

"I know neither of you is local, so do you intend to return to your respective homes?" Mrs Swinton asked, not wishing her daughter to be dragged away to some obscure corner of the globe.

"I am from Roxburghshire," I said, "although I intend to settle in the New Town of Edinburgh once I am established. Charles, I believe, hopes to return to his native island of Barra."

"I could either return to Barra or remain in Edinburgh." Charles had not yet caught on to the game we were playing.

"What is Barra like?" Evelyn asked artlessly. I silently praised her for playing a game of her own.

"It's a beautiful island at the southern tip of the Outer

Hebrides," Charles said. "Most of the people are either crofters, fishermen or sailors. But the sunsets are spectacular."

I could sense the disapproval from Mrs Swinton.

"Is there much society there? Theatres, assembly halls, respectable people?"

Charles shook his head. "No; we only have the church and ceilidhs, which are smoking concerts that can last for days."

"Oh." Mrs Swinton lost interest in the Island of Barra and, by association, with Charles. The day was mine and, in Mrs Swinton's eyes, I had won the hand of the fair Evelyn. Did I want her hand?

I smiled across the table, seeing the girl behind her charm and the woman behind her style. I had never done that before. I had never assessed a woman as I did Evelyn Swinton. Now I summed her up and found her acceptable. She would help me in my climb up the ladder of respectability from a newly qualified doctor to an established practitioner.

Evelyn smiled back at me, as Mrs Swinton glanced at her husband. After that moment, I knew I had found my woman. I leaned back in my seat, strangely satisfied with the way my life was progressing. I knew, somehow, that although Mrs Swinton was on my side, Mr Swinton was less than convinced. When I later retrieved my hat and staff from the maid and left, I wondered how I could turn him around.

"There must be some way," I told myself. "Something will turn up."

I had never eavesdropped before, yet for some reason, that day I lingered when Charles bid me a good evening and marched away, and I heard Mrs Swinton talking. They were in their front room, with the window open, so their voices carried to me on the street outside.

"All our money, Swinton? Are you sure that is wise?"

"Every last penny," Swinton said, "and if I had more I

would invest that, too. It's a certain winner. I know them personally, and I am a legal representative on the board."

"But, all our money, Swinton. It is a huge gamble."

"It is as safe as the Bank of England," Swinton said, "Safer, and with a far higher rate of return."

"Oh, Swinton," Mrs Swinton said. "I don't like the idea at all."

"Nonsense. Constable, the bookseller, is going to rise high. With Walter Scott the novelist backing them, how can they fail?" Swinton gave a little laugh. "Ballantyne the printer as well. Mark my words, Eliza, they'll rise to the heavens. I'll keep my eye on the shares in the financial section of the newspapers; you see if I don't."

I tapped my staff on the ground. I was not aware then, to what depths I could sink, but I somehow knew that I could use that intelligence to my advantage.

When I returned to the West Bow, Miss Anderson was busy at her labours, sweeping the floor with a broom and whistling.

"You are very cheerful, Miss Anderson," I said.

"No sense in being otherwise," Miss Anderson leaned on her broom to talk to me. "But call me Ruth, please."

I hung up my hat and cloak, tapped my staff on the floor and wished I could afford a manservant. "Ruth it is," I said, again noticing what an agreeable countenance Ruth had when she smiled. "You are making this house look extremely pleasant, Ruth." I allowed my smile to work its charm with her. It was strange how I had never had that skill until I moved into my new home.

"I do my best." Ruth began to sweep again, taking short strokes and gathering the dust in a small bucket. I watched her for a while, with my man's eyes following the flow and curves of her body.

"Why is there not a Mr Anderson?" I asked.

"My father is dead," Ruth had the most amiable of voices, deep-toned and slightly hoarse.

"I meant a husband," I said.

"What man would have me?" Ruth stopped sweeping again. "I am anything but a demure wife. I speak my mind and gang my ain gait."

I smiled, stepped to my small sideboard and poured myself a glass of claret, glanced at Ruth and poured a second for her. "Not every man wishes a milk-and-water wife," I said, handing over her glass.

Ruth looked startled at first, but the lure of wine was too strong, and she sipped with more grace than many gentle-women I have met. "Thank you, sir."

"If you are Ruth," I said, "then I must be Martin."

"I can't call you that," Ruth said.

"Then sir it can be, or Dr Elliot, whichever suits you better." I finished my glass, looked at Ruth through the glass and smiled. "Another?"

"Yes, please, Doctor." Ruth tipped back her head, showing an exquisite white throat. "Thank you."

"You are an interesting lady," I said. "You don't seem upset by the unusual rumours and stories." I poured out another two glasses of claret and sipped carefully.

Ruth shrugged. "There's nothing to upset me in an empty house, Doctor. I stopped being scared by bairns' stories years ago."

I smiled. "I was lucky to find you."

"Aye," Ruth said, examining the claret in her glass. "You were." She looked at me, smiling with her eyes. "Are you not afraid to live here all alone?"

"No," I said. "It's only a house."

"You're a brave man," Ruth said.

"It does not take bravery to ignore superstition," I said. "It only takes some common sense."

Ruth smiled. "All I do is sort the wheat of reality from the chaff of popular belief."

I frowned, for such language was not common among the people of the West Bow. "You are indeed an exceptional woman, Ruth."

I am sure she mocked me with her curtsey. "Thank you, Doctor. I shall leave now. Good night."

"Good night." I could not help my brief bow, although one did not bow to servants. "Wait." I stopped her with a hand on her arm. "Who are you, Ruth?"

"Just myself, Doctor," she said.

"You're not an ordinary servant," I said, and on an impulse, I added: "Stay. Stay the night, Ruth."

She shook her head. "That would not be proper, would it, Doctor?"

I felt the surge of rage at being denied. "How dare you?"

"Oh, I dare, Doctor," Ruth stepped away. "What is there that a bold woman will not dare?" She held my gaze, unflinching. "I'll be back to clean tomorrow, Doctor. Good night, to you." As she turned, the candlelight reflected from the brooch she wore on the breast. It was in the shape of a Celtic Cross and somehow seemed out of place in my house.

I stepped away. "Good night," I said.

As I lay down to sleep, I saw the hands on the clock. They pointed to six minutes past six.

It was the next morning that I thought somebody was following me. Drizzling rain dampened me on my journey between my house and my surgery in the pre-dawn dark when I caught a glimpse of a shadowy figure 100 yards to the rear.

Twice I turned, and each time the man, if it was a man, had gone.

"Who's there?" I stopped, gripping my staff, for it was the only weapon I had and that part of Edinburgh could be dangerous in the dark. When nobody replied, I strode back the way I had come, expecting to find some lad waiting to pick my pocket, or at worst a rascal with a blackjack. I saw nobody although I checked the various closes and wynds.

"Let me warn you, I carry a gun," I lied, turned away and resumed my original course. Although I heard nobody, the feeling that somebody was behind me persisted. I deliberately walked into a close, waited a moment, turned and raced out, to find the street deserted. The tall lands glowered down at me, with the sightless eyes of windows staring as I scurried past and close-mouths like entrances to unknown blackness. The misery of the Old Town was apparent as the ugly stench of night-soil filled my nostrils, and the scurrying of rats jangled my already stretched nerves. The rain eased to one of the all-pervading Edinburgh fogs, thick with smoke and harsh on the throat.

My heart was racing when I reached the surgery, and I spent the next 15 minutes peering out of the window, without seeing anybody in the least suspicious. Finally convincing myself that my imagination had been too active, I settled myself for an uneventful day of treating the sick, the helpless and the unrepentant. Although I had hoped for at least a few of the remaining respectable residents of the Old Town, my patients were all of the lowest strata of society, paying in greasy, worn coppers with the occasional flash of a silver coin they had undoubtedly stolen.

"Thank you, Doctor," they said, or grunted, or said nothing at all. Some left muttering under their breath while one or two were spectacularly grateful. Whatever their reactions, they did little to increase the money in my pocketbook. I knew I would not get rich in this area. I needed to find some method of making money if I wished to rise in my profession and the esteem of Edinburgh. Walking to the surgery door, I peered outside into the choking smog. Edinburgh was well named as Auld Reekie when the lowering clouds pressed down the smoke of a thousand chimneys to lie thick and grey among the closes. Perhaps the man who had followed me that morning hoped to increase his fortune by knocking me on the head and stealing my pocketbook. I snorted, for he would be a very disappointed fellow, as I had less than 10 shillings in my possession.

Before the first of the day's patients arrived from whatever hideous close he called home, I stood at my door, peering around me. In the smog, I could not see the castle, although I knew it was up there, rising proudly on its great rock to dominate the city. I had a growing urge to subjugate in the same way, to be somebody other than a struggling doctor with a starvation-thin practice, counting my coppers to see if I could pay the rent.

I tapped my staff on the floor, wondering if the man who dogged me was still there, or if he was merely a product of my imagination, already inflamed by the infantile stories in my house. "Are you there? You there, the fellow who was following me. Are you there?" My voice echoed in the fog, flattened, distorted, lost in the ugliness of poverty and hopelessness.

There was no reply. I had not expected one.

"Aye," I said, reverting to the broad accent of the Border from where I came. "You cannae fright a Teviotdale man like that! We're not scared of men, devils or hounds of hell!"

"I'm glad to hear it, Martin," Charles appeared out of the murk, "although I don't know why you are telling me!"

"Charles!" I grinned for it was always a pleasure to see his cheerful, open face. "Come in, man, come on in!"

Charles stepped inside my surgery, thumping his feet on my stone-slabbed floor.

"Take your hat and gloves off," I said, "hand me your coat for goodness sake, or we can repair to an inn for a warming dram before the day properly begins."

"I am not stopping," Charles said, stamping the chill out of his feet. "I just wished to hand you this." He gave me a folded note, heavily sealed with red wax. "Mrs Swinton was good enough to drop this off at my surgery last night, and I thought I'd catch you this morning before you opened up."

I took the note, instinctively knowing that Evelyn had sent it.

"That was a devil of a noise you were making," Charles said. "Is everything all right?"

"Right as rain," I told him. "I thought somebody was dogging me."

"It's this damned murk," Charles said, touching his cane to his hat. "It makes one imagine things. Well, I must be off before the queue starts to form. I hope your note is good news, Martin."

I felt suddenly lonely as Charles walked away, although I was in the midst of tens of thousands of people. Pushing aside the uneasy feeling that had blanketed me all day, I returned to my desk, broke the seal and unfolded the note.

"Martin,

I hope you do not think me forward, but I would like to invite you back to our house in Queen Street. If it is convenient, please call at seven on Wednesday evening.

Regards
Your friend,
Evelyn Swinton."

It was very concise, yet said all I wished to read. I read it three times, delighting in the natural flow of her writing and smooth formation of the words.

I felt a sudden increase in my heartbeat and knew that we had captured her. *We?* I shook my head. Who were we? Evelyn was mine alone. Smiling, I reread her words, pictured her smile and allowed my mind to wander to other places that only Evelyn and I would share, later, when the time was right, and we were alone with her. When *I* was alone with her, I corrected suddenly, wondering why I had made that same foolish mistake twice.

The surgery was busy that day, with a score of patients, none of whom had more than a few pennies to their name. Although my inclination was to send them away until they could afford my services, I sighed and did my best, knowing that it was my duty as a doctor to help the sick, yet aware that I could never achieve my purpose by dispensing cheap medicine to the terminally destitute.

I needed more than this life, much more, and I had not yet learned how to attain my object.

With the surgery doors closed, I opened the windows wide to clear away the stench of the great unwashed, lifted my staff and walked the streets. I made a couple of home visits, gave some excellent advice that I knew would be ignored and explored my surroundings, wondering at the shadow I seemed to cast. Although I wore a long coat and a low-crowned hat, some trick of the Edinburgh light created a shadow of a man in a flowing cloak with a taller, near conical hat.

On one occasion, I wandered too deeply into a close and

found myself amid a crowd of raggedly dressed boys, the oldest of whom might have been 10 years old. When they began to paw at me, I found my growling did not work, and only when a middle-aged woman came to my aid did I struggle free from that dark canyon.

The Old Town was like that, I learned. It was a mixture of the vile and the genuinely kindly, the embittered, impoverished people who had to claw and struggle just to survive, and the warm-hearted who would part with their last farthing to help a stranger. All the same, it was a place of the defeated and those very few of the older generation who wished to cling to a vanished way of life. Anybody with ambition shunned the ruins of Old Edinburgh and flitted to the refined environment of the New Town. The deeper I explored the dirty closes and broken people, the stronger became my resolve to move northward to the New Town. I stopped outside Fleshmarket Close and looked right and left, along the ridge that marked the spine of the old city. No, I decided. I was better than this. I tapped my staff on the cobbles, with their covering of straw and horse manure. I had not gone through years of penury as a medical student to live in such a place.

I felt the man's gaze on me before I noticed him watching me. He was leaning against a close entrance with a blue tam-o' shanter pulled low over his forehead, and his arms folded across his chest.

"Who the devil are you?" I strode towards him, tapping my staff on the ground.

"A man who is worried about you." The gaunt face was familiar, although I could not say where I had seen it before.

"What?" I lifted my staff to strike him, but there was something about the man's calm demeanour that stilled my hand. "What do you mean? Explain yourself, man!"

"You're heading into trouble, Doctor Elliot." The man had

not flinched from my threat. “If you take my advice, you’ll leave your present abode and seek another home.”

“To the deuce with your advice,” I said. “I know you! You were in the crowd outside my house when I first arrived.”

“Aye, that I was, Doctor,” the man said, not raising his voice in the slightest.

“Were you following me this morning?”

“I was,” the man admitted freely, “and there are worse things than me dogging your footsteps, Doctor.” He frowned suddenly. “Where did you get that stick?”

For some reason, I found myself answering him. “It was in the house.”

The man’s face paled. “Get rid of it, man! If you have any sense at all, you’ll throw that damned stick as far away as possible and run.”

“You damned blackguard!” I said and lifted my staff to thrash him.

“Remember what I said, Doctor,” the man said, withdrawing down the close. “I am

trying to help you.”

“Damn your help,” I said, lowering my staff. I shrugged, but the gaunt-faced man’s words had planted an uneasiness inside me that even half a dozen drams and a stiff glass of claret failed to remove altogether. “If I see you again, my bucko,” I promised, “I’ll make you pay for unsettling me.”

CHAPTER 4

THERE IS something eternally fascinating about a fire. I don't know what it is, although I suspect it is a memory from our distant ancestors when we huddled in caves with only flames keeping us safe from nighttime predators. My compulsion to stare into the fire certainly increased tenfold after I moved into the house off the West Bow. Evening after evening, I fought the shadows of my mind by crouching close to the heat and staring into the orange flames, as if I were a part of the phenomenon that Ruth had created from sticks, paper and coal.

Each night the fire drew me closer, so I could imagine myself standing atop the lumps of black coal as the flames licked around me, with the heat building and people gathered around to watch me gasp and writhe and scream at the unbearable pain. Each night the feeling grew more intense as I burned within the flames, with the stink and crackle of burning hair first, then the searing agony as my skin scorched and my eyeballs melted. I was surrounded by fire, twisting, pleading for mercy that never came, slowly burning to the pitiless interest of the crowd.

I jerked back, aware that I had nearly fallen into the fireplace. That dream, that image was terrifyingly real. Stepping away from the fire, I poured myself a glass of claret, drank it back and stilled my vibrating nerves.

"Doctor Elliot," I told myself sternly, "you must keep control of your imagination. That's all it is, imagination."

Half smiling, I had another drink, lifted a medical treatise to divert my mind on to more practical matters and sat down again, taking the entirely sensible precaution of pulling my chair back from the fire.

Claret seemed to ease my mind, removing my thoughts from these long lapses into the unknown realms, like waking nightmares. Daymares, perhaps, for want of a better name, for it was not yet fully dark outside and I used the fire partly to keep the inherent chill of the house at bay. Whatever I did, the house always seemed cold and clammy, with the occasional, unexplained sound, as if somebody were breathing. Once I thought it was the house itself breathing, but that was when I was newly awake and stupid from sleep.

I wondered anew what that gaunt fellow had meant when he warned me away from this house, and why so many local people recoiled from even entering. Was there some truth to the stories? Some remnant of an old event? A murder perhaps?

I shook my head, resolved to interrogate Ruth the next day, ignored the innocuous shadows and retired to my bed. Only the settling of coals in the fire and the ticking of the clocks disturbed my sleep that night. My mind was as relaxed as any innocent baby's.

~

Evelyn must have been in the hall, waiting for me. I had no sooner rapped on the door of her father's house than the manservant answered, as Evelyn hovered in the background smiling, with an endearing little gap between her front two teeth and her head tilted very slightly to the left.

"Good evening, Martin." Evelyn bobbed in a curtsey, vainly trying to hide her pleasure at seeing me.

"Good evening Evelyn," I responded with a bow.

"You two are very formal." Mr Swinton appeared on the stairs, shaking his head. "I wonder how you'd act if I were elsewhere." His stiff collar looked as if it would cut into his neck while his plain buff weskit was so tight I wondered if it might damage his circulation.

"Father," Evelyn chided him, "we are not children to be overawed in the presence of parents."

"I'll leave you two alone." Mr Swinton left with a mocking bow to me. I liked Evelyn's father with his dry sense of humour, although I suspected he preferred Charles to me. However, I had no qualms that he and I would get along famously after I married his daughter. Only two things stood between us and that happy day. The first was my distinct lack of money, and the second was that I had not yet asked for Evelyn's hand. Looking at her as we stood in the hallway in Mr Swinton's house in Queen Street, so different from my home, I knew I could not ask her yet. How could I justify taking a respectable, elegant lady, used to the finer things in life, to such a squalid locality as the West Bow?

"Well now, Martin." Evelyn might have read my thoughts. "When are you going to show me your new house?"

"When I have it ready for the presence of a lady," I said.

"I am not made of glass, you know." Evelyn gave that smile again. "I will not swoon at a house in disorder."

"You are made perfectly," I said, greatly daring, for I was never good at compliments.

Evelyn gave a gentle curtsey. "Why, thank you, kind sir.

Shall we walk?" That was her kindly way of acknowledging the fact that I was purse starved and a walk was the best I could offer her. I thanked her silently, vowing to treat her like a queen the instant my finances improved.

We strolled the length of Queen Street, with Evelyn's hand butterfly-light on my arm. I could have been in heaven, with Evelyn by my side and the New Town's prosperous bustle all around. Only my poverty spoiled the day. As we turned towards George Street, Evelyn shook her head.

"Not that way, Martin," she said. "I have a small surprise for you," and produced a key from inside her sleeve. "We shall go inside the Pleasure Garden today."

"I thought only residents are allowed in there," I said.

"I *am* a resident," Evelyn said, "and you are my guest. I am sure that nobody will challenge your right to accompany me."

I was equally sure. Evelyn belonged in the dignified squares and terraces of the New Town, with its classical architecture and upright, clean-living inhabitants. Nobody would doubt her right to stroll through the Pleasure Garden of Queen Street, although they may question my presence.

The gardens form a peaceful oasis between the austere stone terraces of Queen Street and Heriot Row, a green space of tall trees, winding pathways and a small pond that remained when the original farm was cleared away.

"This is a delightful place to stroll," I said, "with my favourite girl on my arm and the birds melodious in the trees."

"Your favourite girl?" Evelyn looked sideways at me. "That implies you have more than one. Who is my rival, pray?"

"You have no rival," I said, "nor ever will have." I enjoyed her smile and the way she moved even closer to me, so her hip brushed against mine with every third or fourth step.

We stopped at a large elm. "Is this not the most romantic

spot?" Evelyn asked. "This is the best tree in Edinburgh, with branches that spread out like the arms of a lover."

Above us, the leaves were the bright-green of early summer, rustling in Edinburgh's ever-present wind. I stood still for a moment, savouring the feeling.

"It is a very romantic spot," Evelyn repeated, slightly louder.

Taking that for a cue, I kissed her. Our first real kiss, in the week I had moved into my house in Edinburgh, the capital of Scotland and Evelyn's city. It is a memory I still treasure, despite what happened afterwards. True happiness is hard to find and should be grasped with both hands and savoured against the bad times.

I was surprised how eagerly Evelyn responded. Although she appeared to be a demure, shy girl with the same dry humour as her father, I suspected that there was hidden passion in my Evelyn.

When we withdrew, smiling at each other and somewhat short of breath, I wondered why such an attractive girl from a prosperous background should wish to walk out with me, an impoverished, rather gauche young doctor from the countryside.

"I know what you're thinking," Evelyn said, with her eyes crinkling into a smile.

"What am I thinking?"

"You're wondering what I am going to do next," Evelyn said.

"What are you going to do next, pray?"

"This!" Evelyn said, gave me a push and ran away, looking over her shoulder to ensure that I was following.

Pleasure gardens in Edinburgh are not intended for such unseemliness as young people chasing each other along the paths, over the lawns and around the trees. Edinburgh's douce

New Town frowns on such public displays of affection, so if anybody heard us laughing and saw us frolicking, they would be outwardly shocked. At that moment, I did not care, and enjoyed myself immensely, surprised at the speed at which a young woman could run, even while hampered by long skirts and looking over her shoulder at her pursuer.

After a circuit of the garden, Evelyn allowed me to catch her at the pond. We kissed again, within that magical, peaceful place, and at that moment there was nowhere in the world I would rather have been.

"Oh, Martin," Evelyn said when I released her, and we laughed breathlessly. "This is such fun."

I agreed until I looked up. Only a fringe of low bushes and a wrought iron railing separated the private garden from the public street, and I swear I saw that gaunt-faced fellow watching me from the street outside.

"Martin?" Evelyn was sensitive to my sudden change of mood. "What is the matter, Martin? Have I said something indecorous?"

"No," I shook my head vigorously to reassure her. "Not at all, Evelyn. I thought I saw somebody watching me."

"Is that so bad?" Evelyn took hold of my arm as she scanned the street outside the garden. I swear she was ready to do battle on my account, bless her loyal heart.

I led her away from the fence. "I probably imagined it," I said, and for some reason continued. "I have had some strange experiences lately," I said, "hearing things that are not there."

Evelyn smiled. "That is your nerves troubling you," she reassured me, glancing at the street. "You need not worry about it."

"I am the medical man here," I said. "I know when not to worry."

"What did you hear?" Evelyn asked.

"I heard a clock tick when nobody had wound it up, and a coach-and-four when the street was empty." I told her no more. Not then.

"I would not worry about such things," Evelyn said. "One often hears unexplained things in a strange house. Once you get settled in, you will see that these noises are entirely innocent."

I smiled. "You are probably right," I said and tried to dismiss these events from my mind.

"I do wish you would live in the New Town," Evelyn said. "It is so very much better than the Old."

"I intend to," I said. At that second, the intention was compelling, and I resolved to do everything I could to raise the rhino for better accommodation. I also determined to trace that gaunt-faced man so I could interrogate him.

I sat opposite Charles with the candlelight reflecting from the bottle and the level of claret steadily diminishing.

"There is something very comforting about claret," Charles mused, swirling the contents of his glass. "It is a very satisfying wine, much better than port."

I agreed, although at that moment I was more concerned with the effects drinking claret had on me than anything else.

"One can consume claret in the full knowledge that it helps one's constitution," Charles said. "Unlike port, the consumption of which leads to gout and goodness knows what other infirmities." He looked up, studying me through the shifting red liquid in his glass. "You appear to be in a predicament, old friend."

"I am," I agreed. "I am in the midst of several predicaments, few of which I understand."

"You have a practice with few patients, bills to pay with little income and a girl who appears to dote on you, although God knows why."

"I have all of that," I agreed again.

Charles gave that devil-may-care grin that altered his face from a serious medical practitioner to a likeness of one of his piratical MacNeil ancestors. "We'll have to do something about it, then, shan't we?"

I poured myself another sample of Charles's claret. "I don't know what I can do," I confessed.

Charles's grin widened. "Follow my example, Martin, and teach dissection. I am making money faster than the bank."

A few weeks ago, I would have recoiled from the idea but now I considered the possibilities, rejecting the notion only because of practical considerations rather than moral. "I am no anatomist."

"Nor am I, old friend," Charles said. "All we have to know is the basics, and you got that at medical school. Get yourself a body, advertise that you will demonstrate its workings and a hundred medical students, plus another hundred ghouls, will flock to your premises, all willing to part with their lucre. After all, why should Dr Knox have all the fame?"

Dr Robert Knox is an ex-army surgeon who operates a school of anatomy in Surgeon's Square, attracting many students. I alternately hated and admired him, depending on my mood.

I swallowed more of the claret, enjoying the warm glow it provided. "There is one small flaw in that idea, Charles. Where can I get a human body? It's not as if they fall from the sky, and Dr Knox and his rival John Barclay have the pick of executed criminals and suicides."

"Why, Martin," Charles looked suddenly innocent. "I am surprised you have to ask. You get them the same place as I do;

dig them up at the graveyard. Living in your somewhat nefarious area, I am sure you can find a couple of willing helpers for the price of a glass of whisky."

The thought of digging up graves in some dark graveyard was appalling but no worse than living in poverty as the holes in my shoes expanded. I thought of Evelyn waiting in vain for a man with some prospects and remembered the hope in her eyes as she spoke of me moving to the New Town.

"You might be right," I said.

"You know I am right," Charles said. Leaning across the table, he gave me a hearty smack on the shoulder that nearly knocked me down. "We can work together if you like. Come into partnership with me, and we'll share the patients and profits. What do you say to that?"

I was about to agree. I could think of nothing better than to walk into Charles's established practice and share his wealthy clients. Yet I could not. I had too much pride to live off Charles's reputation and Charles's success. I wanted, no, I *needed,* to prove myself to Evelyn.

To Charles with his wealthy sponsor, grave robbing was little more than fun, a little excitement to earn him pocket money and add spice to his life. To me, it would be the difference between starvation and subsistence with, perhaps, a little over for moving up in the world.

"Well, Martin?" Charles encouraged. "What do you say, eh? You and me together?"

"I might at some time," I said. "Once I have managed to make a success of things."

"As you wish, Martin," Charles said. "Whenever you wish, say the word, and we'll go into the most successful medical partnership Edinburgh has ever known." He raised his glass. "To success and prosperity!"

"Success and prosperity," I echoed and drank the entire

glass in a single draught. In the time it took to drain that glass and replace it on the table, I had made up my mind to follow Charles's lead. Now, how could I find somebody who knew about grave robbing?

I did not know, but I was sure that Ruth Anderson would. She seemed to know everything and everybody in the Old Town. To this day, I wonder why I did not ask Charles.

CHAPTER 5

I WALKED into the public with some trepidation, holding my staff ready in case of a sudden assault. It was situated in a quiet corner of World's End Close and the sign above was ill-spelt and faded, but promised "the best in ales and wines". The clientele watched me enter, narrow-eyed people with haggard faces, some working men and women drinking away their cares, others from the criminal class, seeking an opportunity to prey on their fellows, and a few ladies of the street. One of the latter eyed me, calculating if I were a possible client. I resolved to stay as far as possible from her. Ordering a whisky, I slid on to a bench in the corner nearest the door, wondering what to do next.

The barmaid leaned over me, smelling of smoke. "You're an unfamiliar face," she said, not unfriendly.

"I'm new to the city," I replied, sipping at the whisky, nearly choking at the bite. It was some kill-me-deadly distillation from a hill-still, I guessed, and I doubted it had paid any duty.

"I can tell that." The woman had a broad Edinburgh accent.

"I'm looking for a man named Sandy," I said.

"Lots of men with that name," the barmaid said. "Does he have a surname?"

"Sandy Tait," I said. "Somebody told me he comes in here."

"I'll ask around," the barmaid said. "I'll tell you if he comes in." She moved to another customer, spoke briefly to one of the flashtails and returned to her position behind the counter. I laid my staff on the battered table-top, leaned back on the wall and waited without much hope.

I sat still as more people crowded into the single room, some of whom I recognised. The pockmarked man who had fought outside my door was there, crouched over a jug of whisky and a thick glass that he seemed desperate to fill and empty as quickly as he could. As the night wore on, the noise level rose, and a brightly-dressed flashtail pushed through the crowd to my side.

"Are you the man looking for Sandy?" She was remarkably good looking underneath her face paint, while her tawdry-flash clothes detracted from rather than improved her appearance.

"I am he," I answered gravely, making space for the woman to sit beside me.

"I can take you to Sandy." The woman sat down, pressing her hip against mine. "It will cost you a drink."

"And worth the price." I signalled to the barmaid, who jostled towards us with her jug. "A whisky for the lady," I said. "Fill her glass to the brim." I paid with a flourish, hoping to be thought generous.

"My name is Jenny," the prostitute said.

"Good evening, Jenny. My name is Martin." I bowed from my seat.

"Oh!" Jenny smiled. "You are a proper gentleman!" She gurgled her whisky. "Would you like me to take you to Sandy?"

"I would like that," I said. "I was told he might be in here."

Jenny shook her head. "He's not here today. Come on then, and I'll show you."

"You are a very kind lady." I followed as Jenny made for the door, glancing over her shoulder to ensure that I was following her.

The World's End Close was busy as Jenny led me down the steep slope to the Cowgate, with the buildings deteriorating with every yard we walked. She stopped to wave to another of her kind, a woman in her thirties with a narrow face. "Katie, I'm taking my friend Martin to Sandy Tait's place."

"I'll come along too," Katie said, walking at my other side and exhaling enough whisky fumes to start a distillery. "I know Sandy well."

Side-by-side, we walked into the Cowgate, a narrow, nearly canyon-like street that ran parallel to the High Street at a lower level. At one time, the Cowgate had been the prosperous part of the city, but it had fallen on hard times. Now it was a back-slum comparable to the worst I had seen in Glasgow or anywhere else, a stinking, crumbling horror of a street where broken windows stared out like the sightless eyes of a diseased corpse.

"Sandy's in here!" Jenny took my hand and pulled me into the entrance to a common stair, with Kate a few steps behind. Without lighting of any sort, the stair stank of human urine and dampness, yet Jenny nearly ran up the stairs. "Just two more landings."

Four floors up a stone staircase that a hundred thousand feet had worn to slippery unevenness, Jenny stopped at a battered door, gave a sequence of knocks and patted my shoulder. "This is Sandy's house," she said. "He knows me!"

The instant the door opened, Jenny and Kate escorted me inside. I was in a single, shabby room where a box bed and a broken table took up most of the space. Two chairs and a sea-chest made up the rest of the furniture, all lit by a single tallow candle in a pewter holder.

A man lounged in the darkest corner, with the candlelight highlighting his high cheekbones and the line of his jaw. Although I knew instinctively that this was not the man I sought, I decided to play the game to its inevitable end.

"You must be Sandy," I said.

The man lurched forward. "Aye. Who are you?"

Before I had time to give my name, Sandy punched me hard in the stomach, and Kate wrapped both arms around me.

I gasped. Although I had been half expecting the attack, the speed took me by surprise. I wriggled, trying to kick my assailant as Jenny slid her hands inside my pockets with the deftness of long experience.

"Hit him again, Joe," Kate said, and Joe obliged, landing a solid punch to my midriff that laid me gasping on the filthy floor. He kicked me for good measure until I was sure he had bruised or fractured my ribs. I lay still as Kate and Jenny rifled my pockets of anything of value, laughing when they found the few gold sovereigns in my pocketbook.

I heard the door bang open, and the thunder of feet, a succession of crashes and roars, and then somebody was dragging me to my feet and depositing me on one of the chairs.

"Sit there, Doctor," a deep voice said. "You should have known better, walking into a place like this. What were you thinking?"

Gasping for breath, I massaged my stomach and tenderly probed my ribs. Nothing was broken, but I'd be in pain for some time. "I was looking for a man named Sandy Tait."

"Aye. I heard."

I looked up to see the gaunt-faced man standing over me. Joe was on the floor, curled into a foetal position with a spreading bruise over his forehead, and Jenny sat on the floor, holding her face.

"Here." The gaunt-marked man handed over my pocketbook with the few coins inside, and the silk handkerchief Jenny had extracted from my pocket.

"Thank you. I owe you a debt of gratitude."

"Aye, you can thank me later. Best get away from here before that other hell-bitch brings all her friends. She got away while I was dealing with Joe Maguire."

I nodded, fighting the pain. "Who are you?"

"Sandy Tait," the gaunt-faced man said. "Come on." He stepped over my staff as if it was something lethal, lifted the candle and left the house.

When I regained my staff, Sandy shook his head. "Leave that behind!"

"I will not," I said. "I'm not leaving these people with any sort of prize."

The candlelight only emphasised the foul state of the stair as we descended, and Sandy tossed the candle away when we reached the street. "That light will attract predators as surely as it attracts moths," he said.

"My house is in the West Bow," I said. "I must thank you for helping me."

"I know where your house is," Sandy said shortly. "I would not go there if my life depended on it."

I remembered Sandy had not stepped over my threshold. "Is there a place we can talk?" I tapped my staff on the ground as we walked.

Sandy glanced at me. "We won't talk in a public," he said. "My house."

I wondered if I was being led into another ambush, gripped

my staff tightly and nodded. "As you wish, Sandy. Then you can tell me why you are following me."

"It's just as well I am," Sandy said.

Feeling the ache from my ribs, I did not disagree.

Sandy lived in the third storey of a close off the Lawnmarket, a few hundred yards down from the castle, with windows that looked north towards the New Town. After only a few weeks in the Old Town, I had become used to squalor so I was pleasantly surprised to find Sandy's house neat, clean and well, if simply, furnished.

"Could you leave your stick outside the door, please, Doctor?"

I did as Sandy requested, although with some reluctance.

"Now then, Doctor," Sandy said, pulling back a chair for me, "why do you wish to see me?"

"Ruth Anderson mentioned your name," I said. "She said you had bottom." Now that I saw Sandy in his own environment, I wondered if he was the right man to ask. He seemed out of place amid the dereliction of the Old Town. Although his face was ravaged, intelligence gleamed in his eyes and his clothes were clean and had once been of good quality.

"Aye." Sandy sat opposite me at the walnut table. "Why would I need that?"

I had to gather all my nerves to ask the next question. "I wanted to dig up a body from a graveyard, and Ruth told me you could be the man to ask."

Sandy grunted as he produced a bottle of whisky and two squat tumblers. "Did she now?" When he stared across the table at me, I saw dark shadows behind his intelligent eyes. "Why would you want a corpse, Doctor? Can't you just wait for one of your patients to die?"

About to give an angry retort, I remembered that Sandy

had rescued me and smiled instead. "I am not that sort of doctor," I said. "Could you help me?"

After pouring out two generous glasses of whisky, Sandy nodded. "I can. It will take another man and some organising, tools, a fresh body, somewhere to deposit the corpse, and a route between the graveyard and the depositary."

"Yes." I had not thought of the organisation involved.

"I'll keep my eyes and ears open for deaths and burials," Sandy spoke like a professional. "How much are you offering?"

"Offering?"

"I don't work for nothing," Sandy said. "How much?"

We discussed costs for a few moments as Sandy tried to drain the bottle at a single sitting. When we eventually shook hands on a figure, I left the details in Sandy's hands.

"Now," I said, "there is another matter to discuss."

"You want to know why I am following you," Sandy said quietly.

"That's correct."

"I am trying to look after you." Sandy sipped at his whisky, with his eyes level with mine. "You are not yet ready to hear the full story, Doctor."

"Why is that?"

Sandy placed his glass on the walnut table. "You would not believe me," he said simply.

I took a deep breath, decided I needed this man's help and kept my words to myself. "Tell me when you are ready," I said.

"That might not be long," Sandy told me, standing up. "I'll be in touch about the resurrection," he said, indicating I should leave. He smiled when I looked confused. "That's what we call stealing a dead body."

~

There was a sliver of moon that night, alternately appearing and disappearing behind scudding clouds. Together with the fitful wind, the blinking moonlight added an element of unreality to my nocturnal visit. I stood in the shadow of the ancient kirk of Greyfriars for some minutes, gathering my nerve for the ordeal to come.

"I hope there are no bluebottles around," I said to break the tense silence.

"It's not them you have to worry about," Sandy said. "They've got regular beats to patrol. We lie low when they're due, and they're never any the wiser."

"Do you do this often?" I asked.

"About once a month." The other man, Andrew, rubbed a hand over his face. He was the pockmarked brawler from outside my house.

"It's the grave watchers you have to watch for." Sandy nodded to the watchtower in the corner of the graveyard. "They can be vicious when they choose."

"Vicious?"

"Aye. The watchmen will murder you if it's a relative of theirs you try to lift," Sandy said.

"Remember poor Jimmy Begg." Andrew shook his head.

"Aye." Sandy nodded.

I waited for illumination and eventually had to press. "What happened to Jimmy Begg?"

"He was the gravedigger at the Howff in Dundee just the other week. The mob suspected him of lifting the bodies and damn near killed him, so they did. They tried to bury him alive, him and his wife."

I shivered, imagining the horror of being thrown in an open grave while a howling mob threw spadesful after spadesful of soil on top of me. This grave robbing was more dangerous than

I had thought, and all this talk was increasing my nervous tension. "What are we waiting for?"

"The bobby." Sandy pushed me down. "Keep still."

I lay with my face pressed against the damp grass, yet a shaft of moonlight enabled me to see a policeman's polished tall hat slowly pass by the graveyard. He stopped to peer over the wall, with the beam from his lantern probing the gravestones and small trees. I breathed as quietly as I could, with the grass cold against my face, and then the light clicked off as the policeman closed the shutter of his lantern. I could hear the portentous thump-thump of the constable's heavy boots on the ground, and then he was gone, leaving dishonest folk space to work.

"He'll be back in 30 minutes," Sandy said. "Come on and, for the love of God, keep quiet."

Moving in a low crouch, Sandy left our hiding place and ran to a grave near the very centre of the cemetery. Andrew followed, carrying a heavy bag, and I was in the rear with my heart hammering so loudly I was surprised it did not alert the now-invisible policeman. The gravestones protruded from the grass, some decorated with cross-bones and skulls whose empty eye-sockets accused us of the crime we intended to commit. Once again, I wondered why I was here. I was a respectable doctor, for goodness sake, the son of a kirk elder, not some blackguard ne'er do well from the refuse of society.

"Here's the grave," Sandy stopped at a patch of newly turned earth and checked the stone. "Henrietta Brown. There's no mortstone, thank God. Fate has been kind to us."

"What's a mortstone?" I asked as Andrew opened his bundle and handed out two spades.

"A heavy stone that the relatives place on top of the grave to keep people like us out. Now keep quiet." Sandy and Andrew were already digging, gouging out the dirt at the very foot of the grave. About to ask why they were not working at the grave itself, I closed my mouth, aware it was best to leave such details to the experts.

With two active, experienced men working hard, it took less time than I had imagined to dig a six-foot deep hole just outside the grave. Sandy ordered the loose earth piled up in the lee of two gravestones, hidden from any curious passers-by or lantern-carrying constables.

"Right, Andy," Sandy whispered, and Andrew hauled himself out of the hole and crouched low on the ground.

I heard Sandy swear then, a low-voiced torrent of foul words. "They've laced branches around the coffin."

"What?" I checked my watch. Fifteen minutes had passed since we began. Another 15 and the policeman would return.

"Flexible branches," Andrew said. "It makes it much harder to get into the coffin. We'll have to cut our way in." Without another word, Andrew lifted a pair of heavy shears from his bag and dropped into the hole beside Sandy. I heard the slow snipping of the shears and saw an occasional cut bough thrown clear of the grave.

"Doctor!" Sandy's whisper was urgent. "Take this." He handed up the bough of a tree, complete with a tangle of thorned branches. "Be careful; it's a bloody bramble branch!"

I dragged the branches away, gasping when the sharp thorns tore into my hands. The family of the deceased were undoubtedly making us work for our body.

"That's 20 minutes!" I hissed, checking my watch. "Hurry it up!"

"Here, Doc!" Sandy passed up another bundle of thorny branches.

"*Cave*!" I said, forgetting the Latin word would mean nothing to them. "Careful! Somebody's coming!"

I heard the low murmur of voices before I saw the movement from the watchtower. I saw a yellow oblong as the door opened, the outline of a man against the light and then darkness again as the door closed.

"Still!" Sandy said, and we all froze in our positions, for nothing gives the hunted away quicker than sudden movement. The man lurched out of the watchtower, stopped to light a lantern and began a slow circuit of the graveyard. I watched the yellow circle of lamplight bob closer, lay as close to the earth as I could and prayed for help.

The man was muttering something and staggering as he walked. I saw him stumble, and as he came closer, I could smell the whisky on his breath. I glanced down the hole and saw Sandy lift the spade, holding it like a weapon, and I knew if the watchman found us, there would be bloodshed.

Oh, dear God, I said to myself. *I don't want to add murder to grave robbing. What had I let myself in for here?*

I had my watch in my hand and flicked open the silver case. Twenty-five minutes had elapsed since the policeman had passed. He was due in five minutes, and we had not even got the body out of the grave yet.

The watchman stumbled again and dropped his lantern. The light rolled, blinking on, off and on, with its whale oil sloshing but the wick miraculously remaining alight. The watchman swore, pushed himself upright and stomped to pick his lantern up.

"Halloa there!"

My heart raced at the unexpected challenge.

"Who's that? Who's that in there?' The policeman was two minutes early, peering into the graveyard with the light from his lantern casting long shadows among the gravestones. I heard Andrew take in a long breath.

"It's me, constable," the watchman said. "Jimmy Prentice, the watchman. I dropped my lantern."

"Well, pick it up then and don't be so damned careless," the policeman sounded annoyed at being robbed of a potential arrest. "Is there anything happening there?"

"Not a thing," Jimmy Prentice said. 'All quiet, constable." He lifted his lantern and stomped back to the watchtower, still mumbling to himself.

I waited until the policeman had stalked away out of sight before whispering, "All clear," to my two companions.

"Wait," Sandy hissed. "That constable's no fool. He knows resurrection men are busy this season and he might double back to catch us unawares."

I felt the sweat cold on my spine as I tried to burrow into the earth behind the nearest gravestone. *Here lie the mortal remains of James Arnot*, it read, *rest with the Lord.*

"Right, Andy," Sandy whispered, and they began again immediately, handing up yet another bundle of dangerous thorns before beginning work on the end of the coffin.

"They've nailed the woman in," Andrew said, with an oath.

"Is that bad?"

"Damned right it's bad!" Andrew emphasised his words with a string of oaths, each one more obscene than the last. "I can unscrew screws without noise, but we have to wrench open nails. Let's hope the Lord has not blessed the watchmen with good hearing."

Listening to the choruses of uproarious singing that erupted from the watchtower, I doubted the watchmen would hear anything less than an earthquake that night.

"Give a hand here, Andy," Sandy said.

I could only lie on the ground and watch as Andrew and Sandy inserted a slender jemmy into the foot of the coffin and gradually eased it away from the sides. To my ears, the resurrection men made sufficient noise to wake the dead, but evidently not enough to alert the watchmen, for nobody came to investigate the commotion. At last, the end panel came away, revealing a simple linen endover and the feet of a body, with the shroud rolled back.

"Here we are." Sandy and Andrew struggled up with the corpse of Henrietta Brown, still wrapped in its white shroud. "Take this, Doc."

I helped drag the body from its resting place to the surface and watched in something like horror as my two companions calmly removed the clothes, leaving the body whitely naked on the ground.

"What are you doing?" I asked.

"We're resurrection men," Sandy explained. "Not common thieves. Taking clothes is stealing." He examined the body, removed the wedding ring from the finger and carefully replaced it, with the shroud, inside the coffin. "We'd likely get transported if they found us with that ring," he explained. "Possessions are more valuable than dead people."

With more skill than many a nurse, Andy wrapped the body in a long black sheet, hoisted it over his shoulder and stood in a half-crouch, with the ranked gravestones partly shielding him.

"Come on, Doc," Sandy said. "That's us all done now."

With Sandy carrying the tool bag and Andrew the body, we made our way to the wall where we had entered the graveyard. I cannot articulate the relief I felt as Sandy tossed the tools over the wall and hoisted himself to the top.

"Hand it up, Andy," he held out both hands for the corpse.

"Halloa!" The shout took me entirely by surprise. "You with the body!"

CHAPTER 6

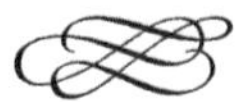

At the precise moment I thought we had succeeded, a host of men exploded from the watchtower and ran towards us. In the heat of the moment, Andy cursed and dropped the corpse. He and I both scrabbled for it, both swearing mightily. The watchmen brandished an assortment of weapons that ranged from an ancient pike that might have done duty at Flodden, to a wide-muzzled blunderbuss.

"There they are!" somebody shouted, his voice slurred with alcohol, "over by the wall!"

"Andy!" Sandy held out his hands again, making long arms as he stretched down as far as he could.

Lifting the body, we thrust it into Sandy's hands, pushing to help him drag it over the wall.

"Jesus," Andy blasphemed, glancing over his shoulder. "There's hundreds of them."

"I've got her," Sandy was the calmest man among us as he grasped the body and, with an impressive display of strength and skill, rolled it across him and lowered it gently on the opposite side of the wall.

"They're getting away!" I heard the despairing wail, and seconds after, the terrible roar of the blunderbuss as the owner chanced a shot.

I felt the sharp sting as something slammed into my arm, and heard Andy yell shrilly as blunderbuss pellets propelled him up the wall. In a second, we were lying on the ground outside, with the corpse amidst us.

"I got them!" one of the watchmen shouted. "I got two of them as clean as you like. They'll be dead before morning unless they're dead already."

"I saw one's head come off!" Somebody else roared. "You killed him, Watty!"

Sandy, unscathed, was first up and still calm. "We can't stay here," he said. "Come on. Can you lads stand?"

I could. My wound was not severe. Andrew was worse, with blood seeping from his thigh and shoulder.

"I can stand." Andrew rose shakily, holding his wounds.

"Come on." Sandy threw the body over his shoulder as if it were a sack of potatoes while I lifted the tools. By the time we got moving, the watchers' heads were bobbing above the wall, with their faces white in the moonlight.

"There they are!" somebody shouted. "Shoot them again, Watty!"

"Move, lads!" Sandy led us into an intricate web of small streets, turning this way and that to evade any pursuit. I was lost within two minutes, and could only follow, helping Andrew as he faltered from time to time.

"We've lost them," I said, glancing over my shoulder.

"Where do you want the body?" Sandy remained the calmest of the three of us.

"My home," I said at once. "It's closer than the surgery."

"I know where it is," Sandy snapped. "We're not going in there."

"Why the devil not?" I was agitated by that time, with my nerves stretched to their limit, and my muscles aching with helping Andrew. The wound where the pellets had hit me was smarting abominably.

"I'm not going in there," Sandy repeated. "I'll take the body to the door, and that's it."

"I can't go much further," Andy was limping heavily, so I had to support him with my uninjured arm.

I looked over my shoulder in case the watchers were following. I could see nothing except the grimy houses. "All right," I said. "Leave the body at the door. I'll pay you tomorrow."

"You'll pay us now."

"The agreement was to deliver the corpse," I said. "That means taking it into my home."

"Damn you, Doctor. The door is close enough, or I can drop the thing here and now and shout out murder!"

I knew a cry of murder in this neighbourhood would either be ignored, or might bring the police with their batons and rattles, and that was the last thing I wished. A doctor caught body-snatching could wave a fond farewell to his career.

"To the door then, Sandy," I agreed, reluctantly, "and damn you for a scoundrel."

Sandy nearly threw the body at the door and waited, with his hand held out.

"My pocketbook's inside," I said, making him wait as I fumbled for a key and entered the house. All was as I had left it, so it was the work of a minute to fish my pocketbook from the locked drawer, extract Sandy's fee and press it into his palm.

"You're trembling, man," I said in surprise after his impressive coolness throughout the excitement of the night.

"So would you, if you knew the truth." Sandy closed his fist on my sovereigns. "I'd not let Andy in there either, Doctor."

"Andrew needs my help," I said, for in truth Andrew was near fainting from nervous shock, pain and loss of blood.

The moment I half-dragged, half-carried Andrew inside the house, Sandy bolted. There is no other word to describe his panic-driven retreat. Leaving his companion in my care, he turned and ran across the courtyard and vanished in the darkness of the echoing close. I told Andrew to sit, hauled in the corpse and dumped it in an untidy heap on the floor, with neither dignity nor respect. Taking red embers from the fire with a pair of tongs, I lit half a dozen candles and arranged them around the room before adding fuel to the fire and holding a newspaper in front to encourage the flames.

"Clothes off, Andrew," I said. He groaned a lot as I stripped him of his clothing so I could see the extent of his wounds. "Now face down on the table."

"You're not too bad, Andy." I was more than relieved to see Andy's injuries were minor, if painful. "About a dozen pellets in your upper leg and shoulder, none of them too deep. Our grave-watching friend did not have a full charge of powder in his gun, thank God. I'll have to pluck the pellets out, and then I'll wash and dress the wounds." My own injuries were paining me but would have to wait. The patient came first.

"Do it quick!" Andrew wriggled, trying to look over his shoulder.

"Lie still!" I ordered and gave him a drink of whisky to settle his nerves and dull his senses. I had nothing else in the house.

Each lead pellet lay in a small swelling, seeping with blood, with some clearly visible and others under the surface of the skin. I used forceps to take out the first and dropped it with a tiny clink into a small dish at my side. "Nothing serious," I said cheerfully as I cleaned up the wound with whisky and Andy wriggled and gasped. "It will sting for a day and then subside to a dull ache. Not a single pellet penetrated deeply enough to cause any problem."

"Thank you, Doctor," Andrew said, again and again. "Thank you, Doctor."

It took an hour to remove all the pellets from Andrew, patch him up and dress him again. By that time, my wounds were aching abominably, and my arm was already stiffening.

"You'd better get off home," I said, pressing Andrew's wages into his palm. "Don't exert yourself for a day or two to give the wounds time to heal."

"Thank you, Doctor," Andrew said again, clutching his money. He looked around the house as if expecting all the demons of hell to emerge from the cupboards and carry him away. As I saw him wend his uneven way across the courtyard and into the close, I wondered if I should escort him to his house, decided that he was old enough and strong enough to manage without my help and retired indoors.

I was exhausted after the labours of the night, but my injuries demanded that I deal with them. Propping a mirror on top of my table, I stripped off my shirt and began to probe for the pellets. There were six of them, half-hidden among a sheen of blood, and, by the time I removed them all, I was shaking and the level of whisky in the bottle had reduced alarmingly. Twice I thought I saw another image in the mirror, a shadowy man with a long nose, but I shook my head, knowing that pain and alcohol can work on the imagination. Gasping, I dressed my wounds as best I could, then lay back in the chair and wondered what to do next.

I knew I had to move the corpse to my surgery, but that was a problem that would have to wait until later. Dragging the body into a cupboard, I left it there and reposed myself to sleep, with my shoulder aching fit to wake the dead.

It was the remorseless ticking of the clock that woke me. I

lay still, listening, confident that I had not wound it up, yet there it was, with that soft, insistent tick. Unable to rest, I forced myself upright and walked to the clock. The arms were the same as before, six minutes past six, yet I had placed them at noon, and there was no sound of ticking. The clock was as silent as any grave. Replacing the arms at noon, I opened the shutters and peered into the courtyard. It was also quiet, with one solitary beggar man sheltering in a doorway.

Convincing myself that I was dreaming, I closed my eyes, ignored the nagging pain from my shoulder and again composed myself to sleep. That was when the singing started. It was low at first, with the occasional drunken laugh, yet soon increased in volume until I threw myself out of bed and ran to the window to quieten down whoever was singing *Maggie Lauder* outside in the courtyard.

Nobody was out there.

"I'm imagining things," I said and returned to bed. I heard somebody laugh and then sleep took me, with nightmares of digging up corpses that giggled and smiled at me, while a shadowy man followed me, tapping my staff to a rhythm that sounded like the rumble of iron-shod wheels on a cobbled road.

I had no patients the next morning. Not one, despite trying to spread the word around the Old Town and the New. Forlorn, I searched for Sandy in Whisky Row and found him sitting alone at a table in Mrs McGuffy's tavern, staring into a glass of whisky as if he was contemplating deep philosophy.

"I might need you again," I said.

"Aye." Sandy did not stir from his seat. "You'll be wanting somebody to help carry the body from your house to the surgery."

"That's right," I said.

Finishing his glass, Sandy gave it a significant look until I beckoned to Mrs McGuffy to fill it again.

"That's the real Ferintosh," Sandy said, as the whisky splashed into his glass.

"Are there any sedan chairs left in Edinburgh?"

"A few," Sandy said. "Some of the older residents like them, and drunken gentlemen prefer the privacy of the closed box."

"Do you know any sedan chair porters that can be trusted?"

"I know the very men." Sandy finished his whisky with a single swallow. "When shall they call?"

"If they come to my house tonight," I began, only for Sandy to shake his head.

"They won't come to that house."

"Why ever not?"

Sandy surveyed me as if working out something. "How many people have warned you about living there?"

"Many," I admitted.

"Well, why don't you take their advice and bloody leave?"

"I'll be damned if I will," I said, wincing as my wound began to bite.

"You'll be damned if you don't," Sandy said quietly. He looked up, his eyes narrow under creased brows. "You told me once that you're not a local man, Doctor."

"I am not," I said. "I'm a Borderer, educated in Glasgow." I signalled to Mrs McGuffy for another refill.

"Have you ever heard about Major Weir?" Sandy asked abruptly.

I admitted that the name meant nothing to me.

Sandy waited until Mrs McGuffy was out of hearing before he continued. "You won't believe much of what I tell you," he said, "but I assure you it is true, and there's much more."

I sighed and sipped at my whisky. "Perhaps you had better educate me," I said.

"You'll know about the seventeenth-century Covenanters," Sandy said, with his voice altering from the local gutter-Edinburgh to something more educated. I wondered, then, from where he came and what his background was. Certainly, he no more belonged in this sink of iniquity than I did.

"I know the Covenanters were extreme Presbyterians," I said carefully. "Very devout men and women."

"That was them." Sandy's eyes were steady as he looked at me across the scarred circular table. Although the public was busy, I felt as if we were the only two there, with the others fading away into obscurity.

"Major Weir was one of the most devout of the devout, a veritable saint among saints, a man who dressed in black yet whose soul and lifestyle was as white as an angel's wings. I have heard that some called him Angelical Thomas."

Sandy's turn of phrase convinced me once more that he was not an ordinary man.

"Carry on, my good fellow." I wondered if drink had been the cause of Sandy's downfall, for he downed his whisky as if determined to drain the bottle dry.

"Well, Doctor, Major Weir was not all he seemed. He was no angel; indeed, he was the very opposite of an angel." Sandy stopped for a moment, staring into his glass, where light from the tiny window reflected through the pale amber of his whisky. "He was the devil himself, the incarnation of evil, a man to whom sin came more readily than prayer, and whose every breath reeked of brimstone."

I raised my eyebrows at Sandy's words, for they smacked of something more than a mere retelling of a folk-tale. They meant something to him.

"What did this Major Weir fellow do?" I asked.

Sandy lowered his voice. "Demonology, bestiality, sorcery and incest," he said. "I won't go into details, Doctor, for they are too horrible even for a doctor of medicine to hear. In short, Major Weir was a warlock. Anyway, his guilt forced a confession and Weir and his sister Grizel were interrogated in the Tolbooth. The judge ordered them to be executed for witchcraft, devil worship and a host of other sins."

I noted Sandy said sins rather than crimes. "His sister as well?"

"I did say incest," Sandy said. "Although she gave more details. She claimed that a fiery coach had carried the Major from his house to Dalkeith, and on the journey, he gained supernatural powers, as well as a carved black staff topped with the likeness of a human head."

I immediately thought of the staff that now lay on the ground at my feet.

"Grizel, or Jean, Weir, the sister, also said their mother, Lady Jean Somerville, was also a witch, and in that period, the 1670s, such things were strongly believed."

"They were," I said. "Not so much now, though."

Sandy looked at me through these remarkably clear eyes. "Perhaps more so than you realise, doctor, particularly among those less educated than you, or rather, those with less formal education than you have."

"Is there a connection with my house?" I asked.

"You are living in Weir's house," Sandy said.

I took another draught of the whisky. "Is that why nobody comes inside, except Ruth Anderson? They are scared of his memory?"

Mrs McGuffy was ready with the whisky even before Sandy finished his glass. She filled it again, nodded to me and filled my glass as well.

"That's right. Major Weir, or the Wizard Weir, was strangled and burned at Gallow Lee, halfway between Edinburgh and Leith, on April 14, 1670." Sandy spoke to his whisky now, rather than to me. "The executioner buried what was left of him at the foot of the gallows there. Before he died, he confessed to incest and refused to ask the Lord to be merciful to him. Instead, he said he had lived as a beast and must die as a beast."

I nodded. "That still does not explain why nobody enters my house," I said. "Weir was evidently mentally unstable. He was no more a wizard than I am and, although incest is detestable, it is not a disease. It cannot be caught, especially after this length of time."

Sandy nursed his whisky. "There are other things, Doctor, things that cannot be explained in that house where Weir lived."

"Nonsense!" I scoffed, too loudly, for I remembered the clock that moved without being wound, the music, and the sound of a coach in an empty street.

"Too many people have seen things for it to be nonsense, Doctor." Again Sandy spoke in his educated, sensible voice and I knew this was no scion of the gutter to believe the superstitious clatter of the masses. "For instance, a long-legged phantom has been seen in the very courtyard outside your front door."

"I have seen no such thing," I said. "Nor do I believe in such an apparition."

"People have seen lights when no earthly inhabitant resided in that house," Sandy said, "and Weir has been seen against the window and sometimes stalking the streets. People have heard dancing, singing, and a howling, like a soul in agony, and the sound of a spinning wheel. The major leaves the close mounted on a black horse, and sometimes a coach is seen, or heard, a black coach and six, as the Devil comes to claim his own."

"I have seen none of these things," I took a somewhat deeper draught of my whisky that time, as I remembered my recent experiences.

"That is well," Sandy said, "for to hear or see the coach is a warning of imminent death."

I avoided mentioning hearing a coach, or the other incidents. "I am too young to die yet," I said with a smile. "I feel I am only now beginning to live." I beckoned for more whisky. "Come now, Sandy, I do not believe that my house has lain empty ever since 1670."

"It has not," Sandy did not respond to my smile. "About a century after the Weirs were executed, a man found the courage to live in that house. His name was William Patullo, an old soldier who had travelled the world and seen all the horrors it had to offer. He looked on any sort of supernatural entities with great cynicism and scoffed at the idea that Major Weir had left anything evil behind."

"A man after my own heart," I said.

Sandy looked directly at me again. "Patullo and his wife moved in with great ceremony, as half the population of the West Bow came to watch. The evening passed without incident, and they went to bed, only for a strange light to emanate from the fireplace and a figure to loom over them, some creature like a calf stared at them, with its forefeet on the bed itself."

I could not repress a shiver at that thought. "Did the soldier Patullo shoot the calf?"

"He left the next morning," Sandy said, "and never returned. You've already lasted longer than him."

"I am a man of science," I said. "I believe in what I can see and touch, not in the tales old women spin to scare bairns to sleep." I sipped at my whisky. "We are a hard-headed bunch in the Borders!"

Standing up, Sandy downed the remnants of his whisky in a single draught. "I'll see you at eleven tonight in your court-yard, Doctor. I'll bring the sedan, you bring the cargo." He gave a small smile. "You will understand when I remind you that we won't be entering that house."

With the body wrapped in a sheet, I propped it up within the open door and waited for the arrival of the sedan chair. As so often, there were cries nearby, as clans of Irish fought each other in a drunken fury. I ignored the sounds, glad they were entertaining each other rather than spying on my rather more nefarious pursuit. A lone seagull circled above, landed hope-fully, realised that the human scavengers had picked the place clean and flew off.

I heard the cursing before the porters appeared in the courtyard, squeezing the sedan chair through the narrow close.

"Are you ready, doctor?" Sandy looked around him.

"Here we are." I pointed to the corpse.

"Come on, then." Rather than the injured Andy, Sandy's companion was a morose Highland Donald with a broad blue bonnet pulled low over his forehead and neatly trimmed whiskers. He favoured me with a glower that might have been intended as a smile. We bundled the body into the sedan, pulled shut the curtains and began the short journey to my surgery.

"How much?" I asked as we unloaded our cargo. The Donald looked around him as though he had never entered such a place before.

"A guinea," Sandy spoke for them both. "Each."

I parted with the money, weighed my rapidly-emptying purse and hoped that this gamble would work.

"Remember what I said about your house," Sandy reminded as he left the surgery, while the Donald stared at me, wordless.

"I'll remember," I said, "although I am not superstitious." I tapped my staff on the floor, planning how to attract students to my small surgery. I pushed Sandy's words out of my head as soon as he left the surgery, for I had neither the desire nor the expectation of seeing him again.

Once students learned that I was giving an anatomy class, they arrived in small numbers. I kept the entrance fee low, to encourage a larger crowd, for I was competing not only with Charles but also with the famous Doctor Knox.

I did not attract as many students as I had hoped, for my surgery did not have the facilities to hold scores of people. However, I charged a guinea per head, the men who did come were enthusiastic, and I pocketed their money without a qualm.

With the blood washed away and what remained of the body buried in a deep pit at the back of the surgery, I counted the takings. I smiled, for although my conscience bothered me a little over digging up a body and dissecting it without the family's permission, the money would undoubtedly help towards more salubrious surroundings of which Evelyn would approve.

My shoulder still pained me, and I had received quite a scare. I wondered if I would try that route again. I sighed, remembering the enthusiastic idealist who had swum out to Cramond Island. What had happened to change me so rapidly?

The reality of life, I told myself, tapping my staff on the

floor. That staff seemed warm in my hand as if throbbing with a life of its own. Even the designs appeared to have altered, for they looked less abstract now as if they were forming a new pattern. I shook my head at the notion, wiped off some splashes of blood and walked back home.

When I looked up, I swear that the man in the mirror was examining me. It was not my face, but that of an older man with a prominent nose, although the features were so blurred that I could not recognise them. I started, trying to awake from what I was sure must be a nightmare.

The eyes held mine. They were brown, with an intense stare such as I had never seen before. I tried to look away, failed, closed my eyes, opened them again and shuddered, unable to escape from that terrible gaze.

"Who are you?" I asked, striving to stand. I could not. I was stuck in my chair as firmly as if somebody had bound me with cords of brass.

There was no reply, nothing except those eyes, fixed on mine like twin gimlets boring inside my head, probing ever deeper into my brain as if the owner had me on the dissecting table and was slicing inside me. I could feel his mind tearing at mine, peeling away layer after layer of my person, stripping me naked before the collected eyes of hundreds, thousands, millions of people. That blurred face came closer until I fancied I saw it emerge from the mirror. The brass bonds prevented me from pulling back as the man entered me, his eyes became my eyes, his mind coalesced with mine, and then he dissipated throughout my body. He emerged again, although I knew he remained inside me, part of who I had become, or who *we* had become.

I lay on the dissecting table, alone, frightened and vulnerable as the people crowded round, generation after generation of people, watching as the long-nosed man who was now part of me bent closer, exposing my faults, sins and weaknesses. I screamed at the blade of his eyes cut me, and the darkness poured out, to merge with the greater dark all around. The inner and outer darkness formed shapes, the like of which I did not understand as music and laughter surrounded me. The crowd was celebrating as I suffered, dancing to the slice of the blade.

"Who are you?" I writhed on the table, peering upwards, until the face that stared into mine altered, the nose shrunk, the eyes became clearer, and the features came into focus. I was looking at myself as I held the steel dissecting saw.

"You're me!" I yelled, pulling at the brass bonds.

The bonds snapped in a fountain of blood, and I sat up on that terrible table with the sweat draining from me. I was in my surgery, although how I got there, I did not know. All the tools of my trade were where I had left them, neat, clean, professional. I lurched to the door, realised I was as naked as the day I was born and cast around for something to wear. My clothes had gone, and I wondered if I had wandered naked from the West Bow to the Grassmarket, and hoped nobody had seen me, for respectable doctors did not walk around in a state of nudity.

I saw a long black cloak hanging from a peg and wrapped it around me. It smelled of acrid smoke. Grabbing my staff, I opened the door, to step into a Grassmarket that was nothing like I remembered, with the cries of hundreds of people rising above the smoke. What were these people doing here at this time of night?

It was not night. It was only evening, and I smelt something nauseating, the hellish scent of burning flesh. Was there a fire? Were these people fleeing from a house fire? No, they were gathered in the centre of the street, shouting, pointing their fingers, chanting something I could not make out.

The words became more explicit. "Hang the witch! Hang the witch!" There was no fire, no flames, only an old woman standing under a gallows tree, screaming imprecations at the crowd.

Hugging my cloak around me, I hurried past, thankful not to be seen as I began the climb up the steep slope of the West Bow. I heard the new sound above the roar of the crowd. It was the rumble of iron-shod wheels on the ancient cobbles, augmented by the drumbeat of hooves. The coach and six hammered down the steep slope until it stopped beside the close that led to my courtyard.

I could smell the smoke again, although it seemed to come from the coach itself, rather than from the Grassmarket. The driver was hunched on his perch, looking at me with the same fixed glare I had seen in the mirror, his eyes missing nothing. He crooked a skeletal finger towards me, indicating that I join him in his coach.

"No!" I shook my head. "No," for I knew the destination of that coach. I would not go there. "You can't have me!"

The laughter came then, coiling around me, mocking everything I had once held dear.

"I am not coming!" I said.

I walked without effort, gliding up the street with my staff tapping on the ancient stones. As I drew level with the coach, the door opened wide, and a man peered out. I knew his face. With those stern brown eyes and that prominent nose, I knew it was the man who stared at me from the mirror, yet there were others behind him, one a woman and the other was me.

I woke with the sweat easing from my scalp to my feet, quickly cooling in the dark of my front room, so I knew I must change my clothes or risk a chill. I must have fallen asleep as soon as I sat down.

With the images still vivid in my head, I quickly stripped off my clothes. Ruth Anderson had made up the fire, so it was the work of a second to strike a spark and set it alight. The comforting warmth and light spread through the room, chasing away the shadows of my nightmare. Pouring myself a glass of claret, I swigged it down, allowing the sensation to relax my nerves before I poured a second. Firelight glistened through the glass, giving life to the red liquid. I drank the second glass more slowly, savouring the flavour and effect.

Although I was awake, I could still feel the intrusion, as if the long-nosed man from my dream was inside my head, and inside my body. I smiled, strangely at peace with the notion I shared everything with another.

The flames were mounting nicely, so I lifted the fireside tongs and added more coal, building it sufficiently to last the night before I sat back, holding my glass. When I was a child in Roxburghshire, it was a little fancy of mine to look into the flames and see what pictures I could devise, and for some reason, I did the same now. I saw a dragon, raising orange wings to fly up the lum, and I saw a volcano, spouting fire. Behind the volcano was something else, something I recognised from a time long past. I saw a woman, poised on a cart with a noose around her neck. Once again, I heard the chanting of the crowd, and the woman looked at me through eyes that were brown and instantly recognisable.

"My sister!" I cried, and, unthinking, thrust my hand into the flames to untie the noose.

The smart of the fire forced me to withdraw with a curse, and I held my injured hand, wondering what had possessed me to make such a foolish move.

"My sister," I repeated and shook my head. "I have no sister," I said.

I spread goose fat over my injured hand and bandaged it, wondering how I could be so foolish. The fact that I, a trained and qualified doctor, had performed such an act of stupidity bordered on insanity.

As I drank my third glass of claret, I looked again at the fire, seeing nothing except burning coal. *I have no sister*, I told myself, although I had a clear image of a brown-eyed woman who was undoubtedly not Evelyn.

Later that night, the noises began again. I lay in bed, heard the laughter of some drunken fool, cursed and pulled the covers over my head to get peace. I got none. If anything, the revelry increased, with hoots of mirth accompanied by singing.

I recognised the song as *Maggie Lauder*, a folk song that must be a 150 years old at least.

"Wha wadna be in love
Wi' bonnie Maggie Lauder?
A piper met her guan to Fife,
And spier'd what was't they ca'd her;
Right scornfully she answer'd him,
Begone you hallanshaker,
Jog on your gate,
ye bladderskate,
My name is Maggie Lauder."

I sat up in bed, cursing. The room was in darkness, with the embers of the fire dead and all the candles doused. I knew I was alone in the house, for only Ruth dared enter, so the carousing must be outside in the courtyard. Staggering to my feet, I lurched to the window, threw back the shutters and stared out.

There was nothing. The courtyard was as bare as a bald man's head.

"What the devil is happening?" I asked myself. "Am I imagining things now? Has Sandy Tait's nonsense influenced me in some way?" I shook my head and laughed again as if such an idea was the most amusing thing in the world.

Lifting my staff, I retired to bed, where we could be alone. The words of *Maggie Lauder* coursed through my head as I fell asleep.

CHAPTER 7

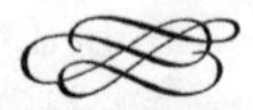

"DOCTOR!" The woman was out of breath and dishevelled as she appeared at the door of my surgery. "You must come quickly!"

I reached for my bag. "Whatever is the matter?"

"There's been a terrible accident." The woman was in distress, with her hair loose beneath her hat and her eyes wild. "She's lying there, all covered in blood."

"Take me to her." I closed and locked the surgery door, for, in the Grassmarket, an open door was merely an invitation to thieves. "Calm yourself now, and tell me what happened."

It was hardly past six in the morning, and I had just stepped into the surgery, with only a few traders' carts in the streets and the closes empty. A stray dog slinked past, intent on its own business.

"It was so sudden." The woman could not be quietened as she gabbled her news to me. "Hurry, doctor." She grabbed my sleeve to pull me along behind her. "It came out of nowhere, so it did."

I followed the woman along the dark canyon on the Cowgate. "What did? What came out of nowhere?"

"Out of nowhere," the woman repeated. "She's along here, all covered in blood."

The blood had flowed along the Cowgate cobbles, dark and thick and already congealing in the growing light. The body lay in a crumpled heap, face down and with both legs at such impossible angles that I knew they were badly broken. Even before I touched the victim, I knew she was dead, for nobody could sustain so many injuries and possibly survive.

"What happened?" I asked as I knelt to feel for a pulse I knew did not exist.

Three women stood beside the casualty, two looking fairly respectable for that locality and the third a typical denizen of the Cowgate, with tawdry ribbons to enhance her short-lived good looks and a skirt too short for respectability. All three women looked at me as if I could bring back the dead.

"It was a coach," the flashtail said. "It came out of nowhere, knocked her down and charged on without stopping."

"Well," I said, "this unfortunate woman won't be seeing any more coaches."

"Is she dead?" the flashtail asked.

"She is dead." I rolled the casualty over on her back and started. Ruth Anderson stared up with her eyes wide open and such a look of horror as I have never seen in a human being before. There was absolute terror in her eyes, while her mouth stretched in a soundless scream. "Oh, dear Lord in heaven," I said.

Even the flashtail, hardened by the sights and experiences of her profession, recoiled at the sight. "She looks like she seen a ghost."

"Aye," one of the other women said. "That's Ruth Anderson. She was aye poking her nose where it was not wanted."

"Can somebody help carry her to my surgery?" I asked.

Only the flashtail, the lowest woman there, stepped forward. I resolved to give her free, or at least cheaper, medical care if the opportunity ever arose. I have noted that in times of crisis, it is often the poorest and least outwardly respectable who come forward first.

Placing Miss Anderson on the examination table, I thanked the prostitute.

"Aye, nae bother," she said, with a sniff, looking around her. "I've never been to a doctor's surgery before."

"You can wash off the blood over there." I pointed to the basin and ewer on my sideboard.

The prostitute glanced at Miss Anderson. "She's been robbed an' all," she said, laconically.

"Robbed? How do you know?"

"See?" The prostitute prodded a dirty finger at the breast of Ruth's jacket. "See where it's torn? I'd wager a golden boy that somebody's ripped something off there. I wager she's not got a penny on her."

The prostitute was right about the torn jacket, but Ruth's purse was still inside her pocket, with seven shillings and three-pence inside it. I remembered the silver Celtic Cross that Ruth had worn at her breast. "Aye," I reverted to the speech of my childhood. "You're right about the ripped jacket." I threw over Ruth's purse. "You'd better have that," I said. "Miss Anderson has no further use for it."

"I'm no' robbing the dead," the prostitute sounded shocked. "That's not right."

I looked at the woman, with her broken shoes and tawdry clothes, the lines of hardship in her face and a life of constant degradation, yet beneath everything, this street prostitute retained a sense of right and wrong. "You're a good woman," I said.

"Good?" Her laugh would have mocked the angel Gabriel. "There's nothing good in this world, doctor. Not one bloody thing." With those cynical words, she left the surgery, leaving me wondering anew at humanity's balance of morality.

When I examined Miss Anderson, I discovered she had more than 20 broken bones, including eight ribs, two of which had penetrated her lungs. Yet although these injuries were severe, none of them was fatal on its own.

Naturally, I sent a boy to Charles for a second opinion. He came after his daily rounds, his honest face clouded.

"A massive heart seizure," Charles said, confirming my own diagnosis.

"She was a fit and healthy woman," I said. "She has no trace of heart disease." I lowered my voice to ensure nobody else could hear us in my nearly empty surgery. "If it were medically possible," I said, "I'd say this unfortunate woman died of fear."

Charles looked up with a smile, which quickly faded. "Perhaps that is not surprising when a carriage was hurtling towards her."

"Perhaps," I said. "Would you agree with my reasoning?"

"It is plausible," Charles said.

We had both seen death in too many forms to be seriously upset, although naturally, I was unhappy that somebody I knew had died in such a manner. I did not say what I really thought, for no sane man or woman would agree with me. I believed that Ruth Anderson had died because she had entered my house, the home of Weir the Wizard. I knew that if I even hinted something so foolish to Charles, the most hard-headed and matter-of-fact doctor would laugh me to scorn.

"Did you find out who drove the coach?" Charles asked. "It sounds as if they were guilty of furious driving."

"I reported the death to the police," I said. "A sergeant and a young constable asked me questions."

"What did you say the cause of death was?"

"Massive heart attack caused by trauma," I said, "in layman's terms. The police said they would seek the coach."

I knew they would not find it. Two witnesses had described the coach as large and black, pulled by a team of dark horses. The flashtail swore there were six horses while the more respectable woman was unsure about the number. The police would never find that coach unless they descended to the nether regions where the devil had carried Major Weir.

I could not tell anybody that strange fancy of mine, and as the day grew longer, I found the very idea more and more ridiculous. By noon the next day, when the sun illuminated the varied life of the Grassmarket, and the sound of raucous voices echoed from the tall lands, I could laugh away my fears.

There was no evil black coach from hell. The idea was ridiculous; a passing notion brought about by nervous tension, the superstition of the uneducated people in the West Bow and the ramblings of Sandy, a common grave-robber. I told myself not to be foolish, scoffed at my stupidity and passed the word around to find a relative of Miss Anderson, whose body I retained in the cold cellar of my surgery.

There was no relative. Miss Anderson had come south from Inverness and had neither friend, spouse, nor sibling. In the hidden recesses of the West Bow and along the tunnel of the Cowgate, from the crazy tenements of the Grassmarket to the decaying lands of the World's End Close, the whisper ran like fire on dry grass. Major Weir claimed Ruth Anderson and sent the devil's coach to take her to hell. I found people looking sideways at me as I walked past, and one or two openly stared, as if at a man already dead.

For some reason, the reactions of other people did not

worry me. If anything, I found them either amusing or quite stimulating. I revelled in the curiosity of the masses, walked with a new spring and tapped my staff on the ground. I felt alive with new confidence as if I was a different man from the shy young Borderer who had recently graduated from Glasgow University.

As that idea grew, I remembered my dream when that strange, long-nosed man had entered my head.

"Maybe that happened," I said to myself, swinging my staff. "Maybe this stranger has given me a surge in confidence." Although I was walking along the crowded Lawnmarket, I gave a great peal of laughter, which caused some passers-by to stare at me as if I was demented.

Perhaps I was, at that, I thought. Ruth Anderson's death gave me another body for dissecting; I realised, cold-bloodedly, and without having to dig one up from the cemetery. In a way, Miss Anderson's death was my good fortune, for the money from the students would come in very handy, particularly if I wished to become engaged to the lovely Evelyn. Yes, I thought, things were shaping up very nicely for me, except for my perennial lack of money.

I looked up from my desk when my last patient of the day stepped through my door.

"Doctor Elliot." He took a seat without asking and looked directly at me.

"Sandy," I replied as my heart began to quicken. I wondered what he wanted, for I guessed it was not something I wished to hear. "You look very healthy to be visiting me."

"As healthy as you are, Doctor."

I could smell the whisky on Sandy's breath and see his eyes, usually so steady, were hazed with alcohol.

"A social call, is it?"

"It's about Ruth Anderson," Sandy said.

I leaned back in my chair, trying to appear calm. "I am afraid Miss Anderson is dead," I said.

"I am aware of that." Sandy breathed his whisky fumes over me. "I heard a black coach and six killed her."

"It seems to have been a black coach," I said, cautiously. "I am unsure how many horses pulled it. I have given the police all the details I know, so I sincerely hope they can clear matters up."

"They won't find anything. It was Major Weir's coach," Sandy spoke with such a tone of finality that it was hard to disagree.

"It was a black coach," I said, "but that was where all similarity ended. Phantom coaches don't run people down, even if some gullible people think they see them. Besides, from what I have heard, Weir's coach comes down the Lawnmarket and the West Bow, not the Cowgate." I shook my head, dismissing Sandy's theory. "Miss Anderson was killed by a solid wooden coach, probably driven by a drunkard. The police will find the driver, charge him with culpable homicide, and the matter will end there."

Sandy licked his lips. "Where in the Cowgate was Ruth killed?"

"About two hundred yards from the Grassmarket," I said.

Sandy nodded. "Beside Hob's Close, at an inset doorway with a carved lintel."

I pictured the scene in my mind. "I believe you are correct," I said.

"That was Major Weir's first house," Sandy said. "Before

he flitted to the West Bow." He licked his lips again. "It's not generally known."

I considered for a few moments before I replied. "If that is true," I said. "It is only a coincidence."

"A bloody unpleasant coincidence, don't you think?" Sandy half rose from his chair. "The only woman to enter Weir's house is hit by a black coach, similar to Weir's outside a house in which Weir used to live?"

I tried to rationalise the facts for, in truth, they unsettled me as much as Sandy. "What makes you think Major Weir lived in that house?"

"I know he did," Sandy looked away. "Trust me on this, Doctor."

I am sure my smile was like the grin of a long-dead corpse. "We can probably find some trace of Weir all over the Old Town if we looked hard enough." I shook my head. "I am sure you are correct that Weir lived there, Sandy. I do not doubt your word."

"Doctor." Sandy leaned across the desk, so his face was close to mine. "I implore you, for the sake of your soul, leave that house."

Before I could reply, Sandy left, slouching out of the surgery and leaving the door wide open in his wake. I closed it, shaking my head, lifted my stick and tapped it on the floor. "You foolish man," I said. "You have no conception of what you are dealing with." I tapped again, creating a rhythm for the song I sang.

"Wha wadna be in love
Wi' bonnie Maggie Lauder?
A piper met her guan to Fife,
And speir'd what was't they ca'd her;
Right scornfully she answer'd him,

Begone you hallanshaker,
Jog on your gate,
ye bladderskate,
My name is Maggie Lauder."

I laughed again, with the sound carrying across the Grassmarket. "Farewell, Sandy Tait," I called, and began to sing again.

Quite a crowd of students appeared for my anatomy lecture on Ruth Anderson, despite the shattered state of her body. Charles had already informed me that some students preferred to view a female rather than a male body and advised me to raise the price for my lecture. By doing so, I managed to amass a healthy sum that would surely help towards my marriage expenses. Although I had not yet asked Swinton for his daughter's hand, I knew he would agree, and my charm had already won Mrs Swinton around. It was only a matter of a few words and raising the necessary money.

The anatomy fees would help, but they were not sufficient, not nearly sufficient to move from the Old Town with its smells and filth, to the elegance of the New. In the New Town, all the prices were higher, and I could raise myself from being a doctor of the impoverished and the few very old members of the quality who clung to their memories. I needed to raise more money to pay the higher rents.

There must be some other methods in a city this size, I told myself when the students drifted away, and then I remembered something that Charles had said that day we swam to Cramond Island. "I am a member of a certain club," he had said, hinting that he made money there. I smiled, running a hand up the shaft of my staff. If a pirate from the Outer Hebrides could make money in an Edinburgh club, then I was sure that a reiver from the Borders could do likewise. Was I not an Elliot, scion of a race that was famed for reiving, robbing and trickery?

I laughed as that other person within me surfaced again, adding his thoughts to mine. I would seek out Charles as soon as I could. I ran my fingers up the length of my staff again, finding them tracing the figure of a woman curled at the base. It was strange that I had not noticed that before. I hummed my old favourite tune of *Maggie Lauder* as I mapped out my plan of campaign.

CHAPTER 8

"Why won't you allow me to visit you in the West Bow?" Evelyn asked petulantly.

I wondered how best to reply. "It is not safe," I said.

We sat in that wondrous oasis of the Queen Street Pleasure Garden, with the sun casting slanting shadows and the birds sweetening the air with their songs.

"I am sure you can protect me against pickpockets and the like," Evelyn said. "Unless I can defend myself. My father was a soldier, remember before he took to the law. He has shown me how to fire a gun. I am sure he will lend you one of his pistols."

"It is not that sort of danger," I said.

"Then what?"

I hesitated, for in the light of such a beautiful summer's day, the story seemed so ludicrous that I could hardly expect Evelyn to understand. She was a very level headed girl.

Evelyn squeezed closer on the wooden bench we shared. "Tell me," she insisted, dropping her voice to a hoarse whisper that would have charmed the birds from the trees.

Lifting a stone, I threw it into the pond and watched the ripples gradually die. "You will think I am a superstitious fool," I said as the water calmed.

"Oh, Martin," Evelyn pushed me, lightly. "I already think that. Tell me." She came even closer, with that hoarse, growling whisper. "Tell me, tell me, tell me, or I will pester you until you do and inform Father that you are keeping secrets from me." She moved back abruptly. "Is that it? Are you keeping a secret from me? Do you have something you don't want me to see? Or somebody perhaps? A woman? Do you share your very private house with a woman?"

"Of course not!" I said as Evelyn manipulated me as easily as if I were a child. "There is no other woman."

Evelyn stood up, stepped away and placed her fists on her hips. "What, then?"

"Sit down," I said. "Sit down, and I will tell you, although I don't think you'll believe it."

Evelyn was beside me in a second. "I knew you'd tell me," she said, smiling in triumph.

I told her. I told her about the invisible coach and the staff and the legend of Major Weir, although I thought it best not to mention the incestuous relationship and some other less salubrious parts. I told her about the death of Ruth Anderson but not about the grave-robbing, or that long-nosed man who I dreamed had entered my head. Evelyn listened with her eyes serious, nodding at all the right places. When I finished, I leaned back on the bench and waited for her mockery.

Evelyn was silent for a good 30 seconds. "How exciting," she said at last. "You live in a haunted house."

"I might," I said. "There could be a rational explanation for everything."

Evelyn smiled, patting my arm. "Did you think I was going to scoff, Martin?"

"Yes," I said.

"I grew up in India," Evelyn said. "We saw many things there that people here would not believe. I will not mock something merely because I don't understand it."

I think it was at that moment that my deep liking for Evelyn altered to love. I saw her differently now, saw new depths I had not noticed before, and wondered anew about marriage, not merely to enhance my career, but to have this woman close to me, to listen to her wisdom and watch every movement she made.

"Although it is exciting to have contact with such spiritual matters," Evelyn said, "what I saw in India also convinced me that it is best to leave well alone. I think you should leave that house. Leave and never look back."

These few words seemed to lift a huge burden from me. I thought of the money I had accumulated from even my two anatomy classes and knew I could afford somewhere better than the West Bow, at least for a while, and then there was Charles's club, with whatever promise that held.

"That is what I will do," I said.

"Take nothing of the house with you," Evelyn said. "Not a single scrap of cloth, not a stick of furniture."

"I will take nothing," I said, "save this staff." I held up the staff.

I swear that Evelyn paled.

"No." She almost snapped the word, so abrupt was her answer. "You must not bring that staff. For all we know, Martin, that is the very staff that Major Weir used."

"I don't think so!" I said. "According to the accounts, Major Weir's staff was burned along with his body. Besides," I said, "ever since I found this stick, I have had good fortune, with the surgery and in meeting you."

"Please, Martin." Evelyn placed her small hand on my arm.

"Please, for me. Leave the staff behind. Leave everything of that house behind. You thought I would laugh at you, but I swear that I understand this more than you, although neither of us understands it at all. The evil in that house, and I believe it *is* an evil, could have tainted everything and anything."

I swithered then, for I felt attached to that staff, and I thought it brought me good fortune. I was tempted to tell Evelyn that I would not bow to her wishes, yet I did not. To my mind, then, it seemed that I had a choice between Evelyn and my staff. It seemed so simple, yet I had an inner turmoil I did not understand. I seemed to be at war with myself, with part of me wishing to cast aside everything connected with Major Weir's house, and another part hoping to build on the success attached to that staff.

"If that is what you wish," I said magnanimously.

"Thank you, Martin," Evelyn said. "And I know you will be glad of your decision."

I smiled although I had no intention of parting from my staff. Holding that length of carved wood increased my confidence in many different situations. I resolved to agree with Evelyn when I could, for she had ignited the flame of my love. However, I would also shield her from anything disagreeable to her sentiments. That way, I could steer a middle course.

"Charles." I stepped inside his surgery, leaned on my staff and admired the modernity of his equipment. "May we talk?"

Charles looked up from behind his desk, looking every inch the successful doctor in his fashionable, nearly sharp clothes and the neatly trimmed side whiskers he had been cultivating as long as I had known him. His grin was the same as ever. "Good e'en, Martin. What a strange question," he gestured me to one of the padded leather seats. "Take a pew."

I did so, tapping my staff on the ground.

"What seems to be the trouble?" Charles leaned back, placing a hand under his chin. "Is there some medical problem with which I can help you? Gout, perhaps, or haemorrhoids?"

"Neither, thank God," I said. "Do you remember the day we were on Cramond Island?"

"As if it were yesterday," Charles said. "The day you met the amiable Miss Evelyn, whom I love with every fibre of my being."

"That's the day." I hesitated, tapped my staff on the floor and continued. "You mentioned a club where you were a member."

"Ah," Charles leaned forward. "Cash strapped, are we? The beauteous Evelyn draining all the gold from your purse? Just say the word, old man, and I will take her off your hands."

I smiled at Charles's poor attempt at humour. "Do you still attend that club?"

"The New Wig Club?" Charles dropped his jocularity. "I do, Martin. Are you serious?"

"I am."

Standing up, Charles paced the breadth of his surgery. "It is possible to lose heavily if you don't know what you are doing," he said, "and there is a small matter of an initiation ceremony that you have to endure."

"I am willing to endure whatever comes my way."

"Splendid!" Charles stopped pacing. "I'll back your membership, Martin, and act as guarantor to the sum of 100 sovereigns."

"A hundred sovs!" I stared at him. "That is extremely generous of you!" I had no intention of gambling to that extent. I thought that 10 sovereigns was a considerable sum to risk.

"We meet at Brodie's Tavern in Princes Street," Charles said. "If you arrive at eight tonight, I will introduce you to the company. After that, it all depends on you. I cannot help you further." I saw shadows behind his smile. "Be careful, Martin. That's the only advice I can give. Be careful, and never gamble more than you can afford."

"Eight tonight, then," I shook his hand in gratitude as I wondered to what I had agreed.

Princes Street is the southernmost street of Craig's original New Town, a row of tenements and townhouses with a spattering of shops and inns and a view across to the Earthen Mound, the castle and the pleasure gardens that replaced the old Nor Loch. Brodie's Tavern was at the eastern end, hidden in a small lane behind the main thoroughfare.

I expected to find the tavern as dingy a hole as any in the Old Town, but I was pleasantly surprised to find it well-lit, with a horseshoe-shaped, marble-topped bar under a bright chandelier. The clientele included clerks, solicitors and even a High Court judge.

Rapping my staff on the counter, I waited for one of the efficient staff to hurry to me.

"I am here for the New Wig Club," I said.

"Certainly, sir." The man was young, with steady eyes. "What is your name?"

He nodded when I told him. "Pray come this way, sir." He led me through a side door and up a flight of stone steps to a long room, with green curtains covering three tall windows and three crystal chandeliers providing excellent lighting.

Charles sat at one of the three circular tables, with an array of men at each. He lifted a hand to acknowledge my arrival. I saw the playing cards spread across the green baize on the tables, with light gleaming on small piles of gold coins in front of each player. I can only describe the atmosphere as tense, with my nearest approximation the nervous stress occasioned by a university examination.

"Dr Martin Elliot," my escort announced, bowed and immediately withdrew as every eye in that room fixed on me. A tall, hook-nosed man dressed entirely in black rose at my entrance.

"Does anybody speak for this man?" the hook-nosed fellow asked.

Charles stood at once, bless his honest heart. "I speak for him. Dr Martin Elliot is a man of honour and principle."

"Dr Elliot, are you willing to undergo the necessary initiation into the august society of the New Wig Club?" The hook-nosed man asked.

"I am," I said, with my heart pattering inside my chest so I was sure everybody in that room could hear it.

"Stand where you are."

I stood still as members opened cupboard doors and brought out a variety of strange objects. I had no notion what the initiation might be, imagining some sort of ordeal, such as running the gauntlet or being ducked in cold water. Instead, the members produced a box shaped like a naked man, two feet high and with generous anatomical proportions, with an eighteen-inch tall glass shaped like a naked woman. Besides these unusual objects, they placed the longest and heaviest wig I had ever seen, made from coarse horsehair, if I was any judge.

Charles caught my eye and winked.

"Remove Dr Elliot's jacket and weskit," Mr Hook-nose said, and eager hands relieved me of the burden of my outer clothing.

"Wig him!" Mr Hook-nose said, and other hands jammed

the wig on my head as hard as they could, with the weight nearly bearing me to the ground.

I watched as somebody filled the naked woman with claret until it overflowed.

"Drink, Dr Elliot, if you wish to be part of the New Wig Club. And you must drink without losing your wig."

The members began to drum on the tables, a slow, rhythmic beat as I lifted the lady to my mouth. Now, drinking is easy, but drinking while being watched, and while balancing a cumbersome wig on one's head, is entirely different. One cannot tip one's head back so one therefore has to tip the cup, which spills claret down one's front, spoiling one's best white shirt.

I persevered, however, choking and spluttering, much to the amusement of the audience. I finished the lady cup to the dregs without losing my wig, if at the expense of a claret-coloured shirt and loss of dignity.

"Good man!" hook-nose said, and with that simple ceremony completed, I was part of the New Wig Club.

"What's your game?"

I looked at the tables, now aware that each table played a different card game. Until that moment I had not given much thought to the next stage in the proceedings, but after the best part of a pint of claret, I knew I was not sufficiently level-headed to play a hand of poker or indeed anything that required concentration. Perhaps that was the idea of the claret, of course, to befuddle the Johnny Raw.

"Vingt-et-un," I said. That is probably the most simple card game ever invented, where the players have to get at close to 21 as they can. Even a tyro such as I was could play with a moderate chance of success, for luck mattered as much as skill.

"This table." Charles sounded happy that I could play alongside him, while I was certainly glad of company I knew.

"I'll take your coat and stick, sir," an efficient servant carried them to a stand at one end of the panelled room.

There were three others at that table. The first was a smiling man with basilisk eyes, the second a handsome young gentleman with rings on both fingers and the third a middle-aged man with carefully groomed side whiskers. Charles introduced them to me as Sir Bernard Somerville, Cedric Outerston and Jonathan Wemyss, in that order.

"Are we playing or having a social evening?" the handsome man, Outerston, asked, cracking his fingers and allowing the light to reflect from his rings.

"Playing," Charles said. He raised his voice. "New pack!"

The same efficient servant brought an unopened pack of cards, which Outerston grabbed and opened. He dealt them deftly, two cards to each man, while placing one of his face down, and one face up. I noticed with a smile that the back of each card held a picture of a well-proportioned woman who wore nothing except an enormous wig.

"In this establishment, if we wish a card in this game," Charles explained quietly, "we say twist. Stick means keep what you have and fold means you are out of the game."

I nodded, for the rules seemed simple enough, checked my cards and smiled. In place of the usual king, queen and knave, were naked people, smiling openly and wearing wigs in strategic locations, while even the number cards were decorated with shaggy wigs. I was so intent on examining the artistry that I nearly forgot to count my total.

Seventeen. I glanced around the table. Outerston had a 10 on view and opened the gambling with a golden guinea. The others followed, except Wemyss, who upped the stakes to two guineas, whereupon I folded. I was not inclined to gamble on anything less than 18, nor twist with the odds stacked against a small value card.

Outerston won that hand, dragging a small handful of gold in his direction. He won the next as well, as I counted the eight guineas I had left of my original ten and wondered again if I had made a major mistake. Charles tapped a finger on the table, met my gaze and winked.

Three hands later, I wished I had never heard of the New Wig Club. I fingered the last gold guinea in my pocket and surveyed the table. There were three winners and two losers. Charles had a moderate pile of gold in front of him, while Sir Bernard and Outerston were well ahead, with Wemyss and me both looking and feeling doleful.

"Are you all right?" Charles asked. "Remember I can loan you some rhino if you need it."

"I don't want a loan," I replied somewhat testily, for I knew how hard I would have to work to raise another 10 guineas. Pushing back my chair, I stalked away, ignoring Outerston's pointed remark about purse-pinched peasants who should have remained in their rural practices.

The servant stepped aside to give me room. "Coat and stick, sir?" He enquired, holding them out for me. His face was expressionless, so doubtless he had seen many men leave after a single exposure to the merciless truth of the green baize.

"Yes, please," I said, grabbing hold of the stick. "No, damn it!" I said, immediately changing my mind. "I've got enough gold for one more hand." Still clutching my staff, I returned to the table and resumed my seat. "I might prevail on you for that loan, Charles," I said, with sudden confidence coursing through me.

"Good man!" Charles said. "Here's five for a start." He slid five guineas across the green baize to me.

With a recklessness that was alien to my character, I laughed. "Deal the cards," I said, "and let the devil take the loser."

"That's the spirit!" Sir Bernard said. "Deal, Outerston!"

The cards flicked across the table, to settle in front of us. I saw Outerston place a knave face up in front of him with his second card face-down beneath. He leaned back in his chair, smiling, as the light reflected from his rings.

I checked my cards. An eight and a seven: 15. "Twist," I said without hesitation. Outerston flicked a card to me. The three of clubs. Eighteen. Did I twist again? What were the chances of a small number? I grinned. Did it matter? Life was always a gamble, and the cards were no different.

"Twist," I said as Charles looked at me, his eyes narrow in warning.

A two, which meant I had 20. That would do. "Stick," I said, sat back, and watched the others.

Charles twisted and threw in his hand without another word. Sir Bernard twisted, took a five of diamonds and leaned back, expressionless, while Wemyss sat tight.

Outerston opened the betting by pushing forward two guineas, smiling to me, hoping to see me fail. Wemyss met him, while Sir Bernard, blank-faced, added another guinea. I pushed forward my guinea and two of Charles's, tossed in one more and waited.

"Living on borrowed money, eh?" Outerston said, meeting my guinea.

"The banks don't care where their gold comes from," I said carelessly.

Wemyss swore, folding his cards as Sir Bernard pushed forward his coins. "I'll see you," Sir Bernard said, in a suddenly tense atmosphere.

Outerston uncovered his bottom card. A 10; he had 20, and as Banker, he defeated me. As he reached for the pot, Sir Bernard shook his head. "Not so fast, Outerston," he said, slowly revealing his cards. "Twenty-one." Reaching forward, he dragged the pot to him. "Mine, I believe."

I felt Outerston's frustrated anger as he watched Sir Bernard piling his winnings into neat golden columns. Strangely, I was not concerned, for that uncommon reckless streak remained.

"Could I prevail upon you for another 10 guineas, Charles?"

"You could, Martin." Charles looked at me, knowing I was acting out of my habitual cautious character. He counted out 10 guineas and passed them over to me. "Have a care now; my pockets are not bottomless."

"The next hand is mine," I said, stroking my staff with my foot. "Right now. Is Outerston still the banker?"

The cards came again, slower this time, with the same nearly inaudible hiss as they passed across the baize. I could feel the tension at the table between Outerston and Sir Bernard. It added to my growing excitement as I viewed my cards.

I had a queen who hid her modesty behind a wig, and a ten of clubs. I watched the others, saw Sir Bernard as expressionless as before, with Charles raising his eyebrows and Wemyss wiping the back of his hand across his forehead. Outerston ignored me as he looked at Sir Bernard. In Outerston's eyes, I was unimportant, a Johnnie Raw with no possibility of challenging him.

"Stick," I said, tried to look smug and leaned back in my chair. My foot inadvertently touched my staff, and I felt a renewed surge of confidence. I knew I would win this hand.

Wemyss called for a card, viewed it and sat back. Charles sat tight. Sir Bernard signalled for a card, nodded and slumped in his chair, avoiding everybody's gaze as he left Outerston to make his decision. A faint draught shifted the chandelier above us, causing wavering shadows to pass across the table.

The betting began at two guineas. I pushed forward four and waited. Wemyss folded right away, with Charles grunting and doing the same. That left only three of us still betting. Sir Bernard met my four and added three guineas more.

I glanced at my cards again, grinned and pushed forward all my money. "That's all I have," I said with a grin. "Unless Charles wishes to lend me more."

"If you need it," Charles said immediately.

I flicked my cards, allowing the face card to be seen but hiding the other.

"I might need it all," I said, smiling.

My words unnerved Outerston, as was my intention, and he folded, with Sir Bernard looking at his hand and the bland expression on my face. "You're bluffing," he said. "I'll see you."

I showed him my twenty, which defeated his 19, and I scooped the pot. Out of curiosity, I glanced at Outerston's hand. He also had twenty and would have won.

"Hard luck, old man," I gloated as I returned Charles's loan money.

By that time, Outerston was rattled. He gambled recklessly on the next hand, losing again and called for a bottle of claret. Sensing victory, Sir Bernard began to twist the screw, while I played with more caution, slowly building up my winnings as first Wemyss and then Charles left the game. Outerston lost two more hands in a row, recouped a little of his losses on the next and killed half his bottle of claret. His face was growing dangerously flushed.

"Another hand," Outerston demanded, nearly shouting.

"I think that might be all for today, Outerston," Charles said mildly.

"Damn you, MacNeil! I decide when I stop playing."

"I'm game if you are," Sir Bernard said. "How about you, Elliot?"

I ignored Charles's head shake. "Oh, play on," I said, rolling my foot up the length of my staff.

"Let's up the stakes then," Sir Bernard said. "Five guineas rather than one."

"Five guineas it is," I said carelessly.

Outerston's run of bad luck had removed most of his bumptious arrogance. His pile of guineas had reduced in direct proportion to the increase of Sir Bernard's and mine. "You said you were new to cards." Outerston addressed me.

"Beginner's luck." I was relishing my success.

"Five guineas it is." Outerston forced a smile.

By that time, the other tables had cleared, and most of the members had left. Only a few men remained, talking in quiet tones, smoking and drinking claret or the dark Edinburgh ale. As we began to play again, all conversation ceased, so there was only the snick of cards and our strained voices. Charles tried to raise an encouraging smile.

Once again, I was given a strong hand and sat tight with a solid nineteen. Sir Bernard's face gave nothing away, while Outerston alternatively glowed with sweat or grinned foolishly as he thought fate favoured him.

I watched the cards fall, seemingly able to guess the numbers before my opposition calculated their hand. Sir Bernard, I knew, was sitting on a sound hand, either 20 or 19, while Outerston had an eight showing and had another three cards concealed.

"I add another five guineas," I said, casually pushing forward my gold.

"I'll match that," Sir Bernard said.

"As will I." Outerston was falsely bombastic.

"And I'll raise five." The old me would have left the table

half an hour ago, astounded at my success. That night I wanted more and expected more. I rolled my staff from foot to foot and played on.

The golden pot was increasing, with the light from the chandeliers reflecting from the guineas. I leaned back in my seat, sipped at the claret the servant brought and ignored Charles's warning looks. This game was mine, by God, and nothing to do with some doctor from the furthest Hebrides.

"Damn it, let's stop skirting the edges," Sir Bernard said. "Raise 100 guineas."

"Yes, 100," I agreed, knowing my purse was that deep. I counted the coins into 10 neat golden piles on the table. "Easy come, easy go, eh, Outerston?"

"I don't have that much," Outerston said.

"Then fold, damn you," Sir Bernard said. "Or pledge your jewellery." He indicated the rings on Outerston's fingers.

"Damn you for a blackguard!" Outerston said, throwing his rings on to the pile.

"And another 50," Sir Bernard said.

I glanced at Charles, who nodded, although his eyes were worried. He handed over 50 guineas. "Be careful, Martin."

"I have no cares today," I said as Outerston licked his lips, staring at the pile of gold in the centre of the table.

"Outerston?" Sir Bernard said. "Match or fold."

"I have nothing else," Outerston said, with all his previous bumptiousness gone.

"That's a fine silk shirt you wear," Sir Bernard said, "and excellent trousers."

"Will you take my pledge?" Outerston asked.

"You know the rules of the house," Sir Bernard said. "No pledges and all debts to be paid on the nail." He dropped his voice. "Or we take it out of your hide."

"Damn you!" Outerston looked at me, as if for help. I said

nothing, waiting, sure of my forthcoming success. Slowly he stripped off his shirt and trousers, adding his gold watch when Sir Bernard pressurised him.

"Is that worth 50 guineas?" Sir Bernard asked.

The servant stepped forward, feeling the quality of the material, checking the make of the watch. "Thirty-five, sir."

"Your coat as well, Outerston," Sir Bernard said.

The coat and hat made up another 14.

"That's near enough," Outerston said.

"You are a guinea short," Sir Bernard said. "The rest." We watched as Outerston removed the final vestiges of his clothing and sat at the table as naked as the day he was born. "Now, I'll see you."

I felt in my pocket, produced my final, reserve guinea and tossed it on to the pile. "Up another guinea."

That was the first time I saw Sir Bernard show some respect. "Fold," he said. "I'm cleaned out."

"Outerston?" I addressed the naked man. "What can you add now? A few fingers, perhaps?"

"Damn you, Elliot!" Outerston rose from the table. "You know I have nothing left!"

"I glanced at his person. "That is true," I said. "You are nothing at all. Fold then."

There were tears in Outerston's eyes as he threw down his cards. I saw them spread across the table as I dragged the pot towards me.

"As a matter of interest," Sir Bernard said. "What did you have?"

"Nineteen," I said.

"I had 20," Sir Bernard rose from his chair. "Thank you for an entertaining evening."

"My pleasure, Sir Bernard." It was bad form to count my winnings at the table, so I scooped the money into a bag the servant provided, tipped him with five guineas and prepared to leave.

"Martin," Charles was frowning. "How about Outerston?"

"What about him?" I lifted my new set of clothes.

"You can't leave him like that," Charles said. "He can't walk home naked."

"Would he have shown compassion to me?"

"What's happened to you, Martin?" Grabbing the clothes from me, Charles passed them across to Outerston. "Here. Make yourself decent, man, for God's sake."

I felt the respect of everybody as I left the New Wig club a good deal wealthier than I had entered, tapping my staff on the ground as I strode through the dark streets to the West Bow. I even laughed out loud as I felt the weight of gold in the bag at my waist. We had done well tonight.

We? Who were we? There was only me, only one winner. Yet I knew somebody had helped me, and I remembered that unsettling dream when the long-nosed gentleman had entered my mind. Well then, I told myself, if his presence had turned around my fortunes to such an extent, he was very welcome. Tapping my staff on the ground, I walked to our home in the West Bow, where my sister was waiting.

CHAPTER 9

Now that I was no longer teetering on the thin edge of destitution, I had a new fear. Having dragged myself to relative, if temporary, prosperity, I knew I would be a target for the ne'er-do-weels and thieves who infested the sordid wynds of the Old Town. I had no wish to lose my hard-won fortune and needed some better protection than a mere staff against the desperate men and women of the night.

Accordingly, I began to search among the pawn shops that infest the more deprived areas of the city. I know I might have obtained a better weapon in a New Town gunsmith, but I had no desire to purchase a Joseph Manton. I wanted a firearm for defence, not something that announced my social position.

The first place I entered was a damp little pawn shop in the West Bow, a stone's throw from my courtyard. The sign above the shop said Maggie Brown's. The man behind the counter looked me up and down before withdrawing slightly. I could sense his suspicion.

"Good afternoon." I touched the brim of my hat. "I am looking for a pistol."

"We don't deal with stolen property," the proprietor said at once.

I understood. "I am not a policeman," I said.

"You look like a bluebottle in disguise." The man was overweight, with shrewd eyes and rings on both hands.

"I am a doctor of medicine," I reassured him, "and lately I have heard some strange noises around my house."

"You're the doctor in Weir's old house!" The man said suddenly, pointing to me as if I were some sort of apparition risen from the Pit.

"I am he," I agreed.

"No wonder you heard strange noises," the man said.

"You are not Maggie Brown." I tapped my staff on the wooden floor, looking around the shop.

"I am David Brown." The man puffed himself up, trying to look important.

"And I am Dr Elliot, searching for a pistol," I said. "Do you have such an item in stock?" I gave him my conspiratorial grin. "Now that you know I am no bluebottle."

Either the smile convinced him, or my staff worked its magic, for, within a minute, David Brown produced three pistols. The first was like a cut-down Brown Bess musket and unsuited to my purpose, while the others were much smaller, suitable to fit inside my pocket. I lifted the smallest, which had twin barrels and an elegant walnut stock.

"That's a good barker." Brown saw my interest. "It will stop an elephant."

"I don't think an elephant will try to rob me." I tested the pistol for weight and balance, aiming at a tall hat hanging on a peg. "Yes, this will do nicely if you can provide powder and shot."

"I always have a supply of both." Brown seemed pleased to

have made such a quick sale. He hesitated before speaking again. "You are a brave man."

"If I were a brave man," I said, "I might not need to arm myself with a pistol."

"Living in that house makes you a brave man," Brown said. "I would not enter there for a gold watch, no, nor for a hundred gold watches and the crown jewels of Scotland."

I shook my head. "The house is not as bad as it's painted. It's cheap to rent and handily positioned."

Brown waited until I had parted with the cost of the pistol and ammunition before he continued. "A barker won't protect you from what's in that house, Doctor. It's something else entirely that you need."

I thought of the strange sounds and shadows, the ticking of the clock and all the other sensations. "What do you recommend, Mr Brown?"

"This." Delving under the counter, Brown produced a simple wooden cross, sitting on a square stand. Before I asked him what was special about his cross, he explained. "The base is of olive wood, cut from a tree on the Mount of Olives, while the cross is made from a rowan tree from the sacred Island of Iona, blessed with holy water."

I stared at him. "I am not one of your superstitious customers from the dark closes," I said. "Nor am I a Roman Catholic."

"If you were, Doctor," Brown said, and I knew that he was not lying, "you would never have entered that house."

I shook my head. "No, Mr Brown, I won't buy your little cross."

"You don't have to buy it." Brown slid it across the counter. "Take it. It's a gift."

For a second, I was tempted. I pocketed the pistol and

reached for the cross, then shook my head. "No," I said. "I won't bow to superstition." Thanking Brown, I stepped back into the street with my barker heavy in my pocket and my staff firm in my grasp. I saw Sandy across the street, raised my hand in acknowledgement to his lifted hat and walked away. It was one thing talking to such people in the line of business, but one does not wish to socialise with them by choice. I tapped my staff on the ground and smiled. Imagine the nerve of that Brown fellow, thinking I would be interested in a wooden cross. Laughing, I strode to the Lawnmarket and into the heart of the city.

I must have passed the Tron Church 100 times without realising it was there. I knew it was a church, of course, but had taken no interest in it until Evelyn began hinting it would be a perfect location for a wedding.

"Either the Tron or St Giles would be lovely, whenever I decide to marry," she said, as artlessly as only an attractive young woman could. "I know it is more fashionable to marry in the New Town, but I do like the history of the Old." She paused long enough to treat me to a wide-eyed smile. "What do you think, Martin?" We stopped outside the Tron Kirk. "If I ever were to marry, should it be here or in St Giles?"

"I have not given it much thought," I said truthfully.

"Well, Martin," Evelyn said, tapping me with her hand, "I am surprised. I'm sure there must have been a dozen young ladies hoping for matrimony with you."

"They can hope," I assured her quickly. "I have only eyes for one."

"Oh." Evelyn smiled and looked away. "Who might that be?"

"Guess," I said, teasing her.

"Let me think," Evelyn said. "Is she tall or short?"

"She is the perfect height for a wife," I replied solemnly.

"Oh," Evelyn said, "that does not help me much. Is she fair or dark?"

"Fair of feature, dark of eyes, always in the correct proportions," I said.

"Fair of feature?" Evelyn said. "I have been called fair."

"Indeed?" I widened my eyes. "Now, there is a coincidence."

Evelyn twisted her head to look up at me. "Who is it, Martin? Tell me who this girl of yours might be."

I smiled. "Why, you, of course."

"Nobody else?"

"Nobody else," I said.

"Well," Evelyn said, "if you were to marry, ever, where would you choose?"

I pretended to ponder the question. "Should I ever marry..." I said slowly. "A wife would undoubtedly be an asset if I wished to cut a respectable figure, but could I accept the restrictions that marriage would bring?" I shook my head. "I do not know," I said. "I shall have to think about it."

"And when you have thought, will you tell me the answer?"

"I shall," I promised.

"Martin," Evelyn said quietly as we continued to walk down the High Street. "I don't like you in that house."

"I know," I said.

"You said you would leave. When will that happen?"

"When I find somewhere better that I can afford," I told her.

Evelyn faced me directly, with her eyes smiling yet very serious. "If I asked you to do something for me, would you promise to oblige?"

I nodded. "Of course."

"No, Martin." Evelyn put her small hand on my chest. "Please don't say yes and then forget. Will you mean it?"

I could see she was in earnest. "I mean it," I said.

"Do you have a Bible?"

"I don't," I said.

"Then take mine," Evelyn said. "Please, Martin." She fished inside her coat and produced a small New Testament with the leather cover much scuffed and worn with use. When I hesitated, she pressed the Bible into my hand. "Please, Martin. I put my love on the pages."

"In that case," I said, "how can I refuse?"

Rather light-heartedly, I slipped Evelyn's Bible inside my pocket.

"Keep it with you," Evelyn said.

"With your Bible by my side, I shall feel even closer to you," I said. The words came smoothly to me. Evelyn's genuine pleasure interested me. It was so easy to make her smile as I learned the subtle arts of bending people to my will. The staff helped there, of course. With that staff in my possession, I could do anything. Married or single, living in the Old Town or the New, we must never be parted from our staff.

Once I realised that I had a talent for cards, I began to enjoy the thrill of the green baize, where a fortune could be won or lost on the turn of a single card. I was never foolish enough to gamble more than I could afford and always left a 100 guineas in a safe place at home before I ventured out.

After a few weeks, I found the New Wig Club a trifle stale and searched for more exciting sport. I made friends among the fast set quickly, learned a host of new games and plumbed the depths of this city. I had long known that Edinburgh had two faces, but now I found that each face hid multiple personalities, and even the most outwardly respectable of men hid secrets from his wife and friends. Discovery was a sweet joy that afforded me great satisfaction as I found erudite professors consorting with illiterate prostitutes and stern High Court judges attending places of public entertainment that even the police hesitated to visit.

My new friends introduced me to cockfighting, a sport patronised by even the elite, and I made small fortunes at these bloody mains. From cockfighting, I moved on to dogfighting and ratting, where dogs had to butcher a large number of rats in a given time. The same sort of clientele frequented both kinds of event, including some of those people who appeared eminently respectable on the surface. One young man, in particular, seemed to frequent all the places I visited, and the more I saw him, the more he intrigued me.

It was while on a visit to a laigh – low – house in Leith that I saw him in profile and wondered at the delicate shape of his chin. And then the realisation clicked.

"Good God," I spoke aloud without realising what I was doing.

"What's the matter?" my companion, the Honourable Peter Lowther, asked.

"That fellow there," I gestured with my chin. "That's a woman in disguise."

"Oh, her," Peter said. "That's Lady Clarinda Snodgrass. She's well known for a sharp. Sometimes she wears women's clothes, and other times she dresses as a man. I don't know why." He shrugged, tapped his cane on the brim of his tall hat and shouted his bet on the ratting competition we were watching.

Naturally, such a person as Lady Clarinda interested me, and I resolved to get to know her Ladyship better. I found myself standing close to her on many subsequent occasions, and we exchanged greetings from time to time.

Armed with this newfound insight into the reality of Edinburgh society, I was better prepared for the world when I walked the streets, tapping my staff on the cobbles and with my pistol a comforting weight in my pocket. I soon began to be known, with men I met at any of my clubs gracing my surgery with their presence and enhancing my normal fees with a little extra to ensure my confidentiality. Many of these men had the most delicate of conditions that required me to advise them to leave their wives alone for the time being. It was around this time that I again became aware of somebody dogging me.

At first, it was only a sensation, a strange pricking at the base of my spine and the back of my neck, a feeling that things were not right. And then it grew. I could hear the footsteps as though they were echoes of my own, and once or twice I turned suddenly, to see nothing, or a flicker of movement as a dark shadow disappeared into a doorway or a close.

"Who's there?" I challenged more than once. There was no response. "I see you!" I shouted. "I have a gun!" I may as well have bayed to the moon. "Is that you, Sandy Tait? I warn you, I am armed, and I'm not disinclined to shoot!"

Swinging my staff, I continued, and after a few days, I ignored whoever was behind me. Whoever they were, they did not harm me. I strongly suspected it was Sandy Tait, on some foolish notion that he could help me.

When I first arrived in Edinburgh, I had felt like a stranger as I took my daily exercise through the streets, but now I was a weel-kent face. Gentlemen in all walks of life, from lords and high-court judges to the lowest scavengers, touched their hats or forelocks to me with a polite "good morning". With so many of the lower orders being Highland or Irish, I learned Erse and

Gaelic to enable me to converse in their native tongue, much to the surprise of Charles.

"You've learned Gaelic," Charles said when I called into his surgery, reversed his patients' chair and leaned over the back, grinning to him.

"I have," I agreed, and continued our conversation in that ancient tongue.

"You were always poor at languages," Charles said. "I remember how you struggled at the higher forms of Latin and Greek." He shook his head. "You needed crib-notes to pass your examinations, as I recall."

"No longer," I told him. "Languages seem to come easily to me now." I did not inform him about the power of my staff. Sometimes one must keep such truths even from one's closest friends, and the most amiable of one's female companions.

Charles shook his head. "You have changed a great deal, Martin. You are no longer the quiet doctor I once knew."

"And I thank providence for it," I said, rising from my perch. "That naïve young boy has gone for good."

"And perhaps he has taken much good with him," Charles murmured.

It was the Honourable Peter Lowther who advised me about another club.

"The gambling is for higher stakes than the New Wig," the Honourable Peter said as he dressed after an essential consultation in my surgery. "But with your luck, that should not be a concern."

I leaned back at my desk, glanced at my staff in the corner of the surgery and smiled. "Pray, tell me more."

"I thought you might be interested," The Honourable Peter

said as winked and gave me more details. "It's not like the New Wig," he said. "There are many very amiable ladies, as I have just proved."

I laughed. "One must be prepared for the unpleasant result of such amiability," I said. "When shall we visit?"

Whoever had created the club named it The Less Ancient and Most Puissant Order of the Beggars Benison and Merryland, and founded it in a very respectable-looking house in St Andrews Square. I found the name intriguing and the entrance even more so, as a tall footman opened the door for me and ushered me into a collection of spacious rooms that overlooked one of the grandest squares in the New Town. Rather than giving all the details here, I will only say that it was unlike any other club I had tried. However, it boasted the usual card and dice games, plus heavy drinking and other pastimes that would not be suitable for a gathering of kirk elders. Or perhaps they would, given the duality of everything in Scotland's sublimely mendacious capital city.

After the Honourable Peter introduced me, I survived the somewhat childish initiation ceremony, pulled my trousers back where they belonged, tapped my staff on the floor and looked for a game to join.

There were three, all with full tables, so I drifted across to a lipped oval table where men were throwing ivory dice in great excitement. Only when I arrived did I realise that Outerston was one of the players. He gave me a vicious glower, to which I replied with a smile, enjoying his discomfort and already feeling quite at home in this emotion-brittle environment. I saw two large, hard-faced men standing in one corner, heard them converse in Gaelic and knew they were there to remove any members who became obstreperous when the cards turned against them. I nodded amiably to them and, rubbed my hand along my staff.

"Who are these lads?" I asked Peter.

"We call them the two Donalds," Peter said. "They're a pair of Highland stirks, both ex-soldiers who could take care of themselves and anybody else. Individually they would give Tom Spring, the heavyweight champion prizefighter, a run for his money; together they are unbeatable."

"I won't try accounts with them," I said. "What is this game called?" I watched the dice roll and click.

"We call this three dice," the Honourable Peter said. "Throw all three, with the highest total winning."

It was straightforward and quick, so I joined in, leaning my staff against my leg and keeping the stakes low at first until I got to know the players. As well as Outerston, the Honourable Peter joined us, with a flat – a novice – who gave his name as Lord Hugh, although anything less noble than that simpleton would be hard to imagine. A fifth man, a complete nobody, drifted over and threw a few dice before losing interest and leaving with a blast of foul language, and a careful, middle-aged lawyer with wild eyes took his place, gambling heavily. I did not hear his name.

As I expected, the dice rolled my way, so my initial modest collection of gold grew to respectable proportions as the evening wore on. Although I was aware of loud laughter from the other tables, I closed off my ears to any distraction and concentrated on removing the sovereigns from Outerston's pocketbook.

"You're successful again." The voice was too throaty to be a man, although the owner wore a man's long coat and a broad-brimmed hat.

"I am indeed." I did not need to mention Lady Clarinda's name. We both knew who she was.

Lady Clarinda leaned over my shoulder. "This is a game for children."

"It suits me," I said, throwing 14.

"I see that fellow over there is losing as heavily as you are winning." Lady Clarinda nodded to Outerston, who was cursing in a low monotone.

"He is," I said calmly, with my foot resting on my staff.

Lord Hugh threw 11, tossed his hat on the floor and trampled it flat, to my undisguised amusement. The lawyer won that game, pulled the pot towards him and left the table. It would be tedious to hear of every throw, so suffice to say that the others withdrew with small wins or losses, leaving only Peter, me and Outerston.

"I owe you the devil of a lot, Elliot," Peter said.

I agreed. "You owe me more than you can afford, Peter," I said softly. "However, we can discuss it later." One never knows when one can use a debtor. "We are well enough acquainted not to worry about money. You can give me your promissory note after this game."

Peter nodded. "You might do better to withdraw as well, Outerston," he said.

"I'm damned if I'll let a mere doctor best me," Outerston said.

"As you wish," Peter said with a shrug.

"As he wishes," Lady Clarinda said, in a tone of pure malice. She lowered her voice to a whisper that only I could hear. "Destroy him, Martin."

I laughed. "That will be my pleasure, your Ladyship."

So I did. As I knew without thought what each roll of the dice would bring, I allowed Outerston to win the occasional small sum. I enjoyed his brief gloating and then forced him to gamble heavily when the dice rolled in my favour. By the time the clock struck midnight, I had reduced him to pauperism while I had 20 neat piles of gold stacked in front of me.

Outerston stood in the centre of the room. "I'm a ruined man," he said.

"Yes," I agreed, tapping my staff on the ground.

"I've lost everything."

"You have," I agreed.

"Do you have no pity?"

About to relent, I felt a surge of something, I cannot describe what, leave the staff and thrust up my arm. I smiled. "Let's put it to the test, shall we? How about a vote?" I faced Outerston. "Cheer up, man, you are the creator of your own fortune."

"And so are you, Doctor," Lady Clarinda said to me, pointing at my winnings.

"And always shall be," I said, ignoring the chill that ran up my spine.

The other members crowded around, laughing, taunting Outerston as he stood there, humiliated and broken. Lady Clarinda lounged on a chair with her hat tipped forward over her face and her eyes bright.

"Who votes for mercy and pity?" I looked around the faces, some of which I knew well, others that belonged to total strangers. Of the 18 men present, about half raised their hands, with most then looking at their companions, hesitating and letting them fall again.

"Five," I said, at the final count. "And who votes for none?"

A forest of hands appeared, with Peter's high among them and Lady Clarinda lifting a languid finger.

"No mercy wins the day!"

"Throw him out," I said, happily.

"Is that all?" Lady Clarinda said, smiling. "He still has his clothes."

"Shall we let him keep his clothes?" I asked the crowd.

"No!" they roared with great enthusiasm.

Lady Clarinda was first in the rush to strip the unhappy Outerston, and this time there was no Charles to rescue him from that final humiliation.

"How about the gauntlet?" Lady Clarinda suggested. "It seems fitting for a man who cannot pay his debts."

I had never seen a gauntlet before. All the men, plus Lady Clarinda, formed a corridor facing inward, through which Outerston had to pass, with every person kicking, slapping or punching the unfortunate man to help him on his way. Only when he reached the far end did the two Donalds take hold of him by the arms, open the front door and propel him into St Andrews's Square with mighty kicks to his backside.

"And that's that," Lady Clarinda said happily. "Now, Martin, I believe there are some private rooms downstairs where we can be alone. Unless you wish others to accompany us?"

"Others?" I asked, dragging my winnings into a green baize bag.

"The management here can supply as many willing partners as we wish." Lady Clarinda's eyes were bright with promise.

"The more, the merrier," I said, humming *Maggie Lauder* as we made our way downstairs.

CHAPTER 10

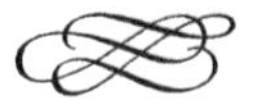

"No, Mr Elliot." Mr Swinton stood with his back to the fire and his legs apart. "I cannot give you permission to marry my daughter."

I stood, stunned, for I had expected an immediate acceptance. "May I ask why not, sir?"

Mr Swinton faced me openly, as square and honest as the man himself. "Now, I am a plain-speaking man, Mr Elliot, and I mean this kindly. I do not think that you two are suitable for each other. I know you are a qualified doctor, and you are working to increase your practice." He shook his head. "But you are not right for my daughter."

I did not reply for a moment as I dredged my mind for something to say. "Evelyn likes me," I said at last.

"Of that, I have no doubt," Mr Swinton said. "No doubt at all."

"Pray tell me why you disapprove, sir?" I felt as if I were pleading when I wanted to vent my frustration at this man who held my future happiness and prospects in the palm of his hand.

Now it was Mr Swinton's turn for silence. "As Evelyn's father," he said, "my priority is the future happiness and well-being of my daughter. I do not believe that you are the best man for her. She is a quiet-living girl, and you are in the fast set."

"Thank you for being so candid." I tried to keep the bitterness from my voice.

"I don't dislike you, Martin." Again, Mr Swinton spoke kindly. "I know my decision must disappoint you, but in a few years you will look back and realise I am right." He sighed. "There is little worse than being in an unsuitable marriage."

"Thank you for your advice, sir," I said, reaching for my hat and staff. "I think it would be better if I left now."

"I hope you don't take this too hard," Mr Swinton said. "I am acting solely in the best interests of my daughter."

"I am sure you are, sir," I said, leaving the room. About to slam the door behind me, I restrained my natural temper and closed it quietly.

"You won't treat us like that," I promised, tapping my staff on the floor.

I had never experienced such black rage as at that moment. I was usually a peaceable man, but my mind filled with images of such violence that I recoiled in horror. Yet something burned within me that I had never experienced before. The more that Mr Swinton tried to deny me Evelyn, the more determined I would be to gain her for myself. I am not sure, now, whether I wanted Evelyn as a wife so much as I hated Swinton denying her to me. The feelings coiled around themselves as I strode, hot-eyed, across the hallway.

The manservant eyed me with sympathy as I left the house, yet said nothing. For all his urbane manners, Swinton was undoubtedly master in his own home. I heard my footsteps echo on the doorstep, walked on to the pavement outside and stopped. Swinton had left the window open, and if I hovered around the iron railings that surrounded the basement in front of the house, I could clearly hear a heated conversation. Mrs Swinton raised her voice in evident anger.

"Why did you send poor Mr Elliot away, Swinton? He is such an amiable, well set-up young man."

Swinton replied without heat. "Yes, he is a well set-up, very amiable man, yet there is something about him I do not like."

"What is that, pray?" Mrs Swinton sounded confused. "I like him, and God knows that Evelyn likes him, more than likes him."

There was a pause. I heard Mr Swinton's footsteps as he walked around the room. "I am aware of that, yet I sense a shadow in him as if he is hiding something, some darkness within him. He has something of the night, indeed, and I have heard some of the most unsettling stories of his attending gambling clubs and the like."

Mrs Swinton made a strange sound, a cross between an unladylike snort and a laugh. "Ha! The only darkness is within your head, Swinton! You are miscalling that fine young man and poor Evelyn will be distraught."

"Poor Evelyn will be better without him," Swinton said, and I heard no more, for a nanny pushing a perambulator came towards me, and I moved away. It would not be done for a respectable gentleman to hover outside a window listening to a husband arguing with his wife.

"Good evening." I nodded to the nanny as I passed.

"Good evening, sir." She gave a little curtsey.

She was a neat little thing, I noted, very trim, and I allowed my mind to drift in a different direction as I paced the next few steps before I began to plan how to gain Mr Swinton's approval for Evelyn's hand. The alternative was to steal her away, elope and marry without her parents' consent. However, I still wished to retain the image of respectability, and Edinburgh doctors do not abduct young women.

I was still plotting when I reached my house, placed my staff in the corner behind the door and stretched out on the nearest chair.

The nightmares had waited for me. Not for them the idea that their victim must be asleep, for they infested the very fabric of the house, lurking in the stonework, embedded in the wood so that they could escape the very second their human victim relaxed his guard. No sooner had I sat down than they returned, circling me with their horrors, gibbering at my ears, revealing themselves in shadow and form, with their harsh laughter in my hearing and their thoughts polluting my brain. I could discern a strange man-beast crouching at the edge of the bed, see a disembodied head floating around the room and hear the whirr and rattle of a spinning wheel, although I had no such machine in the house.

"Begone!" I said, standing up. "Begone! I do not wish you in my house!"

The laughter began somewhere near the fireplace and spread to every room so that it seemed that the entire house was taunting me. That song returned, with a cracked old voice ranting the words.

"Wha wadna be in love
Wi' bonnie Maggie Lauder?
A piper met her guan to Fife,
And speir'd what was't they ca'd her."

I stood up, flailing my arms at the invisible demons in my room.

"You'll never get away." The whisper entered my head.

"You'll never get away. I have you now, and you'll never get away."

"Damn you!" I shouted. "Damn you all!" I might as well have thrown paper to put out a fire as the laughter intensified around me.

"Begone!" I roared, waving my hands in the air. "Get away from me!"

They circled me, these terrible images. I told myself they sprang from my imagination. I told myself they were nothing more than the result of my overwrought nerves thinking about Evelyn, and Mr Swinton, and money, and the risks I had taken when I joined the resurrection men. Forcing myself to reason, I stood up, banishing the horrors from my mind.

"I am a doctor," I said out loud. "I am a man of science, not some foolish superstitious person from the middle of nowhere."

The laughter did not ease.

"Wha wadna be in love
Wi' bonnie Maggie Lauder?
A piper met her guan to Fife,
And speir'd what was't they ca'd her."

Lifting my jacket, I waved it around my head, trying to dispel the images. As I did, something fell from the pocket onto the ground. The laughter ended abruptly.

"What's happened?" I looked downward at the Bible that Evelyn had given me. It lay on the floor where it had fallen, the leather cover scuffed with use and some of the pages dog-eared where Evelyn had pored over the contents. "Oh, dear Lord," I whispered.

I lifted the Bible without feeling any surge of goodness or power. To me, a man of science, it was a book of ancient wisdom and no more. Despite the hundreds of hours I had spent in church as a child and youth, I had long since stopped worshipping or even believing. Yet now, for the first time in years, I wondered.

Was there some world beyond our own? Some further existence on the far side of death? I found that hard to fathom, for when our life force ends; our body ceases to function and sinks into corruption, rather like politicians when they enter parliament.

Holding the Bible, I looked around the room, seeing nothing out of the ordinary. It was a room like any other in the city, a little untidy through use, with books and papers scattered around, the remains of a meal on an unscraped plate, the fire smouldering in the grate, but no supernatural bodies. There was nothing to make the sounds, no voice to sing the songs and undoubtedly no ghost to torment me. All the images, I knew, were in my mind and their ceasing when the Bible fell was only a coincidence.

I shook my head.

What nonsense the human mind can conjure from old superstitions and the imaginings of taut nerves. That's all it was, I knew. I was upset over Swinton's rejection of my attempts to woo Evelyn; that and the gibberings of the uneducated mob in the close had unsettled me. Well then, I thought, I will have to deal with Swinton and learn to ignore the great unwashed. After all, if they were in any way intelligent or successful, they would have risen above their present position and found a more comfortable place to live.

No, I told myself, placing the Bible on the table, there was nothing of the supernatural here.

Test it, I urged. Test it. Step back from the Bible and challenge the dark forces to reappear.

I did just that, taking first one step, then two and five, without effect. There was no resurgence of laughter, singing, or anything else. Satisfied that I had convinced myself of the superiority of reason over groundless fear, I smiled, whistled a merry little tune and checked the time.

Six minutes past six.

Prevent me from meeting Evelyn, would he? Damn the man: Damn Swinton and his ideas. I wanted Evelyn, and I would have her, whatever Mr Swinton or a hundred Mr Swintons may think and do.

I stalked the streets with my staff thumping down on the paving, harder and harder as my mood grew ever fouler. Without realising it, I had walked from the Old Town down the Mound to the New, and even further, so I now stood outside the wrought iron gates of Leithbrae House.

"Good God," I said to myself, "how on earth did I get here? I can't remember a thing about the journey." Pushing open the gates, I marched up the gravel path to the front door, on which I rapped smartly with the head of my staff and waited, humming *Maggie Lauder* to myself.

Leithbrae House is half a mile or so beyond the New Town, on the pleasant slopes that lead down to the sea. The village of Broughton nearby was once an independent Burgh of Barony until the relentless advance of Edinburgh had swallowed it whole while threatening even the policies of the three-storied mansion of Bellevue. Now Leithbrae House stood like a besieged island, a classical house within private grounds as the city lapped at its walled shores.

The butler looked like a man from another age in his powdered periwig and maroon suit. He looked at me as if he wished to deposit me in the ash-pit.

"I have come to see your master." I placed my card on the silver tray he thrust out. "Pray tell him I am here."

"Is he expecting you?" the butler asked, adding "sir" as an afterthought.

"He will see me," I said, pushing into the house.

The Honourable Peter looked slightly wary when he walked towards me, as well he might, given the favours he owed me. I had never mentioned curing him of the pox, let alone the thousands of sovereigns he owed me from the Benison Club.

"Come this way." He ushered me into his gun room, away from prying ears. "To what do I owe the honour?"

I tapped my staff on the ground as I surveyed the array of firearms on the wall. "I believe you have friends in the stock market."

Sir Peter nodded. "That's correct."

Laying my staff on a table, I lifted down a fowling-piece and sighted along the barrel. "Your friends have the power to manipulate share prices, don't they?"

"Yes," the Honourable Peter said, after a slight pause.

"I know nothing about such matters." I swivelled the barrel until it was pointing at his groin and pulled back the hammer. "I hope this piece is not loaded."

"So do I." The Honourable Peter swept his hand sideways, deflecting my aim. "What do you want, Doctor?"

"I want you to clear your debt to me," I said pleasantly, replacing the fowling-piece and lifting a shotgun. "At no expense to you. Is this gun loaded?"

"No," the Honourable Peter said. "What do you mean, at no expense to me?"

"You owe me a great deal of money," I reminded, "and I am sure you have no desire for me to treat you as we treated Outerston."

The Honourable Peter took a deep breath. "Continue, Doctor," he said.

"There is a man I want financially ruined," I said, aiming the shotgun out the window. "I want his stocks to fall so low that he cannot sell them."

"How many does he have?" Peter's erstwhile moral scruples had vanished at my threat to his fortune.

"I don't know," I said. "I know only that he has tied his entire fortune to two particular companies."

Peter nodded without smiling. "Who is this unhappy fellow?"

"That is my affair," I said.

"Is that all you wish me to do?" the Honourable Peter asked. "I have the share prices manipulated, and you forget all my debts?"

"Yes." I replaced the shotgun where it belonged. "Could you do that for me?"

Peter nodded. "I believe so although I don't like to ruin a man for no reason."

"I have an excellent reason," I said, lifting a pair of pistols. "These are well balanced. They might be useful should you become a highwayman if you lose your house." I smiled at him. "But I would own these, too, wouldn't I? I might hire them out to you, for a percentage of the profits, until you are caught and hanged."

The Honourable Peter glared at me. "You're a bastard, Elliot. Do you know that?"

I smiled, keeping the pistols in my hands. "Oh, no. My parents were legally married, Peter. Unlike the little creatures you have sired."

I had no idea whether the Honourable Peter had fathered any illegitimate children but, given his way of life, he probably had. "I am a doctor, old fellow. We learn about such matters." I could see by the expression of his face that he wished to do me harm.

"Tell you what, old fellow." I reversed the pistols and handed them to him, butt first. "I have placed your promissory note in a safe place, in case you are interested. I have given it to my solicitor, with a copy to a very good friend of mine. The solicitor has instructions that if anything happens to me, any debt owed to me is transferred to a third party. Simultaneously, I have given instructions for the lawyer to publish that promissory note in the *Scotsman* and *Caledonian Mercury*." I winked. "My insurance policy, old fellow, in case your natural frustration overcomes your gentlemanly scruples."

When the Honourable Peter said nothing, I sauntered to the door, staff in hand.

"All right, damn you," Peter said. "What is the company name?"

"Constable the bookseller and Ballantyne the printers," I said. "If their stocks fall appreciably, I'll be in touch with the promissory note. If not," I shrugged and looked around me. "I could rather enjoy living here."

CHAPTER 11

I cannot describe the feeling I had when finally I closed the door on that house in the West Bow. It was a mixture of relief that I had escaped and fear that I was stepping into the unknown, a kind of dread that I was leaving some part of me behind. I cannot explain why I should have felt like that.

"You're leaving then, Doctor." The woman remained a good 10 paces from my door.

"I am," I said.

"Did the house chase you away?"

I pondered my answer. "It may have done so," I said.

The woman stepped closer. I did not recognise her, an elderly, wizened thing with hands like claws. "It does that," she spoke in a harsh whisper, like somebody who had not used her voice for a long time. "And sometimes you take it with you."

"It's a house," I said to the crazy old witch. "How can I take it with me?"

I could smell the woman from where I stood, a mixture of smoke, soot and even I didn't know what. "Hell has its methods," she said.

"I'm leaving the gateway to Hell behind," I said, without a trace of irony. I, the scientific doctor, the man proud of his rational thought, the graduate of Glasgow University, was leaving a house because of superstitious fancies that a warlock had once lived here. Looked at seriously, the idea was not only ludicrous, but it was also untrue. I told myself that I was not leaving the West Bow because of the stories, but because the New Town address would advance my career. All the other events, the strange noises, dreams and happenings, were flights of the imagination brought on by strained nerves, or the creaking of an ancient house in the wind, nothing more.

"That may be true, Doctor Elliot, Dr Martin Elliot," the old woman said, "but in my master's kingdom, there are many doorways."

"What?" I asked. "What the devil do you mean by that?"

What ever the devil the old woman had meant, she slipped back into her doorway, and although I was only a few steps behind her, she had vanished before I reached her. In such a labyrinth of passageways, closes, wynds and courtyards as the Old Town, there was no point in trying to find her.

Leaving the carriers to convey my belongings away from the house, I decided the old woman was crazed and stepped away from that place for the last time. I tapped my staff on the ground, humming *Maggie Lauder* as I sauntered up the West Bow. When I reached the Lawnmarket, I turned for a final look at the street where so much had happened. I was leaving the black coaches and invisible visitors behind as I bid a final farewell to the Old Town.

"Wha wadna be in love
Wi' bonnie Maggie Lauder?
A piper met her guan to Fife,
And speir'd what was't they ca'd her."

Living in the New Town was undoubtedly different from living in the old. The gracious Georgian streets were wide and elegant, the neighbours were so respectable they were afraid to raise their voices lest they break the outward serenity of the area, and even the birds were polite as they greeted the dawn.

It was good to leave my new house at the corner of George Street and Hanover Street without stepping over the sleeping bodies of the destitute and I did not miss the stench of urine and worse that filled the courtyard in the West Bow. It was pleasant to stroll along George Street and Princes Street with its exceptional view to the castle and to tip my hat to the graceful ladies and smart gentlemen who swept past me.

All this was fine enough but tame. One new source of amusement was reading the financial sector of the newspapers. From a high, the shares of Constable the bookseller commenced a steady slide, slipping in value day by day, while Ballantynes followed, slowly but certainly reducing Swinton's fortune. Every morning I read the newspaper, partly to smile at the falling stocks, but also to restore my strength after the night's now-expected horrors. I had thought that leaving the West Bow would end the nightmares. I was wrong. They continued night after terrible, sleep-tearing night.

I was in the surgery, regaling myself with the latest downturn in the fortunes of Constable when the door banged open, and Evelyn appeared, gasping for breath.

"I'm sorry, Doctor Elliot," my latest servant said, trying to restrain her. "She just burst in."

I smiled as Evelyn ran towards me. "That's quite all right, John," I said. "This lady is always welcome."

I had hardly seen Evelyn since Swinton had denied me the chance to propose. I avoided Evelyn partly because our meetings would be too painful, and partly because there seemed little point until I had Swinton where I wanted him. Besides, I was trying to charm the father of a smart little redhead as an alternative to Evelyn if my present strategy was unsuccessful. Oh, don't misunderstand me – although the redhead was a bouncy little piece, Evelyn was still my first choice.

"Martin." Evelyn began speaking even before John withdrew. "I know you can't help and probably don't wish to, but I don't know where else to turn."

"I'll help in any way I can," I reassured her. "Now, don't distress yourself, and tell me what's wrong."

Evelyn closed the door in John's face before she sat down. "It's Father," she said.

"What about him?" I hid my joy, guessing what was coming.

"He's in a bad state with his nerves, alternatively in hysterics or plunging into black moods."

"Ah," I said. "Do you know what brought this on?"

"Yes," Evelyn said. "When I asked Mother what had occurred, she said Father is in terrible financial trouble."

"Ah," I said again, looking concerned. "If you ask your father to come here, I could prescribe something to lift his spirits."

"Would you?" Evelyn asked.

"Yes, of course."

"Even after he denied you my hand in marriage?"

"He was doing what he thought was best," I said magnanimously. "I do not agree with him, but I cannot blame him for trying to look after his daughter." I gave what I hoped was a long-suffering sigh. "At some time, I hope to convince your father to change his mind. I have not given up yet."

Evelyn made a long arm and touched my sleeve. "Nor have I, Martin, and God bless you. May I bring Father here?"

"My door is always open to your father."

I swear I saw tears in Evelyn's eyes when she left my surgery. "You are a good man, Martin. I hope that father appreciates your forbearance."

It was not until the next day that Mr Swinton came to my surgery, white of face and bowed of shoulder. In short, he was quite unlike the bold, confident man of only a few weeks before. I greeted him like an old friend.

"Mr Swinton! How good to see you again. Come, give me your hat and coat." I ushered him to the chair opposite mine, with the desk in between.

"Sit down, Mr Swinton and tell me what seems to be the matter." I had the newspaper before me, neatly folded, with the financial section uppermost. "I perceive that you are unhappy and prone to fits of melancholia."

Swinton sat, keeping his shoulders bowed and his head down. "Thank you for seeing me, Doctor. You are right in your diagnosis."

I nodded understandingly. "You are so unlike your old self that I suspect some outside source has caused this downturn in your health."

Mr Swinton looked at me as if I were the new Messiah. "Yes, Doctor."

"So then, if we remove or repair the source, we shall soon restore you to health." I pronounced my antidote with a smile.

"Yes, Doctor, you are correct," Swinton said, "although I fear that removing the source is quite beyond your capabilities or anybody else's."

I nodded sympathetically. "I will not know that until you take me into your confidence." I leaned back in my seat, looking stern. "I know enough about human nature to know there are only three things that can so suddenly affect a man in such a manner. One is a matter of the heart, such as a family dispute or trouble; the second is a matter of physical health, and the third is a matter of finances."

Swinton nodded again.

"All right then," I continued, sagely. "I know you and Mrs Swinton are as devoted a couple as it is possible to find, while Evelyn would never dream of going against your will, as I know to my cost." Let that little barb sink in, I thought. "That leaves physical health or financial concerns. So, Mr Swinton, I will give you a thorough examination before we go any further."

"There is no need, Doctor." Swinton demurred, as I knew he would, for no man would wish to undergo an intimate inspection by the very fellow he had rejected as his daughter's suitor.

"There is every need," I insisted solemnly. "Come on, man, off with your clothes!"

I watched as Swinton removed his clothing, and proceeded to give him the most thorough and prolonged medical examination of his life. After such an investigation, a man in such a state as Swinton would be in no condition, mental or physical, to resist my plan, I reasoned, and correctly, as it turned out.

"Now, sir," I said, without giving the fellow time to dress again. "Sit down and tell me what ails you. Physically you are tip-top, without a care in the world."

At last Swinton faced me. I had degraded him in every possible way, so I was in total control of the situation, and him.

"I have financial problems, sir," Swinton replied in a muffled tone, without meeting my eyes.

"Good God, sir." I shook my head. "Is that all? Why Mr Swinton," I reached into the top drawer of the desk and withdrew the pocketbook I had placed there earlier. "Why, sir, if you say how much you need, I am sure I can help."

Swinton coloured and looked away, shuffling a tear from his eye. "You are too kind, sir, too kind indeed."

I produced a sheaf of banknotes and handed them over. "That is 100 pounds, Mr Swinton. Will that help?" I knew his losses were very much more.

"Sir, Doctor Elliot, your kindness overwhelms me."

I pushed across the money. "There now, you are Evelyn's father."

"Sir," Swinton said, "I appreciate your help, but I fear I am deeply in debt."

"Ah." I settled back in my chair. "Put your clothes back on, Mr Swinton, and tell me everything. I assure you it will go no further."

I listened to the tragic story of how Swinton had expected a high return on both Constables and Ballantynes, but when the price of shares had collapsed, he had lost everything.

"Everything, Mr Elliot," Swinton said. "I was so confident that I took out a loan from the bank, with the house as security."

"I see," I said, gloating inwardly.

"Now the bank wants to foreclose and call in the loan."

I already knew that, as the bank manager happened to be a member of the New Wig Club and was in my debt. "That's terrible," I said. "How much is the loan?" I produced another bundle of banknotes. "There is 200 there, Mr Swinton. That is all the ready cash I have in the world, so you were right to stop me marrying Evelyn."

"I fear there is no hope, Elliot," Swinton lowered his voice to a whisper. "I am 3,000 in debt."

"So much?" I said, shaking my head. Standing up, I walked to the door and opened it. "John," I said to my man. "Close the surgery for the day. I have an urgent case here." I waited until the doors were closed and John was gone, while Swinton sat in despair, entirely at my mercy.

"Mr Swinton," I said. "There may be a way to raise your money, but it will not be to your liking."

"Mr Elliot," Swinton said. "I will do anything, anything at all, to keep a roof over my wife's head."

"You may have to compromise your principles," I said.

"I fear I have none left," Swinton said sadly. "Not when my wife and home are threatened."

"Have you heard of the New Wig Club?" I asked. "It is a gentleman's club where money can be won and lost at the tables."

"I have none to lose," Swinton said.

"You have that 200 pounds," I said, "and I can scrape up a reserve of 250 more, with luck." I gave him my best devil-may-care grin. "Come, cheer up, sir, all is not lost."

I was fortunate that I knew the gamblers present at the New Wig when I escorted in Mr Swinton. "This gentleman is a friend of mine," I said, "so we are both novices at the card tables."

Most of the men there were in debt to me, so smiled ruefully at my words, and none was foolish enough to disagree. If they had, I would have called in their obligations or sent the porters to their door. Although the New Wig had nobody as formidable as the two Donalds, they employed a trio of hard-faced men who ensured a relatively peaceful atmosphere.

"Set up the table," I said. "My friend is named Smith. John Smith." I winked at Mr Swinton. "And I am Mr James Brown."

Once again, nobody would deny my word, so as Smith and Brown, we sat at the table as the house dealer set out the cards for poker. I will not go into tedious details over every card in every hand, but with my staff leaning against my chair, I once again began to bring in the money. Swinton was only an average card player, but games of whist with Mrs Swinton had taught him how to read the fall of the cards, so he did not disgrace himself.

Slowly, we built up our winnings, with my usual luck carrying me through and Swinton dogged, with the candlelight reflecting on the sheen of sweat across his face. We were fortunate that the other players were no more skilled than Swinton, and more fortunate still that an eager young flat joined us. I knew immediately that the newcomer would be our gull for the day. He came with a smile on his face and no attempt at concealment in his expression.

"Good evening, sir," I said. "I have not had the pleasure of playing with you before."

"No, Mr Brown," he said. "This is my first time here."

"Us too," I said with the beaming smile of the truly innocent.

I gave him a quick introduction to the game of poker, told him he was very welcome and asked him quiet questions about himself.

"I'm 21 years old," he said, in a North Country accent.

"A man indeed," I said, watching his eyes brighten as he read his new cards. I recognised him as a mammy's boy, freshly released from the apron-strings and eager to try out everything the city has to offer.

By alternatively raking in his rhino and encouraging him with an occasional small victory, I gradually reduced my gull's fortune until he had only a few golden guineas in front of him. I had long learned not to flout my winnings, so kept them at a small side-table, hidden under a green silk handkerchief. On the last hand of the evening, I saw an exultant expression on my gull's face and knew he had a strong hand. I played that for all I was worth, cursing and blinding when I turned my cards and throwing down my money as if I expected to lose.

Swinton watched me through worried eyes, although I

knew his hand was at least fair. The gull fell for my ruse, of course, murmuring, "Hard luck, old fellow," as he raised me to the limit of his fortune and added his gold signet ring in an attempt to make me fold.

"Look here," I said. "This is a queer do. I think you're bluffing and have a bad hand. That's the sort of fellow you are, I think."

"Me, sir?" my flat asked.

"You, sir," I said. "I fancy you're a sharp, one of those fellows who try to look innocent while you gull respectable men like Mr Smith and me."

The flat grinned, pleased that I thought him a sharp.

"All right," I said, glancing at my hand in apparent disgust, "I'll call your bluff, sir and raise you." Without more ado, I put 50 guineas on the table.

"I don't have that much in readies," the fool said. "But I have it at home."

"You'll not sharp me, by God," I said. "Not James Brown of Netherby Hall. Double or quits, if you dare, card sharp or not."

By now thoroughly convinced that I had a queer hand, my gull doubled, and doubled again, until I knew he had promised his entire fortune and probably that of his children and grand-children as well. Swinton had sensibly folded, while the other players gathered around, well aware of my ploy.

"There we are then," I said at last. "It's the knackers yard for me and damn you, sir, for a villain."

I threw down my cards, face down.

My dupe was grinning like a mountebank when he showed his hand, a reasonable knave-high flush. Now I had him in the palm of my hand, I dropped my act and turned my cards. "Four kings, old fellow. My pot, I think." I took his promissory note.

The youngster stared at me in mixed dismay and horror. "That's my father's house and lands," he said.

"My house and lands now," I told him.

"It's worth 10,000 guineas."

I nodded, allowing him to suffer for a minute out of pure devilment. "I'll tell you what, old fellow, I'll go easy on you. Find me three thousand, and we'll forget the rest."

I saw Swinton look up in surprise. "What a noble fellow you are, Mr Brown," he said.

The flat grabbed at this offer with both hands, as well he might for I was saving his skin, but what would I want with an estate somewhere in the wilds of Perthshire or Ross or the devil knows where? Hundreds of acres of heather-moor and wet rock, for God's sake, with sodden tenants who could not even speak an intelligible language. My love affair with Gaelic had been short-lived.

"Thank you," my broken youngster said, thoroughly humbled.

"That's all right, old fellow," I said. "I want you to hand over the money to my banker, in the name of Mr Swinton." I felt Swinton's eyes swivel to me. "It's not my name, of course."

"Swinton," my youth said. "I'll do that." He hesitated. "It might take me a day or two."

"Two days," I agreed, clapping him on the back in false bonhomie. "As you are a Highland gentleman, I know you won't let me down."

I watched him slouch off, having learned his lesson not to play outside his league. "Now, Mr Smith, I think we should celebrate with our winnings."

"Good God, man," Swinton said as we left the New Wig club and sauntered along Princes Street with the wind fairly biting at us and the lights of the castle glowing across the gardens. "What have you done?"

"Helped a friend," I said.

"You have no idea how grateful I am to you," Swinton said.

"You've loaned me three thousand guineas. How can I ever repay you?"

"It's not a loan, Mr Swinton," I said. "It's your money, paid into your bank in your name. You are debt-free. Now, let us celebrate with our other winnings. I happen to know another establishment where the company is cheerful, and the wine flows free."

When Swinton looked at me with the gratitude warm in his eyes, I knew he was wondering if I might, after all, be a suitable match for his darling daughter. However, I had another ploy yet for the oh-so-respectable Mr Swinton.

"I've never been in here," I said, pausing outside the door of an establishment where I was a frequent visitor, "but Charles MacNeil tells me it is the most amazing establishment with the best of wines imported directly from France and the most refined of company."

"I cannot say no to the most generous of men I have ever encountered." Already Swinton walked straighter as if I had removed a heavy weight from his shoulders.

"It's this way, I think," I said as if I had never trodden the route. The Waverley Club was named after the famous Waverley Novels as a blind to disguise its real purpose. There was no connection to the author except the name and the glass-fronted bookcase in the lobby of the Rose Street building. Once through the arched door, one entered the most secretive and best-run brothel in Edinburgh.

I conducted Swinton into the front room, where half a dozen gentlemen lounged on comfortable chairs, while smartly dressed women offered them the most varied selection of drinks in the city.

"My name is Brown," I announced, introducing myself to the oldest of these ladies, who knew me of old. "And this is Mr Smith."

Swinton looked at me sideways, as if wondering why I did not use our correct names in such a respectable establishment. However, he followed my lead and sank into a chair.

"I am Mrs Lightfoot," Madame Dora told me, straight-faced. "What can I do for you gentlemen today?"

"A glass of claret for me, Mrs Lightfoot, if you please, but my friend Mr Smith has cause to celebrate."

Madame Dora produced her most innocent professional smile. "Will it be the finest of our French wines?"

"That will do," I said, "I'll pay for a bottle. No." I changed my mind. "Champagne, I think."

"No, I insist on paying." Swinton put a hand on my sleeve. "You have already been too generous."

"We must share your good fortune," I said as Madame Dora looked from Swinton to me and back, trying to work out my plan.

We sat at a private table, with Swinton gradually relaxing as the exotic champagne worked its magic. After an hour, I sought out Madame Dora again, leaving Swinton to enjoy the ambience.

"Do you still work the Edinburgh crimp?" I asked, keeping my voice low.

Dora nodded. "Yes, I can drug unpleasant clients and smuggle them on board a Leith ship bound for India or some other far-flung destination. Do you wish to send your Mr Smith on a long sea voyage?"

"I want to play a joke on him," I said, and explained my idea.

Madame Dora listened, smiling. "I believe I can arrange that," she said.

"I don't want him hurt," I said.

"He won't feel a thing," Madame Dora promised.

"I'll leave things in your hands," I said.

"As long as you pay the piper," Dora said.

I passed across 10 guineas. "Don't let me down," I said.

I had no fear of that, of course, for Dora was a professional. "When do you want it done?" she asked.

"The day after tomorrow," I said. "I want no connection with me at all."

Dora secreted away my gold. "None, Mr Brown." Her wink was as good as a signed and sealed document from the highest legal minds in the land. Probably more secure, for I have met many of the highest as they gamble and cavort in the most unsavoury places. I told Dora Swinton's home and business address and left her to work out the details.

Swinton was half-seas-over when one of the other clients in the room began to have a convulsive fit. By the time I had helped him recover, Swinton was nearly asleep.

"Come along, old fellow," I roused him with a gentle shake. "It's time we were heading back home. Your good lady will be wondering where you are."

Dora was there to help Swinton on with his coat and handed him his hat and gloves as to the manner born. "I hope to see you again, Mr Smith," Dora said.

"I hope so too," Swinton said, as I escorted him back to the street with my plan hatching very nicely. I had proved myself the very best of friends, advanced my case for matrimony, hatched a plot with Madame Dora and made a tidy sum of money. The day had been a success. I whistled *Maggie Lauder* as I manoeuvred Swinton to the green door in Queen Street.

CHAPTER 12

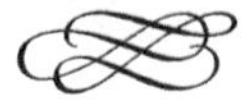

"Mrs Swinton! I have good news, the very best of news!" Swinton lurched into his house, swaying in the grand hall as he looked around him. Mrs Swinton hurried out to meet him.

"Swinton! What time do you call this? Have you been drinking?" She noticed me and stopped, with one hand over her mouth. "I do apologise, Mr Elliot! What must you think of us?"

I realised she was in her nightclothes, smiled and politely turned my back. "It's quite all right, Mrs Swinton, you are perfectly decent, and I am a doctor."

"Father! Are you all right?" Evelyn was also in her night-clothes and a very captivating sight she was, with a night-cap not quite succeeding in controlling all her hair and her bare ankles and feet protruding delicately. "Oh! Martin!" She stepped behind a high-backed chair to hide her extremities.

I remained with my back to the family as Swinton tried to explain the evening's events. As it happened, there was a mirror on the wall that afforded me an excellent view, but one must observe the niceties.

"All is well," Swinton said. "Mr Elliot has come to our aid. Oh, what a splendid fellow he is, simply splendid."

I agreed with that, of course, although I shook my head in denial.

Evelyn clapped her hands and emerged from behind the chair. "What has happened, Father, pray, tell me!"

"Come into the parlour," Mrs Swinton said, flapping her hand. She had thrown on a dressing gown, although Evelyn, I was glad to see, had not copied her example. "Come on, come on. You too, Mr Elliot."

I followed, partly supporting Mr Swinton, who was swaying, partly through the effects of over-indulgence in alcohol, partly through the excitement of relief.

Evelyn watched me, gently smiling, although I could sense her confusion. Her dishevelled hair and bare feet made her even more attractive in my eyes.

We trailed into the parlour, with Mrs Swinton sending a tired servant back to bed before she demanded to hear the news.

"Come on, Swinton! Out with it!" Mrs Swinton perched on the edge of a chair.

"Yes, Father." Evelyn sat comfortably close to me, with her hand only an inch from my leg. I did not move, preferring to watch the by-play between the Swintons. For one second, I wished I could be part of such a close circle, glanced at Evelyn and wondered if that could ever happen.

Talking at a great pace, Swinton related his exciting evening, praising me at every opportunity as he spoke of the end of his money troubles and my magnificent generosity. I waved away the Swintons' gratitude while accepting the small hand-squeeze by Evelyn, which was the best prize I could have had.

"Three thousand pounds!" Evelyn's eyes were wide as she

stared at me as if I was some new Messiah. "Does that not leave you destitute, Mr Elliot?"

"It was money won in a card game," I said, truthfully. "I did not possess it this time yesterday, and I shall not miss it tomorrow."

Evelyn squeezed my hand again. "I knew you would help," she whispered.

After a round of gratitude and congratulations, I spoke again. "I am sorry to break up this happy gathering," I said, "but I'm afraid I must leave now."

"Mr Elliot, Martin," Mrs Swinton said. "You must stay the night. You are the hero of the hour, the Wellington of the finances, the very prince of generosity. Of course, we will pay you back."

"It is a gift from God," I said, "not a loan." I decided to lay it on thick. "I have never been to that club before and prayed for help. It was all the Lord's work." There, I thought. Now you have rejected a suitor who is God-fearing man as well as generous.

I felt their eyes on me as I left their house and marched, straight-backed, along Queen Street. I knew it was best to perform the apparently good deed and depart without milking the Swintons' gratitude. With nothing to tempt me home, I spent the rest of the night in Dora's establishment, having already picked out a shapely lady with a roving eye. Dora was pleased to see me and delighted to see the gold I passed into her already swollen coffers.

I returned to my new home only as the first grey streaks of dawn lightened the eastern sky, changed hurriedly and walked to the surgery. Despite being so tired I could hardly see straight, I was smiling, and *Maggie Lauder* had never sounded so tuneful in my ears.

I heard the sharp rap on the door only moments before I left my bed. "That's surprising," I said to myself. Foolishly, I checked the time, saw the usual six minutes past six and made my unsteady way to the door, picking up my pistol en route.

When I opened the door, I found a note pinned outside, with the address of a house in the Cowgate and the single letter "D".

"Oh, very cryptic, Dora," I said. "But our mutual friend will have to wait until I am ready to rescue him."

I washed and dressed in a leisurely manner, wondering at the difference between this light and airy house and the darkness of the last, ate a simple breakfast and lifted my staff.

"Now, Mr Swinton," I said, "let me see how amenable you are to reason." Stepping across to the mirror, I checked my appearance, brushed a few hairs from my coat, nodded in satisfaction and was about to turn away when I saw the figure standing behind me.

"What the devil are you doing here?" Thinking it was one of the servants, I turned, prepared to thrash him.

The room was empty. I fought the shiver that ran down my back. "I have my Bible," I said firmly. "You can no longer scare me."

There was no reply, nothing except my voice resounding in that room. Taking a deep breath, I returned my attention to the mirror, to see the figure behind me, peering over my shoulder.

"You cannot hurt me," I said. "You cannot influence me in any way."

The figure was not as indistinct as it had once been, for I could now make out features. It was a tall man in a long cloak, with a prominent nose and a pair of stern brown eyes. I knew he was the same man who had entered my dreams in the West Bow, the man who had merged with my mind.

"I see you," I said, "but I do not fear you." With my gaze fixed firmly on the mirror, I stepped backwards until I reached the small table on which I had placed the Bible. Lifting it in my left hand, I held it up. "There, you see? I am protected."

I had heard the laughter during the night. That was the first time I heard it in daylight, and although I held the Bible high in the air, the laughter continued, mocking me as I withdrew out of the door and into the outer hall, where weak sunlight streamed through the semi-circular fanlight above the door.

"We're still here," the voice said as I opened the door and blundered outside into the reality of George Street.

"Are you all right, Doctor?" The hawker stood in a corner, staring at me.

"I am," I said. I nearly ran down Hanover Street and climbed the Earthen Mound at such speed that the muscles of my legs complained. When I reached the Lawnmarket, the world had awakened with harsh voices, the cheerful clatter of traffic and a riot of colour.

Gripping my staff firmly, I avoided the steep slope of the Bow and descended a dark wynd into the chasm of the Cowgate, with its bitter memories of the death of Ruth Anderson. I had walked only 100 yards when I rechecked the address, and stopped, with the breath catching in my throat.

I was outside the exact door where the coach had run Ruth down, the close where Weir had lived before he moved to the West Bow. I am no doubter of coincidences, but this was one too many.

"Oh, dear God in heaven," I said softly. For a moment, I contemplated walking on, leaving Swinton to his fate, but that would ruin my plan. I had gone to great lengths to ensure I could manipulate him, and I would not allow a long-dead man spoil them, for I was now confident that Sandy was correct and Thomas Weir, in some form or other, was influencing me.

With my heart hammering, I gripped the Bible firmly within my pocket as I entered the stinking close and negotiated the turnpike stairs to the third floor. I heard raised voices behind a door, male and female. Without hesitating, I pushed inside, to see Swinton lying on a filthy bed, trying to cover his nakedness as two harpies of the lowest possible type screeched at him. Swinton looked terrified, as well he might in that company, and I swear he had been weeping.

"Dr Elliot! How are you here?" Swinton's voice was strained.

"Mr Smith!" I shouted. "What the devil is this?"

The women screamed vituperation from poisonous tongues and swung wildly at me with nails like filthy claws. A few months earlier, I would have recoiled at such devil women, but my time in the West Bow had hardened me.

"Get away from me, you vile creatures!" I swung my staff at them, enjoying the thrill of contact. "Leave that man alone! He is a gentleman!"

"A gentleman, is he?" the closer of the women, a wild-haired monster with a gaunt face, screamed. "He owes us for last night!"

"Owes you?" I held my staff ready for any fresh assault.

"He hasnae paid us for last night," the second woman, a skeletal-thin girl who might have reached her 14th winter, said, adding a string of obscenities to strengthen her case. "If he doesnae pay we'll scrape the hide off him!" She went into anatomical details that would have turned a marine's hair white.

Swinton stared at me, pale-faced and evidently terrified. "I have to get away, but somebody's stolen all my money."

"I wonder who?" Raising my staff, I faced the harpies. "Never mind, let's get you out of here."

"He hasnae paid," the younger creature repeated, holding a wickedly-long knife in her hand. "If he doesnae pay I'll..."

I did not wait for the details. "How much does he owe?" I asked the women. "Here!" I spun a golden guinea over to them. "Come on, Mr Smith. Let's get out of here."

Bundling up his clothes, Swinton nearly ran from that sordid little room and down the stairs before he paused to drag his clothes on, sobbing.

"What happened?" I asked him. "How did you end in such a terrible predicament?"

Swinton looked bemused and embarrassed, as well he might, given the place from where I had rescued him. "I cannot explain it," he said. "I had a new client visit me at the office, a handsome, well set up gentlewoman who wished to show me her property with a view to having me sell it for her."

I listened as we walked along the Cowgate, learning how Dora tricked her gulls. "And what happened, Mr Swinton?"

"The gentlewoman showed me her property, a fine town-house in Frederick Street, and I was valuing it when she asked if I wished a glass of claret. I accepted, and the rest is a blur, sir, a blur. I do not recall very much except those two terrible women being with me."

I nodded. "I understand, Mr Swinton. Your gentlewoman drugged you. Even the best of gentlemen can fall into the worst of company, purely by misadventure."

Swinton shook his head. "I assure you, Mr Elliot, that I was not searching for such women."

I nodded. "Some concerned person – I don't know who – left a note than my friend Mr Smith was at that address." I stopped as we entered the Grassmarket. "Mrs Swinton will be most concerned that you were out all night."

"She will indeed," Swinton said. "I will hurry to her forthwith."

I tapped my staff on the ground. "Then there is the other matter, the most delicate of matters."

Swinton looked at me. "What is that, sir? I am afraid I do not understand you."

I stopped as a cart rolled past with its wheels lurching on the uneven cobbles. "Your wife, sir. You seem to have spent the night with two unfortunates, two prostitutes. You may have picked up some disease."

Swinton stared at me with what remained of the colour draining from his face. "You don't think that I..?"

"I do not know, Mr Swinton," I said. "You have a choice now; you may make a clean breast of things to Mrs Swinton or find an excuse not to expect your marital rights until you know you are free of any contagion."

"Oh, my God," Swinton said as the full enormity of his position came to him.

"I am not a married man, as you know," I continued, "but I suggest that confessing everything to Mrs Swinton may hurt her and weaken your marital bonds."

Swinton said nothing, shaking his head in wordless horror. As I tapped my staff on the ground, I knew I had him secure in the palm of my hand.

"Come to the surgery," I said. "I can recommend a course of mercury pills or a new iodine treatment recommended by a Dublin doctor named William Wallace."

"Whatever is best, Doctor." Swinton sounded faint, as well he might.

"Come now," I said, reassuringly. "I can cure you if you trust me. I'll send my servant to Mrs Swinton with a message that you have had a nasty turn and will be home shortly."

I had Swinton where I wanted him. He would be dependent on me until I pronounced him cured, which would be whenever I had Evelyn as my intended, with her father's blessing.

"There is one more thing," I said, casually increasing Swinton's worries after I had inspected him. "Do you wish me to inform the police?"

"The police?" Swinton looked even more shocked. "Good God, no!"

"As you wish." I withdrew the suggestion immediately. "But they may find out anyway. Somebody has worked out that I was Mr Brown, so they may also know your identity."

I let him ponder that for a while, handed him some mercury pills I kept in the surgery and advised he keep them hidden from his wife. "Just in case of complications," I said. I was quiet as I accompanied Swinton across the North Bridge to the New Town, where the gale had us both staggering.

Mrs Swinton was all a-fluster when I brought her husband back, explained that he had suddenly been taken ill and needed some time to recover.

"Oh, Dr Elliot," she nearly sobbed. "You have proved our saviour yet again."

"Nonsense," I said. "I am caring for one of my patients and a good friend." I tipped my hat to Evelyn as she appeared at the head of the stairs, waving to me. "Good morning, Miss Swinton."

Leaving Swinton in the care of his wife, I returned home, tapping my staff on the ground and humming *Maggie Lauder*.

I expected Swinton to call into my surgery, and he came the very next day. He arrived with an awkward smile, removing his hat as though to a lord, and not to a man he had pronounced unsuitable for his daughter's hand.

I greeted him with a professional smile and an invitation to sit down.

"Thank you, Dr Elliot," Swinton said and lapsed into silence.

I allowed him the luxury of peace, watching him with my eyebrows raised.

"Dr Elliot," Swinton said at last. "I owe you an apology. I have done you the gravest of injustices, and I must rectify matters."

I waited, enjoying his discomfort. "You have done nothing of the sort, sir," I said.

Swinton shifted his feet. "When you asked for my daughter's hand in marriage, I rejected you."

"You did," I said, heaping coals of fire on his head. "You were acting as any father would do, in the best interests of his daughter. I assure you I bear you no ill-will over the matter and will not bother Miss Swinton again if that is your desire."

"This is very embarrassing," Swinton said. "I am not making myself understood. I have not come to reinforce that decision, but to rescind it, Dr Elliot." He stood up. "I was mistaken, sir, vastly mistaken. When I was at my lowest ebb, in despair, contemplating ending my life, sir, you stepped in and pulled me from the abyss. I owe you more than I can ever repay." Swinton shook his head. "Why, Dr Elliot, Martin, if I may be so bold, I did you the greatest of injustices, and you responded with nothing but kindness, not once, but twice."

I said nothing, savouring his humiliation.

"Dr Elliot, Martin," Swinton said. "I withdraw my previous words and fully give my permission for you to court our Evelyn, and there's my hand on it." When Swinton held out his paw, I could see he was shaking, as was to be expected, for, in essence, he had sold his daughter. If I had been purse-pinched and unable to lift his financial troubles, Mr Swinton would never have agreed to transfer her care to me.

"You are a gentleman, sir," I said, shaking his hand heartily, "and I thank you from the bottom of my heart. I assure you that, should Evelyn agree to my proposal, I shall treat her with the same respect you do." *As a chattel to be sold to the highest bidder.*

"That is all any father could ask." Swinton had not yet released my hand. "Sir, you have saved me. You arrived like a guardian angel."

"I am no angel," I said truthfully.

"You are," Swinton said. "I swear that you are."

I did not argue a second time, although inwardly I wondered what colour my wings would be if ever I were to achieve angelic status. Would they be red to reflect the flames of hell? Or black to show the colour of my soul?

The thought of fire brought that old image into my mind. I was sitting alone, unable to move as first the smoke and then the flames rose around me. I felt the heat rise to unbearable heights and wriggled and writhed to escape. There were voices in the background, somebody laughing, others cheering, and the sound of crackling as wood expanded and exploded in the heat. I could hear somebody singing in the background, the song familiar as it mocked my predicament.

"Dr Elliot?" Swinton was leaning over me, his face concerned. "Dr Elliot? Martin, are you all right?"

I pulled back from my torment. I had experienced that vision frequently, but never in company. "Yes, thank you." I raised a wan smile. "I am tired. I must have been overdoing things."

"Yes," Swinton said. "Yes, that must be it. You need a rest, I think."

I put on a brave smile. "I have too much work to do." I hid my worry, for I had hoped these burning nightmares would end when I left the house in the West Bow.

"You work too hard, my boy." Swinton was all smiles and good fellowship now. I often found that, of course. People were inclined to friendship with men who could further their ambitions, which makes one doubt the sincerity and depth of such attachments. "I am a plain-speaking man," Swinton said, which I rather doubted as solicitors worked with legal terminology that only other lawyers could decipher, "and I will say that I have always liked you."

I bowed at these words, knowing them to be as false as a politician's promise. "Thank you, sir," I said.

He shook my hand again, jerking my arm as if it were the handle of a reluctant pump. "I will do everything in my power to encourage Evelyn to agree to your request, my boy."

"Thank you, sir," I said. I had Swinton wrapped around my finger, thanks to my staff. "Now, Mr Swinton, I would like to examine you again, to see if there are any burgeoning signs of disease." I enjoyed his dismay. "Pray lower your clothing."

It was a small step from receiving Mr Swinton's permission to approach Evelyn to physically asking her. I had resolved on a romantic approach, something to appeal to Evelyn's love of the dramatic, or at least to her liking for Walter Scott's novels. I had no intention of dressing up in Highland fripperies as in *Rob Roy* or wearing a suit of armour, such as featured in *Ivanhoe,* but I did think of a romantic spot to propose.

I needed to present a token of my affection, so scoured the shops. At one time, there were tiny shops named locken – or locked - booths opposite St Giles Kirk, but city improvements had cleared them away. The name survived in Edinburgh's Luckenbooth brooches, which sweethearts frequently presented as love tokens. I had no knowledge of such things, so I made enquiries before my purchase. These Luckenbooth brooches have been popular in Edinburgh since the 16th century for, as well as a declaration of undying love, they protected against the evil eye and malevolent spirits. Such an all-encompassing piece of jewellery could only be welcome, so I chose the most expensive I could find. I liked a piece with two intertwined silver hearts surrounding a diamond and ruby, surmounted by a crown garnished with a small garnet.

"That's a fine piece of craftsmanship," I said when I viewed my selection.

"Your young lady will prize it highly," the seller said.

"Do you have it in gold?" I asked, and he shook his head.

"No, sir. They are traditionally silver."

"Then silver it shall be," I said, parting with the purchase price and adding a few shillings in the spirit of generosity.

"If you don't mind me saying so, sir..." The jeweller leaned across his counter to speak in a conspiratorial whisper. "When your union is blessed with children and the lady's time draws near and her baby is due, you can pin this brooch to her petticoats at her left thigh. It eases the pangs of childbirth."

"Ah," I said, wondering if I could add that information to my medical knowledge.

"It also ensures a steady supply of breast milk," the jeweller said. "If you place it on that part of her body."

"Thank you," I said solemnly. "Is there anything else?"

"Yes, indeed," the jeweller said. "When the blessed arrival comes, pin the brooch to the baby's shawl, and the fairies will not transport him away."

"Thank you," I said solemnly.

"One final thing." The jeweller seemed reluctant to part

with his creation. "You will notice I have placed a single garnet within the crown."

"I noticed," I said.

"Garnets influence the heart," the jeweller said. "They show the constancy of a man towards his intended."

I left the shop filled with new knowledge, and wondering at the superstition I met in every corner of this city. I had known such beliefs since childhood in the depths of Teviotdale but had expected the capital city to be more enlightened. It seems that Christian piety and the triumphs of rational thought were only a surface covering on much deeper, vastly older beliefs.

I shrugged, tapped my staff on the ground and made steps for the New Town, where such simple superstitions could have no hold. With the brooch in my pocket, I called for Evelyn, bowed as if she were the Queen of Sheba and invited her to stroll with me.

"Why, of course, sir," Evelyn accepted with a graceful curtsey that did not hide the sparkle in her eyes. "Where are you taking me?"

"Out," I said, and left her to make what she liked out of that. I had hired a gig for the day, took the ribbons and drove south of the city and on to the ancient romantic ruin of Craigmillar Castle. There, in the shadow of a place once used by Mary, Queen of Scots, I knelt on one knee and proposed.

"My dear Evelyn," I said, looking into her eyes. "Will you do me the honour of becoming my wife?"

"Yes," Evelyn said simply, and that was the matter resolved, there and then. She examined her brooch. "It's beautiful," she said. "It's the most beautiful thing I have ever seen."

I helped pin it on her breast, with much giggling and not a little fondling. One must take whatever opportunities one can.

With that little formality out of the way, all we had to do was inform the Swintons and make the arrangements for the wedding. The first part was easy, with both parents expecting nothing else, and once they had made all the correct noises and Mrs Swinton had nearly swooned with happiness, she advised the servants of her daughter's new elevated status. They crowded around, of course, admiring the brooch and wishing the young mistress all the luck in the world.

"Tomorrow," I proclaimed, "we will look at churches and decide which one we will grace with our wedding."

"Yes," Evelyn agreed at once, and then, being a woman, changed her mind and began the process of changing me from the raw man she claimed to love to the husband she hoped I would become.

"First," Evelyn said with a smile, "we'll look at your house. At last, I'll see the property in which I will live as a married woman."

CHAPTER 13

I HAD no fear of showing Evelyn my abode, for my New Town house was everything that a woman could desire. On the corner of George Street and Hanover Street, it had a basement for the servants, a ground floor in which Evelyn decided I should have my surgery and an upper floor in which we would live after our marriage. Even better, in Evelyn's opinion, we were only a short walk from Queen Street and her parents' house.

As soon as I had stepped in the door, I had felt as if I belonged. I felt that I was coming back to myself, which made no sense at all to the rational, scientific side of my brain, while my old, misunderstood, irrational side danced for joy in some primitive fashion.

With such a prestigious address, and Evelyn pushing all her parents' friends towards me, my list of patients proliferated. After only a week of Evelyn's encouragement, I was challenging Charles for patient numbers and after three weeks, I had overtaken him. Every few evenings, I visited the New Wig Club and each time left with a sizeable addition to my purse. Naturally, I did not inform Evelyn of my nocturnal activities, for she was already fulfilling her purpose, and I did not need to include her in other aspects of my life.

"Your fortunes have certainly improved," Evelyn said, as I came to her door dressed in the very best clothes available.

"Indeed they have," I agreed.

Evelyn and I promenaded along Edinburgh's most fashionable streets, met the most prestigious people, danced at the Assembly Rooms and sat in the best seats in the theatre. Life was better than I had ever imagined. Even my patients helped. Rather than men and women crawling with lice who paid in stolen coppers, I treated gentlemen for gout and ladies in delicate conditions who paid in gold and were grateful to be seen by the most fashionable doctor in town.

"I think I should buy a carriage," I said to Evelyn one Saturday evening as we returned from the theatre in Shakespeare Square.

"A dog-cart?" Evelyn asked.

"Good God, no." I shook my head at the idea. "A coach and pair, at least."

"You've changed, Martin." Evelyn looked at me sideways, perhaps with new respect in her eyes. "You were not like this when first we met on Granton beach."

"I remember," I said. "I was a callow youth, wasn't I?"

"That was only six months ago," Evelyn reminded me.

"Is that all it was?" I laughed at the memory, twirling my staff. "It seems like a different life. I could not imagine swimming from Granton to Cramond Island now."

"Or running through Queen Street Pleasure Gardens, laughing with me?" Evelyn said.

I shivered. "It wasn't dignified, was it?" I said. "Hardly the correct behaviour for a man in my station."

"Perhaps not," Evelyn said, "but it was fun."

Raising my staff, I hailed a cab, pushing in front of a shabby-looking fellow with a limp.

"That gentleman was before us," Evelyn pointed out.

I laughed. "He's barely a gentleman. We are more important than he will ever be."

Evelyn frowned. "But Martin..."

"Come on, my girl." I pushed Evelyn into the cab. "George Street," I told the driver. "And quick about it."

Evelyn was very quiet on the journey home, and although I offered to introduce her to my latest French wines, she declined brusquely and had the driver take her to Queen Street. "I want to go home," Evelyn said and clamped her mouth shut on further conversation.

After Evelyn's rejection, I was not in the best of tempers when I stepped into my house, to find my manservant half asleep in my chair in the living room.

"What's the meaning of this, by God?" Naturally, I tipped him off the chair and on to the floor, where he sprawled in some confusion. "Did I give you permission to sit in my chairs?"

"No, sir," he looked up at me.

"Then stay off them!" Placing my foot on his chest, I pushed down hard. "Now get to your room." Only then did I become aware of the maid watching me from the open door. "And what are you staring at?"

As the girl scrambled away, I landed a solid kick on my man's backside, resolved to get rid of him as soon as I could find a replacement, and poured myself a healthy drink. I still favoured claret, although exposure to the Old Town had given me rather a taste for highland Ferintosh, with French brandy when the mood was on me. That night, after Evelyn's unaccountable moodiness, I punished the bottles rather heavily and had no bad dreams.

I felt better the next day, once I had put both servants out on the street and hired a couple of replacements, a man in his early twenties with shoulders like an ox and a lively young girl with dancing eyes and the figure of Venus.

"You." I pointed to the man, Walter as he called himself although I was damned if I could be bothered to remember his name. "If you enter my living quarters without my express permission I'll end your employment without a reference."

"Yes, sir," Walter said, too smoothly for my liking. He gave a small bow.

"And you." I pointed my walking cane at the girl. "What the devil is your name again?"

"Amanda, if it pleases you, sir." The girl gave a prim little curtsey that did not match her bold eye. I knew then that she was one to watch.

"It pleases me if you do as I say," I growled. "You are to keep my rooms clean and tidy at all times, do you hear?"

"Yes, sir." Another curtsey, another bold look from under demurely lowered eyelashes.

"But if you value the skin on your backside," I said, "do not touch my staff."

Amanda-if-it-pleased-me looked at my carved staff. "No, sir," she said.

"Right, be off with you," I said, watching as Amanda swayed away.

I had a short surgery that day. My male patients were a young man with a swollen finger and a gentleman with a delicate disease that he swore he had caught from his wife. My female patients included one lady who needed nothing more than company and reassurance and two young women who wanted to meet the new doctor in town. I gave them all the very best of my attention, took their money and closed up my practice.

"I'm going out," I said to Walter.

"Yes, sir." He bowed again.

After Evelyn's strange behaviour, I was less inclined to visit the churches for our wedding, but there was little choice. A wife would further my image of a respectable member of society, and that meant going through with the ridiculous farce of a wedding.

Or did it?

I did not know from where the idea came.

I could elope or merely live in sin. As I left my house to cross Hanover Street, I tapped my staff on the ground. Eloping would solve a multitude of problems, as well as saving me the uncomfortable experience of standing at the altar before the gaze of a congregation of damned hypocrites.

No. I shook my head. People had to view me as a conventional, traditional married man. Edinburgh expected such a thing, and in Edinburgh, appearances mattered more than reality. With that decided, I set about finding a suitable location for our wedding.

The Tron Kirk is ancient, with a steeple that is a significant landmark. I must have passed it 50 times without ever entering, and now I wondered if I could marry there, as Evelyn wanted an old church. I struggled with the idea before nerving myself to enter.

Why was I nervous about entering a church? I had grown up in a God-fearing family and had survived thousands of Sunday services by the banks of the Teviot. Only when I left home for Glasgow University did I slide away from the kirk, and when both my parents died, my church attendance ended completely. Hefting my staff, I pushed open the door and stood at the entrance. I tried to step inside and stopped.

I could go no further. My feet would not obey my brain's orders.

"What the devil!" I stepped back and tried again, with the same result.

Whatever I did, I could not enter the Tron Kirk.

"Come in, man!" A kirk elder stood by the pews a few steps inside. "You're letting all the cold out!"

Although I tried to move, my muscles refused to operate. I stood as if paralysed, with the elder looking concerned. "Are you sick?" An elderly man dressed in sober grey, he hurried to me. "Come in and sit down."

"I can't," I said. I had never experienced anything like it before, complete paralysis of my limbs, preventing me from moving even an inch.

The elder put his arm around my shoulders. "I'll help you," he said. "Just allow me to help."

Perhaps he had some spiritual strength that I lacked, for with his touch I could step into the church, although my head began to spin and I felt nauseous. Escorting me to a pew, the elder bent over me.

"You're safe in the Lord's house now," he said. "I'll fetch you a drink of water."

I may have been in the Lord's house, but I was an unwanted guest with nausea rising in my throat and a terrible noise, like the rushing of a thousand birds, filling my head. I could not remain in that place, so the instant the elder left, I staggered to the door and into the street again. Immediately I did so, the power returned to my limbs, and I walked away as quickly as I could.

I stopped at a dram shop, forgoing my favoured claret for a whisky. The denizens were not used to having a gentleman in their establishment until somebody whispered that I was a doctor, and immediately they told me their various ailments as if I was their family physician. I stayed only a few moments, gave some free advice, suggested the rest could attend my surgery on the morrow and escaped, slightly refreshed if still concerned.

If the Tron would not have me, then I would try the High Kirk. With whisky-confidence coursing through my veins, I strode toward St Giles, which stands in the centre of the High Street, grey, defiant and so old one can feel the history seeping from every stone.

Holding on to my confidence, I pushed open the massive iron-studded wooden doors and stepped inside. Or rather, I tried to. Although I pushed forward with my left leg, and then my right, I could no more enter that church than I could fly to the moon. It felt as though some invisible barrier had sprung up between me and the interior. I could see inside St Giles. I could see half a dozen people on the pews and the minister standing talking to one of the kirk elders, but whatever I did, I could not enter.

I blasphemed quietly and then with more force as the unseen power prevented me from stepping one inch inside St Giles.

"Let me in!" I yelled. "For God's sake, let me in!"

The minister stepped forward with a concerned frown on his face. I could see his mouth working as he spoke, and I could see the elder turning to face me, yet I could hear nothing except the roaring that filled my ears, rather like the beating of a thousand wings, a powerful waterfall, or a huge fire.

The closer the minister came, the louder was the roaring, until it became too much for me to bear. I turned away and ran down the High Street with the breath burning in my lungs and the burghers of the city staring at my distress. I was nearly at Holyrood Palace before I stopped, leaned against the wall of Queensberry House, that asylum of destitution, and gasped to regain my strength.

"Are you all right, sir?" The man looked about 80, with one

eye and one leg missing. I immediately knew that he was an old soldier, and expected some whine about being a veteran of Waterloo or Maida or some such decades-old battle.

"I'm perfectly well," I snarled.

"Here," the oldster offered me a drink from a small bottle. "Have a sip. It's all I have."

The whisky was pure kill-me-deadly that burned my throat all the way down. I had a couple of swallows and decided that was enough for anybody. The veteran seemed to understand, for he sloped off, round-shouldered, into one of the wynds, leaving me still panting on the border between the city and the environs of the royal park.

What had happened? I asked myself the question as I blundered on, walking into the park where a hundred workmen were carving out a path around the red cliffs of Salisbury Crags. I had tried to enter two different churches, and both had repelled me. I swore, softly and then with increasing force. God himself had rejected me, for some inscrutable reason of his own.

I stood at the base of the Crags, watching the labourers toil to earn themselves a pittance, and I tapped my staff on the ground. "Well then," I told myself. "If God does not want me, then I do not want him."

As I spoke, there was a loud rumble from the Crags, and a huge section of rock broke from the cliffs and rolled down the steep slope towards me. I remained static, knowing that even if God had rejected me, some other power would protect me. The rocks tumbled and hammered down the slope, with the foremost coming to a halt only three feet from where I stood.

"Was that you speaking to me, God?" I asked. "Was that you expressing your anger with me for gambling and drinking?"

The dust of the rockfall settled without any supernatural agency replying to me. I walked into King's Park, tapping my staff on the ground and shaking with a mixture of fear, guilt and anger. I was fearful that I had angered God to such an extent that He could deny me access to His holy place. I was also guilty that I had let Him, and generations of my family, down, and angry that anybody, mortal or immortal, should treat me in such a manner.

Well then, Lord God, if you would not allow me into your blessed building, I would marry Evelyn elsewhere, for I needed a wife to create a mask in this city where a veneer of respectability was required to conceal the dark underbelly. Reaching St Margaret's Loch, beneath the ruined old chapel of St Anthony, I stopped again, swinging my staff in frustration.

"Damn it all," I thought as my original plan of elopement returned in force. If need be, I would throw Evelyn over my shoulder and flee with her to Gretna Green. The romance of the abduction of a willing bride would hardly reduce my reputation. More likely the reverse in a city that revered the novels of Sir Walter Scott.

By God, that would be fun!

CHAPTER 14

I HEARD the footsteps as I lay in bed, in the half-awake-half-asleep state that often brings ideas and strange fancies. Opening the drawer beside my bed, I lifted my pistol. Knowing it was already loaded, I cocked both hammers and slid out of bed.

Footsteps in the house meant one of two things: either Walter or Amanda was wandering around at night, or there was an intruder. I wished neither, so stealthily opened the door and slipped outside my bedroom. The house was in darkness, with only the fading embers of the sitting room fire providing a modicum of light as I padded from room to room, pistol ready to blast any impudent intruder. YORLING

I saw the shadow as I entered the drawing-room. It was a glimpse, nothing more, and I whirled around, pointing my pistol. There was nothing there, only darkness outside the faint glow of the fire. I shook my head; how could I see a shadow in the dark? The idea was ludicrous, yet I was convinced it had happened.

Withdrawing into the darkest corner of the room, I waited,

listening for footsteps or the sound of breathing, looking for a flicker of movement. There was only stillness. I was alone in that room. Walking to each corner in turn, I pointed my pistol at the darkness, nodding as I reassured myself there was nobody there.

I knew my house would be a natural target for thieves. My fame as a successful practitioner had spread, and my luck in the New Wig Club was known among a particular sector of Edinburgh's society. The criminal class would soon learn where I lived, and I did not doubt that they would be wild to rob me. That was the price of success.

Lighting a candle by the last embers of the fire, I placed it in a brass candlestick, held it in my left hand and continued my patrol. The yellow light created darting shadows along the walls, made tables into crouching lions and chairs into waiting murderers. Twice I thought I saw figures waiting in the corner of a room, and each time I was mistaken. One was a folded curtain and the other my staff, leaning where I had left it. I tested the front door and the shutters and all was secure.

My house had three storeys and once I had satisfied myself that the upper and ground floors were clear, I stepped on to the stairs to the basement. As in all the houses of the New Town, the stairs leading to the servants' quarters in the basement were functional rather than decorative, with plain metal railings and no walnut bannister.

The candle bounced light along the walls, leading me downwards into a chillier atmosphere. I knew that a burglar would have little reason to visit the servants' quarters, for there was little there to steal, but I reasoned that he might be hiding there. I grunted – perhaps it was no burglar but an illicit night-time visitor for the bold-eyed Amanda with the swivelling hips. I checked the kitchen first, finding all in order and the shutters correctly locked.

By that time, I was reasonably confident that my imagination had taken control, and there was no intruder in the house. I opened Walter's door quietly and allowed the candlelight to penetrate. Walter was on his face, sleeping alone. Closing the door, I checked Amanda's room.

"Who's there?" Two terrified eyes stared at me. "Walter, is that you?"

"It's only me." I had no desire to frighten my servants. "Dr Elliot. I thought I heard somebody."

"It will be the ghost." Amanda blinked in the candlelight, with one hand shielding her eyes.

"The ghost?" I placed the candlestick on Amanda's table, beside the basin and ewer, and sat on her chair, close enough to be seen while at a sufficient distance to maintain decency. "What ghost?"

"The ghost in the cellar, sir." Amanda pulled her knees up to her chest, still lying in bed.

"There's no ghost." I tried to sound reassuring, for I had no reason to dislike the young creature. "I'll look into the cellar, Amanda. Get back to sleep." I patted her shoulder and left the room.

There were two cellars in the basement. In one, I stored wine and food, while the other was mostly empty, for I had not lived in the house long enough to accumulate a collection of unwanted objects. Shining my candle into the stone chamber, I ascertained that nobody was hiding inside, shut the door and entered the wine cellar.

"Is anybody here?" I lifted the candle, watching the shadows play among the bottles and stored flour, bread and meal. Strangely, I could nearly understand why Amanda thought this cellar haunted, for there was a chill in the air that the previous chamber lacked, while my voice echoed from the rough stone walls.

I stood alone, allowing the atmosphere to wrap around me, nearly enjoying the sensation of fear. But why fear? There was nothing in this room to cause anxiety. For a moment, I pondered snuffing the candle and standing alone in the dark, as I had done as a child when I wished to test my courage. Shaking my head at such a strange fancy, I examined the walls, where the builder had slapped on the black-speckled mortar between rough-hewn stones.

Satisfied that there were no spirits, I left the cellar, checked that the basement and garden doors were both locked and returned to Amanda's room. She was lying awake, as I had expected.

"There is no intruder," I said, uncocking my pistol. "And no ghosts. You can sleep sound."

"Thank you, sir." Again Amanda's wide eyes stared at me. I winked at her and withdrew.

When I returned to my bedroom, the candlelight caught my image in the mirror, although I would not have recognised myself. Some trick of the flame gave me a more prominent nose, and I swear I was walking with a pronounced stoop. When I looked directly at myself, I gasped, for it was not my face that stared back at me but that of an older, hollow-cheeked man.

"Dear God!" I said. In stepping back, I dropped the candle, which rolled on the floor, sending flickering light around the room. When I picked it up, the image in the mirror was gone, and my reflection stared back at me, slightly pale and with dishevelled hair.

"Imagination," I told myself. "I need a tonic or some fresh air." I returned to bed, placed the pistol in its drawer and was about to blow out the candle when I hesitated. "I'll leave it lit tonight," I decided. "And tomorrow I'll close the surgery early and walk up Arthur's Seat. Fresh air will clear my head and chase away all these fantasies."

I woke late, with the candle a mess of melted wax, threw back the bedclothes in a foul mood and ate breakfast without a word as Amanda served me quietly.

"Walter!" I growled. "You did not wind the clocks last night!" I realised both my clocks were silent. "That's one of your duties."

"I did, sir," Walter said.

"Listen!" I rose from the table. "Not a sound!" Pulling my gold watch from my waistcoat pocket, I checked the time. "It's ten minutes after seven, and what does the clock say?"

"Six minutes after six, sir," Walter said quietly. "I don't understand it unless the mechanism is faulty."

"What time?" I started. That was the same time as the clock in the West Bow had stopped.

"Six minutes past six, sir," Walter said.

"Did you put the clock at that time?"

"No, sir," Walter said.

"Did you?" I demanded of Amanda, scarcely more gently although she already looked terrified.

"No, sir! I would never touch your clocks, sir."

"Well, somebody has, by God!" I said. "Put them right, Walter, and if you neglect your duties again, I'll put you on the streets."

After the scares of the previous night, that little incident rattled me, so I retired to my surgery with shaking hands. I needed a stiff glass of claret to steady my nerves, and added a little brandy for good measure.

"What the devil is wrong with me?" I looked in my surgery mirror, glad that it was my own familiar face that peered back. After the church incidents and the upset the previous night, my nerves were stretched beyond the bearable. I could feel myself still shaking, took a deep breath and prepared to meet my first patient.

"Martin," Charles said as he stepped inside my house, throwing his hat and cane to Walter. "We must talk."

"Of course." I ushered him into my front room, where sunlight streamed through the tall windows and my new furniture spread across the Persian carpet. "Drink? Brandy, claret or some fine smuggled Ferintosh."

"Claret." Charles settled himself in one of my armchairs. "You are certainly doing well for yourself now, Martin."

"Life is taking the course I had hoped," I said, pouring us generous glasses of claret and resolving not to mention my nighttime scares.

"I cannot agree with that," Charles said.

"Why ever not? We are both successful doctors with thriving practices and a growing social circle," I said.

"Cast your mind back only a few months," Charles said, "when we swam to Cramond Island. Do you remember?"

"I do," I said. "The day I met Evelyn."

"Before that," Charles said. "Do you remember our conversation on the island?"

I drank deeply from my glass. "Yes."

"We were going to do good and help people," Charles said. "What happened?"

"We are helping people," I said, smiling. "We're helping ourselves."

"You would never have said that before," Charles sipped at his claret, with his gaze steady on me.

I shrugged. "Maybe I have realised that I am as important as anybody else."

"You did not become a doctor to enrich yourself," Charles said. "You've changed, Martin, and I worry about you."

I could not control my amusement. "Changed? I'm no

longer the idealistic young student you knew. I am a doctor now, Charles. If you don't approve of who I am, then please refrain from visiting. Good day to you."

"Martin?" Charles lifted his head. "I think we should discuss this."

"There is nothing to discuss," I told him.

"As you wish, Martin," Charles lifted his hat and cane as he left, and I slammed the door behind him. What did I care for his sanctimonious lectures, prosing at me as if he were somebody important? I finished my glass of claret, filled the glass again, drained it and stamped away, shouting at the maid as I left to get the damned place cleaned up.

Bloody Charles bloody MacNeil! What right did he think he give me orders? I had a good mind to visit his surgery and take a horsewhip to him, the damned scoundrel. I played with that image for a few moments, enjoying the feeling of power I would have, and the pain I would inflict, and then decided I wished something more than mere fantasy.

The New Benison was open for me, with dice and cards, but I opted instead for a prizefight that people had mentioned. It was not one of the major bare-knuckle competitions between skilled men in the peak of condition. Instead, it was a grudge match between a carter with a foul temper and a blacksmith with a herculean stature and the face of a young Greek god. YORLING

"Welcome, Doctor," the Honourable Peter greeted me with a smile.

"Thank you." After Charles's gloomy words, the churches' rejection and Evelyn's moodiness, it was refreshing to be somewhere I was wanted.

"Good afternoon, Doctor." Lady Clarinda gave me her best smile as she stood beside me at the front of the makeshift ring. "I wondered if you would be here."

I lifted my hat politely, as one must do to the aristocracy, even when we meet in the most unlikely places. "Good afternoon, your Ladyship," I said.

"Who are you betting on?" The contest took place at the back of Blackford Hill, south of the city.

"The carter," I said, after only a glance at the pugilists. They were stripped for action and sitting on the knee of their seconds.

"The blacksmith is the larger and more powerful." Lady Clarinda ran an appreciative eye over the torso of the blacksmith. "Quite an impressive figure of a man, and so handsome." I could hear the naked desire in her voice.

"It is that handsome face that will prove his nemesis," I said. "Look at my man." The carter was smaller, lighter and more wiry than muscular, but there was a force within him that the placid blacksmith lacked. "If he can channel his temper into aggression, he will win." I had good odds on the 10 guineas I put on the carter and stepped back to watch the fight. I was only slightly surprised when Lady Clarinda came so close to me that I could feel the heat from her body and hear her short, panting breath. I knew that blood sports – and pugilism was nothing if not a blood sport – excited some women. Evidently, Lady Clarinda was of that ilk. Well, that was nothing to me – any personable woman was welcome to press her hips against mine whenever she chose.

When the pugilists came up to scratch, the blacksmith loomed half a head taller and much broader than his opponent. However, the carter was the livelier and looked more pugnacious.

"Now we'll see," Lady Clarinda said as the blacksmith opened the contest with a wild swing that would have taken my carter's head off his shoulders had he not ducked. The carter retaliated by boring in with three jabs that bounced off the blacksmith's ribs as if they were pats from a kitten.

"My man is much the stronger," Lady Clarinda said.

"And much the more clumsy," I responded as my carter landed a facer that spread drops of blood from the blacksmith's nose. "There's the claret flowing."

I saw the excitement in Lady Clarinda's eyes as she watched the blacksmith shake his head, spraying his blood on to the audience. "Get him, Blacksmith!" She raised her voice, so it carried clearly to the fighters, encouraging her fancy to launch a two-fisted attack that drove back the carter half a dozen paces. The carter rested a while on the ropes, ducking, dodging and weaving as the blacksmith's great fists whooshed through the air all around him. It was only a matter of time before one made contact, and when it did, the carter fell like a stone.

"Well done, Blacksmith!" Lady Clarinda called, looking at me in triumph.

"The fight is not over yet," I warned, for I understood the tenacity of my man. If his will matched his frame, the carter would recover quickly and be all the more aggressive in his pugilism.

The corner-men revived the carter with smelling salts and cold water, glowered at the posing blacksmith and pushed their man back into the ring, to the cheers of the crowd. Although financial gain by gambling was the excuse for this prizefight, most of the fancy enjoyed watching two courageous men battering each other senseless. They wanted claret – blood – and plenty of it. They cheered whenever a punch landed, and blood flowed, laughed when one of the carter's blows knocked a tooth from the blacksmith's jaw and watched in glee whenever a man fell to the bloodied turf.

After two hours of courage and carnage, it was evident that

both men were tiring. Their movements were slower, their punching less crisp and they took longer to recover from a blow.

"We're nearly done now," I said. "One more round." I studied both combatants, then tapped my staff on the ground. "My man will win."

"Your man's face is all smashed up," Lady Clarinda said. She was correct. The blacksmith landed few punches, but when one made contact, the force caused considerable damage. A swelling purple bruise hid the carter's left eye, his nose was spread all over his face, and I could see his left cheekbone was broken.

On the other hand, the carter had landed so many body blows that the blacksmith was barely able to move. I estimated that three, if not four, of his ribs, were broken and others cracked or bruised.

When the carter fell again, the crowd gave more of a groan than a roar, with few expecting him to rise. He surprised them all by returning to the mark, blinking through a film of blood as he strove to see the blacksmith.

The end came quickly. As the blacksmith advanced, swinging his massive roundhouse punches, the carter ducked, landed two quick blows, right-left, into his opponent's damaged ribs, and finished with a tremendous uppercut. I heard the jawbone snap as the blacksmith crumpled.

"My victory," I said, and knew by Lady Clarinda's expression that I had won more than gold after that bout. The moment I collected my winnings, I joined her in her dark closed carriage, with the coachman impassive on his perch. Once again, my Lady proved she was adept at many things and suppler than any woman I had previously met. I did not think of Evelyn that night.

CHAPTER 15

Although my days were lucrative, my nights continued to be a torment. Every evening, I set the clocks, and every morning the hands pointed to six minutes past six. Whatever I did, however carefully I arranged them, the result was the same. I no longer blamed Walter, for one night I decided to stay awake and watch the long-case clock to see if perhaps there was a conspiracy among the servants to choose that time.

"I'll not have servants treat me as a fool," I said, coming into the living room with my staff in my hand. "By God," I told myself. "If anybody comes into this room tonight, I'll have the hide off them."

With the servants in bed, I doused the lights and settled into the largest chair in the room. I chose that chair because its high back ensured nobody would see me until it was too late and I would catch them in the act. Tapping the end of my staff in the palm of my hand, I watched the last of the coals settle, and the embers gradually fade from orange to dull red to nothing more than a glimmer.

I heard the soft footfall of somebody trying to disguise his steps, accompanied by a strange tapping I recognised but could not immediately place. I frowned. I knew that sound – it was the sound my staff made as I walked along the road.

"Now he's coming." I gripped my stick firmly, preparing to swing it at Walter. I smiled without humour, imagining the expression on his face when he saw me waiting. "Come on, man, and see what I've got for you."

I did not hear the living room door open, only the footsteps that came right up to my chair. I took a deep breath, counted to five and sprang up.

"Caught you!" I roared, swinging my staff.

The staff hissed through empty air, nearly unbalancing me.

"Where are you?" I looked around the room, quickly lit a candle from the embers and held it high. The yellow light pooled around the room, revealing only the furniture. There was no servant there, nothing to account for the footsteps I had heard.

"Doctor!" The door burst open, and Walter stood there in his nightshirt with a stout cudgel in his hand.

"Sir? Are you all right, Doctor? I heard you moving about."

"I thought I heard somebody," I said.

Walter looked around the room. "There's nobody in here, sir. Perhaps he fled."

"Did you pass anybody in the corridor?"

"No, sir."

The maid stepped in then, with her night things loose around her and holding a candle in her left hand and a heavy pewter ladle in her right.

"Amanda!" I pointed my staff at her. "Did you see anybody out there?"

She shook her head, close to tears. "No, sir," she said.

"You are lying!" I said. "You are both lying. This is a trick, a deception to unsettle my nerves."

"No, sir!" Amanda shook her head again, with her blonde ringlets flying around her face.

"Somebody, one of you two, came into this room," I said.

"No, sir," Walter said steadily. "We heard you shouting and came upstairs directly."

I opened my mouth to contradict him but closed it again. I had heard the footsteps before the servants entered the room, and anyway, the door had been closed.

"You did," I said. "I must have had a nightmare." I nodded to them both. "I apologise for miscalling you."

The maid looked shocked that I had apologised, while Walter grunted.

"Do you wish me to search the house, sir?"

"No," I said. "No, thank you. I am sure there is no need. You two get back to bed and thank you for responding so quickly." I watched them leave the room and heard the murmur of their voices as they returned to the basement.

"Well," I told myself. "At least the servants won't move the hands of the clock today. I must have imagined the footsteps." Shaking my head at the fickle tricks one's imagination could play; I glanced at the clock to see what time it was.

Six minutes past six.

Oh, dear God in heaven!

Next morning, Walter left my employment. Amanda remained, although she was nearly in tears every time I asked her to enter the wine cellar. She left three days later.

Servants never remained long in my house, some claiming to have seen or heard a ghost in the basement, and others leaving without any excuse. I tried everything I could to persuade them to stay, doubling the normal wages, allowing them days off, even permitting the male servants to bring their sweethearts home and the females their beaux. That experiment resulted in a drunken rampage that I ended only by throwing the whole lot out of the house at one o'clock in the morning.

With the house cleared of people, I removed the keys from both the grandfather and grandmother clocks. My reasoning was simple. If nobody wound up the clocks, they could not tick, and I would have a night of undisturbed rest.

Yet throughout all my problems with servants, I had other, more important things on my mind. One was Evelyn's and Charles's increasing coolness towards me, and the other was my inability to enter a church. I knew I must address both if I were to establish myself as the most fashionable doctor in the city. As the lesser of my worries, I put Charles aside temporarily and decided to tackle the question of Evelyn.

In Edinburgh, one does not need to announce a visit in advance. One merely raps or knocks on the door and walks in, for few houses are locked during daylight hours. I walked into the Swinton's house with casual ease, for Mrs Swinton to greet me with her usual friendliness, although with a shadow in her eyes.

"Good afternoon, Martin. I hope you have not come to see Evelyn."

"I rather hoped to find her in," I said, tapping my staff on the floor. "We have not been on the best of terms of late, and I hoped to resolve our differences."

Mrs Swinton shook her head. "That is a very laudable ambition, Dr Elliot, for Evelyn has been moping around as if her world had ended. However, she is out at present. I believe she is visiting Elaine, her older sister."

"Ah, thank you." I bowed. "That is unfortunate. Pray tell her that I called."

I was slightly discomfited when I left the house, for I had wished to talk to Evelyn, but I could walk faster without her, and Arthur's Seat was still available. There was a drizzle when I walked down the Canongate, past the old Palace of Holyroodhouse and on to the rough ground around Arthur's Seat, the 800-foot high hill that overlooks Edinburgh. I don't mind the rain, and that afternoon it suited my mood as I followed the Radical Road, the road that the unemployed were building around the base of the Salisbury Crags. They were not working today, so nobody disturbed my perambulation as I turned into the old duelling ground of Hunter's Bog and the path up to Arthur's Seat itself.

Twice I thought I saw somebody following me. I knew I was foolish, for there was no reason for such a thing to happen. Sandy did not need to dog me, as he could walk into my surgery at any time. I increased my pace, nearly marching into the drizzle that altered into thick, drifting mist as I climbed higher. Sheep moved around here, but I was a Borderer so I understood them. Their bleating, distorted by the mist, did not distract me any more than the sudden gleam of their eyes. The footsteps continued behind me, with the occasional glimpse of a figure. Twice I turned around to peer through the mist, and each time I thought I saw him, waiting, or ducking behind one of the wind-battered bushes that line the rough track.

"Sandy!" I shouted. "Is that you?" The mist distorted my voice, so it sounded flat, with neither timbre nor resonance. The man made no response.

Although the King's Park and Arthur's Seat is right beside the capital city, it can be a lonely place when the weather is foul. When the unemployed were destroying the magnificent red cliffs of Salisbury Crags to earn their pittance, the park echoed with the clatter of picks and the hoarse sound of their voices, but when they were gone, only the bleat of sheep and the call of wild birds disturbed the silence. I knew that, if any man were following me, there was no help up here. I was alone.

Gripping my staff firmly, I increased my speed. Having been brought up around the Border Hills, I fancied myself better at hill-craft than any city-bred townie and deliberately made noise, so my dogger would follow, then I stepped off the path to the greasy ground at the side. Here, the grass muffled the sound of my feet, and the mist shrouded my shape. Moving swiftly, I took 15 long steps and halted to listen.

My pursuer continued up the path, with his feet urgent, sliding on the loose stones, scuffing as he tried to catch me but unable to see much in the murk. I allowed him two minutes to get ahead before I returned to the path. Now I had a choice. I could hurry back to Edinburgh and leave my mysterious follower to flounder on the path, chasing shadows, or I could follow him and see who he was.

Although the first was the sensible option, I chose the second. I wished to find out who the devil was following me, Sandy or somebody else. Remembering the days of my early youth, when I used to dodge the gamekeepers to poach the tributaries of the River Teviot, I walked as quietly as I knew how in the wake of my erstwhile pursuer. The mist grew ever thicker as we climbed higher, the man in front evidently wild to catch me, while I was equally keen to find him. I saw him ahead now, a smudged figure in a flowing coat, sliding as he trudged up. I stopped when he stopped, and I saw him try to peer from side to side, searching for me in the murk.

When he moved, I also moved, keeping the same distance between us.

We reached a broader part of the path, where a mound rises another 15 feet or so to afford the best of views on favourable days and nothing at all that day.

"Halloa!" I shouted. "What the devil do you mean by following me?"

When the man turned around, I still could not make out who he was. Enveloped by a voluminous cloak, he had pulled his hat down over his face and turned his collar up against the weather. For an instant, I thought it was the large-nosed man I had seen in the mirror, and then a shift of wind cleared the mist.

"You!" I stepped back in surprise. "Outerston!"

"You ruined me!" Outerston said. "You took everything I had. Every penny, every possession."

"You gambled and you lost." I gripped my staff tightly, prepared to defend myself. "Why are you following me?"

"I'm going to destroy you," Outerston said. "I'm going to expose you for the charlatan you are."

"By following me?" I laughed out loud. "You're a fool, Outerston."

"You're no doctor," Outerston said. "You're a gambler, a rake, a member of the fast set."

"As were you," I reminded.

"I am no hypocrite!" Outerston was close to tears, or perhaps to violence. I was not sure which.

Perhaps it was because I laughed again that Outerston lunged at me. I stepped aside. "Go home, Outerston," I said. "Go home."

"I have no home!" he screamed, waving his fists as he launched a blundering attack that would have been laughable even in a school playground. I sidestepped with ease, laughing as he floundered around in his rage.

"You gambled and you lost," I taunted, waiting for his next rush, dodging aside and waiting again. I had no fear of him, for a man in his mental state posed a threat only to himself. Rather, I enjoyed his anguish. I remembered the old Border rhyme when Johnnie Armstrong approached King James V for a pardon, only for the king to order him hanged.

"I have asked for grace at a graceless face,
But there is nane for my men and me."

I was the man with the graceless face as I tormented that unhinged fellow who swore, ranted and raved at me on the mist-shrouded slopes of Arthur's Seat, flapping his fists in clumsy attacks that availed him nothing. After a few moments, however, I tired of it all, for tormenting a fool is poor entertainment.

"Begone now," I said, pushing Outerston away. "I will have nothing to do with you."

"I will not!" He rushed at me again, with his fists working like windmills in a gale. Laughing, I turned my back and strode up the hill into the mist, hearing him cursing me for everything he could think of and resorting to pure obscenity when his vocabulary failed.

The mist thickened then, clinging to me like a grey blanket, obscuring anything more than 10 paces distant and distorting all sounds so that the bleating of a sheep could have been from two feet or 200 feet. It was only by the merest chance that I kept on the correct path and reached the summit without any mishap. The peak thrust out of the mist, an ocean of clarity enclosed within a grey cocoon.

Outerston stumbled after me, still shouting. He emerged from the mist, hatless and wild-eyed.

"I'll kill myself!" he yelled, standing on the edge of the steepest part of the hill. "You've left me nothing."

"You're getting very tiresome," I said. "If you wish to end your life, then do so. I certainly won't stand in your way."

He ran towards me then, shouting something incoherent. I

do not know if he intended pushing me over the edge, or if he genuinely wished to commit suicide. Whichever it was, I stepped aside as smartly as I could, Outerston stumbled and plummeted into the abyss. At that point, the summit of Arthur's Seat is little more than the lip of a cliff and down he fell. I heard his voice for a second or two, a sickening crunch as he landed on the rocks, and then silence save for the bleat of a solitary sheep.

I cannot describe how I felt at that moment. Relief that it was Outerson and not me that had fallen, guilt that I had been in some measure responsible for his death, sorrow for a wasted life and, underlying all, a thrill of excitement that I could not understand. With my medical training forcing me to care for the sick and injured, I immediately made my way back down the hill but, in the mist, I was unable to locate Outerston's body. I spent a long hour searching in the scattered rocks and bushes, before returning home to face the rather more pressing problem of what to do about Evelyn.

It was on the journey back that for some strange reason I thought I felt my staff move beneath my hand. When I looked, I saw a human shape along the shaft, where yesterday there had only been geometrical designs. Wondering how I could be so mistaken, I resumed my walk home, with the words of *Maggie Lauder* resounding through my head.

I had intended to walk straight home when I left the King's Park, for I was wet and miserable, and slightly shaken by my encounter with Outerston. I tapped my staff on the ground, and for some reason, changed my mind. It felt as if something guided me along Princes Street to Shakespeare Square.

I was passing the Theatre Royal when I saw her. Evelyn

was wearing a long bottle-green cloak I had never seen before, with her hat at an acute angle, partly concealing her face, yet I would recognise her in a crowd of thousands. I looked for her sister in the street, not knowing what she was like but sure I would see any family resemblance. Instead of one of the Swinton clan, I saw Charles, emerging from the theatre, swinging his stick and with a tall hat on his head.

I was wondering who to approach first when Charles stepped across to Evelyn and took her arm.

CHAPTER 16

I CANNOT DESCRIBE how I felt seeing my most particular friend with my girl, my intended, my Evelyn, outside the theatre in what was obviously a pre-arranged assignation. Slipping into a doorway, I watched with a mixture of anger and sick despair as they walked down the street together, deep in conversation. My first instinct was to challenge them and demand an explanation.

No, I told myself. Evelyn and Charles might be innocent of any wrongdoing; their meeting could be the merest coincidence. I fought the sudden rage that consumed me. Should I follow them, as Outerston had followed me? I shook my head. No; that was not the act of a gentleman. Yet although I wished to turn away and leave my suspicions behind, I found myself dogging the pair of them, keeping well back, letting my feet hit the ground the same instant as Charles's to disguise my footfall.

Wherever did I learn that trick? It seemed to come as naturally as hugging the shadows and pushing down the brim of my hat.

Charles and Evelyn were close, walking side by side, occasionally touching each other as they turned corners or passed other people. Each time that happened, I felt a surge of jealousy, although I knew that I was now far richer than Charles and therefore more attractive to women. I could buy and sell him if I wished.

When the happy couple entered Queen Street I lagged further behind, for the street is broad, with few places in which to hide and if either of them turned around, they could not fail to see me. I waited under the shadow of a tree from the Pleasure Garden as they stopped outside Evelyn's door, and watched as Evelyn opened the door and stepped inside. I nodded grimly, gripping my staff and fought my desire to rush across the road and belabour Charles as he stood. Not only was that man trying to tell me how to live my life, but he was also trying to seduce my girl, and from right under my feet as well.

Breathing heavily, I turned on my heel and paced the full length of Queen Street before I managed to control my anger. All right then, Charles Roderick MacNeil, I thought, if that's the underhand game you wish to play, then I understand how the cards are dealt. I returned along Princes Street, tapping my staff on the ground as dark thoughts filled my head. I had dealt with Swinton when he stood in my way, and I would not hesitate to deal with MacNeil as well.

I was in a foul mood when I got home and not at all prepared to receive visitors. I snarled when somebody knocked loudly at the door and swore when my new servant informed me who it was.

"There's a mister Alexander Tait to see you, doctor."

"Tell him I am not at home," I ordered, wondering what else was going to happen that day.

"That may be truer than you realise." Sandy pushed past the servant without as much as a by-your-leave. "You'll have a minute to spare for me, Doctor."

"The devil I will," I responded.

"The devil you must," Sandy said seriously. "I don't think you realise the danger that you are in."

"Danger? I am in no danger." I felt the weight of the pistol in my pocket as I removed my coat. Was Sandy Tait going to try and lecture me as well?

"I believe you are in the greatest danger imaginable, Doctor Elliot."

"Pray return when you are more coherent," I said. "For you appear to be under the influence of drink."

"Come with me, Doctor." Taking hold of my sleeve, Sandy guided me into the drawing-room. "Please listen to what I have to say."

"I will do no such thing." I opened my mouth to call for the servants to eject the impudent fellow when Sandy stopped me with a few words.

"I know too much about you, Doctor. Resurrection men are not popular."

I sat down with on a hard chair with a painful bump.

"What do you want?" I asked. "Money?"

Sandy continued to stand, a rather shabby figure in my room, yet at that moment, his presence dominated the whole house. "No, Doctor. I am here to help you."

"Then help me by leaving my home." I tried to regain the initiative.

"That would not help you at all," Sandy said.

"Who the devil do you think you are?" I asked, wondering if I could throw this man out physically. Remembering how he had handled himself on previous occasions, I rather doubted I had the strength or skill, so remained sitting. Extreme alcohol consumption and late nights do not make a man physically fit.

"Alexander Tait," Sandy said. "Drink?" He offered me

some of my own claret, poured himself a glass and handed one to me. "You'd better take it, Doctor, for I think you will need it."

Something about his attitude warned me not to push this man too far. I accepted the glass and drank deeply as Sandy watched, nodding. He sipped his claret, with his gaze never straying from my face.

"In a previous conversation, Doctor, I told you something about Major Weir and his sister."

"I remember," I said shortly, for his presence unsettled me, and I was upset about Outerston and angry after seeing Charles with Evelyn.

"There is more to the story," Sandy said.

"I have no more interest in that fable," I said, refusing to admit my fears.

Sandy sipped again and refilled my glass. "Perhaps you should develop an interest," he said, "for it concerns you and everything you do."

"I have left Weir's house," I reminded him, "and have no intention of ever returning."

"You already have," Sandy said.

I could not repress my shudder. "What do you mean, sir?"

Still holding his glass, Sandy began to pace the floor, walking back and forth as he spoke. "I told you that Major Weir was executed at the Gallow Lee, halfway between Edinburgh and Leith."

I nodded, bracing myself for bad news. "You did."

"And the good people of Edinburgh believed that was the end of things."

I nodded. "Being executed and one's body burned normally signifies an end," I agreed.

"After Weir was burned, his ashes were buried on the mound where the gibbet stood," Sandy said "That's the gallows-tree."

"I know what a gibbet is, damn you!" I said.

"Good," Sandy said calmly. "It was the tradition to bury murderers, witches and the like in unconsecrated ground, thus continuing their punishment after death."

I sighed as my patience stretched beyond breaking point. "If you have nothing to add to my knowledge, Sandy, I'd thank you not to waste my time."

Sandy continued to pace. "Decades later, Edinburgh expanded as the New Town was built, and the then-owner of the Gallow Lee sold the sand for the mortar. He made huge sums of money, most of which he spent on drink."

I poured myself another glass of claret, for I was becoming more uneasy.

"Weir's ashes were mixed with that sand, of course, and could still be seen as dark stains in the mortar. I heard that two of the carts carrying Weir's ashes overturned and killed one of the drivers. The other suffered terrible injuries as the cart landed on top of him. However, eventually the sand, together with Weir's ashes, was used in mortar for several houses."

I guessed what was coming next. "Where were these houses?"

"Here." Sandy stamped his foot on the ground. "This corner of George Street."

I said nothing, although my hand began to tremble further. I finished my claret and poured another, with Sandy joining me.

"Tell me, Dr Elliot, have you noticed anything unusual in this house? Anything untoward?"

"Damn you, Tait," I said.

"I am trying to ensure that you are not damned, Doctor," Sandy said. "Have you noticed anything unusual? Any untoward occurrences, sights, sounds, smells even?"

"I have noticed nothing out of the ordinary," I said.

"May I speak to your servants?" Sandy asked. "They often keep things to themselves."

Before I could reply, Sandy had risen and was descending the stairs two at a time. I followed, cursing the man for his impudence. Naturally, the noise alerted the servants, and Sandy ushered them into the kitchen with surprising firmness.

"Your master has kindly allowed me to ask you some questions," Sandy did not waste time with a preamble. "Have any of you heard or seen anything unusual in this house?"

I now kept three servants, and all came forward with their stories, to which Sandy listened with apparent interest.

"There are noises in the cellar," my younger maid said, "and once I seen a skeleton, all in white."

"I heard a man singing," the older maid said, "and there is a queer feeling in the wine cellar. Fair scares me, it does."

My man looked stern. "I've not heard nothing," he said. "I've only seen that man in the cloak."

"Where did you see him?" Sandy asked.

"In the wine cellar," the servant said. "And coming out of it sometimes."

When everybody had drained their imaginations, Sandy thanked them solemnly.

"These tales focus on and around the cellars," Sandy said when we stood in the basement corridor. "May I look inside?"

I scraped a light for the candles I kept immediately inside the cellar door, and within a minute, Sandy pointed to the dark flecks I had already seen in the mortar.

"There we have the source of your servants' stories," Sandy said, holding the candle-flame close to the mortar, "and there we have the mortal remains of Major Weir."

I shook my head. "You are jumping at shadows, Sandy. This mortar may not have come from the Gallow Lee, and even if it did, those ashes, if indeed they are ashes, might not belong to Weir."

Sandy looked up at me from his kneeling position. "They do, Doctor, believe me, they do."

"How the devil do you know that?"

"I know as much as any man living about that creature," Sandy said, "and more than I wish."

"How?"

Sandy stood, with the flame of his candle sending wavering shadows along the wall, so for an instant I fancied a man was watching us, with his long nose poking towards me and his cloak hanging loose from his shoulders. Then I looked away, and the fancy was gone.

"I may tell you some day," Sandy said. "In the meantime, Doctor, I would advise you to leave this house."

"I have already left one house," I said. "I will not leave another because of the possibility there may be human ashes in the cellar."

"Then seal them in," Sandy said, urgently. "Seal that cellar so that nobody can enter."

I admit that Sandy's words, coupled with the strange events of the past few weeks, unnerved me. Although I was not willing to believe in spirits from an alleged warlock whom the authorities executed a hundred and fifty years before, the surfeit of coincidences worried me.

"How would I do that?" I asked.

"With something holy," Sandy said. "Not with stone and cement."

I had no idea what holy thing could reassure the servants that their fear of the cellar was groundless. When Sandy left the house, I began to pace, trying to put my thoughts in order.

I had many problems. First and foremost, there was Evelyn, who seemed to prefer Charles to me. Second, there was

Charles himself, and third was the mystery of the cellar. Well, I could either dispose of Charles or win back Evelyn and enjoy his frustration, which was the much more pleasurable option.

Dispose of Charles? I shook my head. What was I thinking? I tapped my staff on the floor, resolving to woo Evelyn anew. With that achieved, and I did not doubt my ability to turn Evelyn's head, then I could think about the problem of the cellar.

~

In the event, winning back Evelyn proved even easier than I had imagined, for no sooner had I knocked on the green door in Queen Street than she was there.

"Oh, Martin!" she said and immediately threw both arms around my neck. "Mother told me you had come to apologise."

I had never mentioned an apology, but Mrs Swinton was a cunning woman who understood how to mend a quarrel.

"Are we friends again?" I asked, after a kiss that may have shocked the neighbours in douce Edinburgh and certainly entertained the servants. I gave Evelyn another for good measure.

"Of course we are friends," Evelyn said. "We were never unfriends! We were just so worried about you, that's all!"

"We?" I asked, placing my staff in the hall stand with the other canes.

"Charles MacNeil and I," Evelyn said. "We both see changes in you."

"Have you been talking to him?"

"Yes," Evelyn admitted at once.

I took a deep breath. If Evelyn were cuckolding me, she would not have been so quick to confess. "I will try to give you less to worry about in future," I said.

"And I will not be so moody," Evelyn replied at once.

I had not realised that Mrs Swinton was watching us from the inner hall. She was smiling as we walked together, arm-in-arm and hip-to-hip, to the drawing room.

With my disagreement with Evelyn resolved or at least patched over, I walked the streets again, tapping my staff from the cracked paving stones and battered cobbles as I contemplated my next problem. Having moved from one unpleasant house to another, I found myself in a similar situation, except this time, I had a possible avenue of escape. If I could find something spiritual to block the entrance to that uncanny cellar, I might cure my nightmares and retain my servants for longer. I shook my head; one would think that a city the size of Edinburgh had a vast pool of servants, yet each one I hired seemed less suitable than the last. I would soon be dragging the dregs of the barrel and end with some slutty wench and squint-eyed rogue from the depths of Tanner's Close or the Happy Land, where the worst scoundrels in Scotland lived.

No. I shook away such thoughts. Today I would find a way to lock that door permanently and perhaps retain my present servants.

My first idea was to visit a church, but after my previous experience, I shied from repeating that experiment. There must be other places and other people who would know what to do. I had already discovered that if one walks the streets of Edinburgh long enough, and pokes diligently into every close and wynd, one can usually find what one seeks. I started with the pawnshop in the West Bow, where I had obtained my pistol.

"Good evening, Doctor." Mr Brown recognised me immediately. "Have you come for another weapon? I have a fine

Highland dirk here, as used by Rob Roy MacGregor, according to the fellow who brought it in, but more likely borrowed from the depot of the Gordon Highlanders!" He laughed at his poor joke.

"No, I am looking for a religious symbol," I said at once, peering around the shop with its amazing collection of worn shoes, gaudy clothing and no-doubt-stolen household objects.

The dealer was immediately on guard. "What sort of religious symbol?" He glanced toward the back shop in evident guilt. "We don't deal in stolen property here, Doctor. I heard about a theft at St George's kirk, but I wouldnae touch anything stolen, my oath on it."

"I'm glad to hear it," I said dryly. "I am no police detective, and I am not interested in stolen church items. I want something that the people in the old days might have used to keep evil away."

"I already showed you my cross," the dealer said. "That's gone, though. A most respectable young lady bought that. She came in with that friend of yours, the other doctor."

"Dr MacNeil!" I smiled. "I am glad he has finally found himself a lady. Do you have any other similar pieces?"

"I don't," the broker said. "Your best chance would be with old Mother Marwick. She's a queer old soul, her and has all sorts of queer old stuff."

"I don't know the lady," I said, tapping my stick on the floor. "Where could I find her?"

"Morocco's Land," the dealer said. "Tell her that I sent you."

Morocco's Land is a six-storey-high building near the foot of the Canongate, a substantial building of some antiquity to which unlikely stories of Barbary corsairs and distant romances are attached. I ventured there forthwith, ignored the angry shouts of a carter as I stepped in front of his wagon, cracked my staff across the backside of an impudent young fellow who refused to give me passage and stopped at the close that burrowed under the Land.

I had seen many worse entrances in Edinburgh and Glasgow, but for some reason this low-roofed close made me pause. I could sense that something monumental was waiting for me, although I did not know what.

The pawnshop was in the deepest part of the close, with two steps leading down to a near-subterranean cave filled with the strangest collections of items I had ever seen. The only source of light was a smoky, unsnuffed tallow candle set in a greasy tin candlestick, which added to the unpleasant aromas of the shop. The darting shadows showed silver-grey cobwebs hanging from a ceiling whose once-beautiful decoration now flaked painted and stained plaster.

I rapped my staff on the floor. "Mother Marwick?"

A dark-visaged woman appeared from the shadows of the shop. "That'll be me." Her eyes were deep-set, glowing like polished coal in a tanned face. "What do you seek, Doctor Elliot?"

"You know me?" I asked.

"I know who you are," Mother Marwick said. "I don't know you. Do you know you?"

"I know me very well," I retorted.

"I wonder about that." Mother Marwick was of medium height, with no grey in her black hair and the most direct gaze I had ever seen in any woman. I started, for I realised that I had seen her before. Mother Marwick was the very woman who had spoken to me in the West Bow courtyard.

"In my master's kingdom there are many doorways." I repeated what she had said to me on that occasion.

Mother Marwick's lips twitched in what might have been a

smile. "That's correct, Doctor, and you seem to have stepped from one of them into another."

I grunted. "I am not sure what you mean," I said.

"You know full well," Mother Marwick said, "if you allow yourself to push aside your science and admit your feelings." She lowered her voice to a croak. "Our feelings are the product of 10,000 years of ancestry, blood and experience. Don't neglect what you sense."

I grunted, disregarding the words of this silly old woman, and explained why I was here, and who had sent me.

Mother Marwick reached under her crowded counter to pull out an ancient book. "This might be what you want," she said.

"What is it?" I eyed the torn and stained cover with distaste.

"Open it," Mother Marwick suggested.

I had never seen anything quite like the images inside that book. Some were geometric designs of interlocking lines and curves, others were beautifully worked, yet simple, pictures of animals and people in strange clothes.

"This book will be influential to somebody important to you," Mother Marwick said.

I do not know why I bought that battered book. The title read *Images from Stones*, which meant nothing to me. Mother Marwick's eyes were extremely persuasive as I parted with a shilling for the book.

I don't know what made me scan the contents of that pawn shop. Perhaps it was simple curiosity, or maybe something compelled me to look. Either way, the glitter of candlelight on silver caught my attention. "What's that?" I pointed to the little object, half-hidden underneath a pile of satin ribbons.

"Nothing to interest you." Mother Marwick shifted the ribbons to conceal the object of my attention.

"I am interested," I said, using my staff to shove aside the ribbons. A silver Celtic Cross gleamed at me. I started, knowing I had seen that cross before. "Where did you get that?" I asked.

Mother Marwick shrugged. "Somebody brought it in," she said. "They come, I buy, no questions asked."

"I'll take it," I said. "How much?"

Mrs Marwick's eyes glittered as she looked me up and down. "Six shillings and sixpence," she said, "and cheap at the price."

It seemed a strange price to pay, and too high, but I tossed the silver coins across the counter and grasped the cross in my hand. I knew that Ruth Anderson had worn that same cross.

I could feel Mother Marwick watching me as I left and something cold crawled up from the very base of my spine to settle around my heart.

I had been beguiled, of course, for what good could a book of strange designs do? The minute I got home, I flicked through the images and threw the damned thing on to the table. It was worse than useless, the cover was filthy and the images obscure, entirely without meaning. I held the silver cross for a moment, wondering who had stolen it from Ruth Anderson, shrugged and tossed it beside the book. I had bought it on a whim and now regretted my impulsiveness.

Where should I go now? I had wasted the day so far when I had the answer at the tip of my fingers. I had always known the very person to ask, and, pushing the problem of Charles to the back of my mind, I lifted my staff and strode directly to Queen Street.

"Come, Evelyn!" I interrupted her as she prepared some charity work with Mrs Swinton. "We must walk together."

"But mother and I are preparing to help the poor," Evelyn protested.

"The poor are with us always," I said, holding out my hand.

Mrs Swinton smiled. "Matthew 26:11," she said and gave Evelyn a little push. "Off you go, Evelyn. I can manage without you, while Dr Elliot needs you, I believe."

"Thank you, Mother," Evelyn stood, brushing her skirt with her hand. "Martin, you are a perfect tiger when you command something."

Hardly waiting for Evelyn to change into outdoor clothes and don her boots, I nodded to the servants and left the house, I was so impatient to speak to her.

"Whatever is the hurry?" Evelyn asked, almost having to run to keep up with me.

"I need your advice," I said, knowing that the words would win her around.

"Oh, Martin!" Evelyn beamed at me. "You've never asked for my advice before. What is it?"

"I don't want you to laugh at me," I said, and explained the situation in its entirety. "I don't believe in such things," I said, "but it might help to settle the servants down."

I led Evelyn to the Botanical Garden down in its new location by Inverleith. It was a pleasant walk past the old Barony of Broughton, across the echoing bridge that spanned the Water of Leith at Canonmills and onward to the lawns and trees of the garden.

"I won't laugh," Evelyn promised. "Thank you for trusting me with such a delicate matter."

"I knew I could trust you." Except with Charles MacNeil, I thought, and pushed that picture away. I have resolved that situation, I told myself, and I had no cause for concern.

"Did my Bible help?" Evelyn asked as we paused under a

spreading oak tree, from where a lone blackbird sweetened the air with its melody.

"I believe so." I did not wish to admit my reliance in anything other than science. "I am more concerned about the servants."

"Then there is your answer," Evelyn sounded delighted that she could help. Without hesitation, she slipped her arm inside the crook of my elbow. "Put a Bible in the door, and that should keep any unpleasant spirits, or whatever they are, inside the cellar." She pulled me closer. "Come on, Martin, let's find a bookshop and buy you a Bible. We'll buy two, so you can have one for yourself and give me mine back."

"Thank you," I said, and kissed her where she stood. When a passing matron frowned at such an unseemly display, I kissed Evelyn again, laughed away her scandalised protests and kissed her a third time. On a whim, I fished Ruth Anderson's silver cross from my pocketbook and pinned it to her breast. "There," I said. "A small thank you for your help."

We bought two Bibles, as Evelyn wished. One for me, a rather workaday volume with a plain black leather cover and a minimum of decoration, and a much larger Bible for the door. In truth, this latter was a magnificent creation, the crowning jewel of the bookbinder's art, for the cover was of tooled leather, hand sewn with gold thread and each letter hand-printed and golden. Inside were coloured illustrations, the first I had ever seen in a Bible, while the price would have fed the average family for three months, and still left change to pay the church its tithe.

I have noticed that people who have lived with poverty and come into money veer in one of two directions. Either they retain the habits of a lifetime and hoard all they have, becoming so purse-proud they are veritable misers, or they are the opposite and spend lavishly to prove their escape from penury. I was one of the latter, a cheery, spendthrift fellow who delighted in spreading my good fortune to all and sundry, as long as I retained plenty for myself.

"If that Bible does not do the job," I said to Evelyn as we skimmed through the pages, "then nothing will."

She squeezed my arm, although whether in affection, in awe at the price or to compare my muscle with Charles's, I did not know.

I am not a man of my hands, so I hired a workman to take down the old cellar door and create a new one, with a special enclosure for my new Bible. I tried to supervise the work, but Evelyn had become houseproud and instructed the unfortunate carpenter in the minutiae of the trade he had spent a seven-year apprenticeship learning. However, the fellow was patient and, between the two of them, they created a more-than-serviceable door, despite a catalogue of unfortunate accidents when the carpenter lost some of his tools and once even cut himself so severely that he required my attention.

"I've never placed a Bible inside a door before," the carpenter said, watching unmoved as I stitched his hand together. "Especially one as well-presented as this."

"It's just a fancy of ours," I deliberately included Evelyn in my words. If she thought of us as a couple, she might be less inclined to chase after Charles.

I watched as the carpenter finished his job by adding two heavy bolts and a padlock sufficiently large to restrain a wild elephant.

The carpenter stood up. "That's me finished, sir. Shall I send the account here?" He faced me honestly, for people with money tend to make tradesmen wait for their wages, or neglected to pay them at all.

Aware that Evelyn was watching, I fished in my pocket and

produced three guineas, which was a phenomenally generous amount for a single piece of work.

For the first time since I entered that house, I had a full night's sleep. There were no unexplained footsteps, no strange dreams, no visions of being consumed by flames and no unwanted images in the mirror. In short, Evelyn's idea of placing a Bible to contain the restless spirit or merely to calm my nerves had succeeded.

Next morning the atmosphere within the house had altered, with the maid singing as she made up the fire and set the breakfast table and even the footman less surly than usual. "That is a beautiful Bible," the maid called as she scrubbed black lead into the kitchen range. "I've never seen a better."

"As long as it keeps your fanciful delusions away," I said, "then it does its job."

"It must have cost a pretty penny, sir," the maid continued, smiling at me over her shoulder.

"It did." I was never loath to proclaim my wealth, now I had some.

"Just wait until I tell my folks that you've stuck a fancy Bible inside a door," the maid said. "They'll think I'm working for royalty!"

I smiled. "You tell them all you like," I said.

I left the servants with a wave of my staff and checked the time with my watch.

"Ten minutes off the hour," I said, quite cheerfully for I had dreaded finding it was six minutes past six. "I will be back shortly after seven tonight." I had a full day ahead of me, visiting a clutch of regular patients who needed my help with a variety of ailments, mostly self-inflicted or purely imaginary.

I was not accurate with my timing, for, after my final call, I paused for a couple of quick hands at the New Wig, won a comfortable 30 guineas, tipped the porters two guineas each and returned by way of Queen Street. I had an inclination to call on Evelyn, who was surely pining for my company, but instead, I saw Charles leaving the house with a wave and marching briskly along the street as if he had every right to be there.

I almost stopped breathing when I saw Charles, my old and trusted friend, again emerging from the green door. I felt sick, physically sick, at my betrayal by him and Evelyn. This time I had no doubt, for there was no reason for any liaison between the two.

Turning away, I followed Charles, tapping my staff on the paving as I walked, with the anger surging through me to explode inside my brain. After everything I had done to gain Evelyn's favour, she was betraying me with a man I had known for years.

For the life of me, I could not see what appeal Charles could have. True, he was a charming man and romantic with his Hebridean antecedents, but I was five times richer, with a prosperous practice. I had money safe in the bank and shares with the best and most reliable of companies. Was I not sufficiently handsome? By God, I could alter that! I could hire a couple of Donalds or Irish from Tanner's Close who would mark Charles' face so that no woman would ever look at him without a shudder. There were scores of old soldiers or navigators who would kill a man, let alone disfigure one, for the price of a drink.

No. I shook my head. That was a stupid thing to contemplate. Charles was my friend and Evelyn my intended. Neither of them would betray me. I was overwrought, overtired or affected by recent events.

I looked up. Charles was heading down Hanover Street, whistling and swinging his cane as if he had not a care in the world. I watched as he bid a cheery good evening to a married couple before he eventually arrived at Abercrombie Street. What on earth was Charles doing there? I was not aware he had an acquaintance in that street. And he was not visiting a patient, not without his medical bag.

I followed, keeping my distance, with my thoughts so confused, I felt as if my head might explode. One moment I thought that Charles was my friend, and I could trust him, and the next I knew he had betrayed me with Evelyn. I hated myself for the distrust I knew was justified, and loathed Charles for what he had done.

Sheltering under a tree, I watched Charles rap at a dark-painted door. A servant opened, they had a brief conversation, and Charles entered the house.

Now what was happening? What the devil was MacNeil doing?

From across the road, I kept watching as a slow rain wept from the heavens and water dripped on me from the spreading branches of the tree. Ignoring my discomfort, I had the occasional glimpse of Charles moving inside, clear through the tall windows. Twice I saw a woman, dark-haired, elegant and evidently quite at ease in Charles's company although I only saw her back view.

"Who is that?" I asked myself. "Are you walking out with two women, Charles?"

Confused, frustrated and angry, I waited outside that house for two hours as the rain increased and my temper worsened by the minute. It was dark when I returned home, with nothing resolved in my head.

"Damn you, Charles MacNeil," I said, putting a light to the fire. "Damn you for a Gaelic Donald of the worst sort."

As I stared at the fire, I could see him burning, with the flames curling around him. I knew the agony that would bring, for I had been there, I had been within the flames, writhing and screaming, choking on the acrid smoke as the crowd watched, pointing excitedly.

No!

I pulled back.

That was nonsense. I had not been in the fire. From where did that idea come? I shook my head. We had banished such horrors when we blocked the cellar down below, had we not?

We? What did I mean by *we*? I was only myself, until the moment I wed Evelyn. And I could not perform that single act unless I entered a church, and would not feel properly married as long as Charles MacNeil stalked the streets, preying on women, preying on my woman. With that thought, the circle began again. I stared into the fire as the long hours passed and the street outside echoed only to the wind and rain.

I did not retire to bed that night. I think I dozed on the chair, although my mind was so confused, I am not sure. I only know that in the morning I was befuddled with lack of sleep and so dizzy I could barely walk.

CHAPTER 17

SANDY CROSSED HIS LEGS, sipped at his claret and surveyed me over the rim of his glass. "I understand what you are going through, Doctor."

I shook my head. "I would doubt that, Sandy. I am a qualified medical doctor, and *I* don't understand. How can you know?"

Sandy sipped again, with his gaze never straying from my face. "You have an internal struggle, Doctor, between what you know to be right and what you feel you want to do."

I considered while the fire roared in my ears. The older of my maids added coal, for the evening carried a chill. "That is correct. How do you know?"

"I've had the same all my life."

I reached for the claret bottle, hesitated, and poured myself another glass. "You are an interesting man, Sandy. You live in one of the poorer parts of the city, yet you are undoubtedly educated. What happened? Was it a bad business deal? Or was it this?" I indicated the bottle.

"Neither," Sandy said, unsmiling.

"Then what? And how do you know so much about Thomas Weir, and how he affects people." I saw no profit in hiding the truth from Sandy.

Sandy stared into the fire for a long time before he replied. "I know too much about Thomas Weir, Doctor," he said. "I doubt there is a man living or dead who knows more than me."

"How is that?" I asked. "And why is that? Why are you interested in such an unpleasant fellow?"

"Come, Doctor." Sandy gave a twisted smile. "Is that any way to talk about my ancestor?"

I started at that. "Your ancestor?" I shook my head. "Thomas Weir was not married. Did he have a child out of wedlock?"

"Worse than that, Doctor," Sandy said. "It was much worse. He had a child with his sister, an incestuous child."

I had heard of such things but never encountered them in my professional career. "I was unaware of that," I said, slowly. "What happened to the child?"

"They brought it up secretly in the house in the West Bow," Sandy said. "And then later claimed that somebody left it on their doorstep."

"Poor wee mite," I said, as my rational side battled with a feeling of anger that our secret was known. *Our secret?*

"Aye." Sandy spoke as if he remembered the incident personally, rather than referring to a child who must have lived and died more than a century ago. "That boy was my great-great-grandfather."

I nodded, trying to digest this new information. "Did that knowledge give you the interest in Major Weir?"

"More than the knowledge." Sandy sipped at his claret. "I try to alleviate the harm and steer folk away from him."

I grunted. "I thought I was the first to live in Weir's house for years."

"You were," Sandy said. He sighed. "You are also the first to move from that house to this one. I think you are in great danger, Doctor."

"I've locked up the cellar where the ashes are," I said, "and sealed it with a Bible."

"Aye," Sandy said, "but you've kept the staff." He glanced at my stave, leaning against the fireplace. I seldom left it out of reach.

"It brings me luck," I said.

Sandy was quiet for a moment as he gazed into the fire. Taking a pipe from his pocket, he stuffed the bowl with tobacco, lit it with a glowing ember and tapped the staff with his foot. "What sort of luck, Doctor?"

"All sorts of luck," I said.

"Wine, women and song?"

I nodded. "And money."

Sandy finished his claret, shaking his head when I offered him more. "The sort of luck you would not expect a respectable man to have."

I nodded again. "Perhaps."

"You are entering establishments you would never take a kirk minister into."

I thought of the New Wig, the Waverley and the Benison. "Yes, indeed."

"The staff is not bringing you luck, doctor. The staff is leading you the wrong way, the easy way. Wide is the gate, and broad is the road that leadeth to destruction. Matthew, chapter seven, verse 13." Sandy poked at the fire with his foot. "It's altering your personality, Doctor." He sighed. "We all have two sides, a good and a bad, a duality of person, if you wish. The staff seems to have the ability to emphasise the bad side and suppress the good."

I had already guessed that the staff was not a benign influence, but the love of money had seduced me to evil ways, as it had seduced millions before me. I studied the black staff again, with its geometrical designs and those two naked human figures writhing around the lower half. Then I thought of the gold piled in my name in the bank, and the comfortable life it would gain for Evelyn.

"You are confused, Doctor," Sandy said. "I only hope that my words have helped you."

"This cannot be Major Weir's staff," I said, running a finger along the carvings. "His staff burned alongside him."

"Did it?" Sandy asked. "Does the devil burn in Hell?"

I remembered my nightmares, with the flames licking around me, the acrid bite of smoke and the scorching, unbearable agony.

Sandy stood up. "I will leave you to work things out in your mind, Doctor. I can only remind you how you obtained peace in the house by blocking your cellar."

I spent the next hour alternately staring into the fire and glancing at the staff where it leaned, dark, mysterious and yet so full of promise. I was uncertain what was best to be done, so I thought of my life before I found that staff, and my life after. I had gained friends, prestige and money, yet my mind was troubled. Did my gains counterbalance my losses? Would I, could I, keep Evelyn if I were poor?

Would she want to be married to an impoverished doctor with few prospects? Would she wish to be married to a passionate gambler who whored and cavorted with the fast set of the city?

I paced the room, listening to the thunder of my thoughts until my head positively ached, and my legs were weary. I did not mark the passage of time, so I was surprised when I heard a timid knock on the door, and the maid poked her head inside the room.

"You are up early, Doctor," she said.

"I have not slept," I admitted, running a hand across my bristly, unshaven jaw.

The maid bobbed in a small curtsey. "May I make up the fire, sir?"

I realised the embers were dead and cold. "Yes, of course." I tried to muster a smile. "Tell me," I said, "what do you think of my walking stick?"

The maid shook her head. "Begging your pardon, Doctor, but I think it's a hideous thing with all the devil's carvings on it and those people with no clothes."

"You don't like it, then?"

"No, sir. It scares me."

"Ah," I said. "We can't have that, can we?" For some unknown reason, this simple young girl's words carried great weight that morning. I know I had been wrestling with the burden all night, and was undoubtedly weary, so her slender help was sufficient to tip the scales in one direction or the other. By disliking my staff, she made my decision for me.

"Thank you, my dear," I said, which words surprised her greatly, but not as much as the grateful kiss I planted on her forehead. "You are a girl of great perspicacity."

"Thank you, sir." The girl looked confused, as well she might for I doubt she understood the meaning of the word.

Evelyn had urged me to part with that staff, Sandy had warned me of its malign influence, and even my younger servant girl feared it. At that moment, my love for Evelyn overcame my love of money. Lifting the staff, I strode out of the house for, with my mind made up, I determined to act on the matter with the least delay. I knew that burning was of no use with this black staff, so determined to see if the converse element would succeed. At that hour of the morning, the streets were empty, with not even a single tradesman's cart, and nobody witnessed me marching northwards, down past the old Barony of Broughton and down to Canonmills and the single-arched bridge over the Water of Leith.

As luck would have it, the rain had continued all night, so the river was in flood, hissing against the grassy banks and churning a creamy brown beneath the bridge. I knew that hesitation might prove fatal to my enterprise, so hardly looked over the parapet before lifting that fearful black staff and launching it to eternity. As a child, my friends and I had played a game where we threw sticks over one side of the bridge in Hawick and then rushed to the opposite side to see whose stick was first through. Now I did the same, stepping to the downstream side of the Canonmills Bridge to watch my staff charge downstream.

I saw it bob with the racing current, snag on the branch of a fallen tree, remain static for a moment with the water breaking white around it, then work itself free and race on, out of my sight. I had expected to experience mixed emotions, yet there was nothing but relief and a sense of elation that I was free of its malevolent influence. I had sufficient money in the bank to carry me for quite some time, and as long as I could build my practice, life should be sweet.

I stood on the Canonmills Bridge for some time, watching the flow of water with the trees on either bank dipping and curtseying as the river dragged at their lowest branches. The feeling descended suddenly, like some revelation from on-high.

I was free.

"Evelyn."

"Evelyn." I said her name once more, unable to restrain my smile. "Evelyn Swinton, or Mrs Evelyn Elliot!" I smiled at the coincidence of alliteration and nearly ran back up the slope of Broughton Street to the New Town and my George Street house. I washed, shaved and dressed with a light heart, and was about to open my surgery when I decided on a small experiment.

Even since I had collapsed in the Tron Kirk and failed to enter St Giles, I had avoided churches and eluded all Evelyn's attempts to coerce me into worship. Now, I dashed out of my house and along the road to the nearest church, St Andrews, in George Street. With hardly a pause, I stormed through the doors with neither let nor hindrance. I stood for a second within the holy site, opened my mouth and shouted: "Hallelujah! Praise the Lord!"

Two worshippers stared at me, for the kirk frowns upon such unbecoming behaviour. One old man muttered that I must be demented, which was the very opposite of the truth. I treated the worshippers to a smile, blessed them both and left, to march back to the surgery.

"George," I shouted to my manservant, scribbled a concise but heartfelt note, sealed it and handed it to him. "Take that to the Swintons' house in Queen Street," I said.

"Will there be a reply?" George asked.

"Not immediately," I said. "There is no need to wait." On a whim, I passed him a half crown as well. "Buy yourself some refreshment on your way back."

"Why thank you, sir. That is very generous of you."

I laughed as George closed his fist on the silver coin and waited for my first patient of the day. Now that I was without my lucky staff, I knew I could not rely on the cards to provide my primary source of income. I would have to increase my practice and become a full-time doctor again. Well, I told myself, that was the reason I had studied so hard at Glasgow University.

As I had hoped, my letter to Evelyn drew her to my house. She arrived within the hour, slightly out of breath and with loose strands of hair escaping from the ridiculous hat that seems to be all in fashion for women these days.

"Is everything all right, Martin?" Perhaps Evelyn read my mind, for she removed her hat, revealing a new hairstyle, parted in the centre, with prim rows of curls in the front and dressed high at the back.

"It could not be better," I said. "And I like your hair."

"Oh." Evelyn's hand strayed to her head. "You did not ask me here to compliment me on my hair!"

"Indeed I did not," I said, smiling, and raced on. "I once contemplated eloping with you. I believe I mentioned the idea. I want you to forget all that nonsense, Evelyn. I must have had a fever on the brain. We shall have a fine wedding in the church your family attends, with everybody there whom we want to be there." I watched her face glow with happiness.

"Will you worship with us on Sunday?" Evelyn asked nervously.

"With the greatest of pleasure," I said, and knew her cup of joy ran over. "I have thrown away that black staff."

"Oh!" Evelyn said.

"I took your advice," I said and kissed her.

The next few days were undoubtedly among the happiest I had ever experienced. I attended St George's Church in Charlotte Square with the Swintons, and the minister and congregation welcomed me as if I were a long-lost brother, or the black sheep newly returned to the fold, which I was, in a way.

With the spiritual and physical barrier to my entering churches removed, I had no objections when Evelyn next asked which church we should marry in. "I had wished for an old church," she said, "but you were correct. We should marry in the family church of St George's."

"Why then," I said, "that is the church we shall use."

And that was the end of that discussion.

I will skip the next few weeks as the banns were read and Evelyn decided who should attend the wedding. I will say only that the George Street house remained quiet, the servants were contented and increasingly efficient, and arrangements for the wedding proceeded apace. I also made a point of examining Mr Swinton once more to proclaim him free of any infection.

"Are you sure, sir?" Swinton asked, with the beginnings of hope in his face.

"Perfectly sure," I said. "The mercury treatment I prescribed was only a precaution for we do not know what occurred that unfortunate night. Either my treatment worked perfectly, or you were not infected, or indeed nothing untoward happened." I smiled. "I am sure Mrs Swinton will be glad to have her husband back."

"Doctor! Martin!" Swinton took my hand and shook it vigorously. "I cannot say what relief your words have given me. I have heard that one could be infected for years."

"Not in your case, Mr Swinton," I said. "I can pronounce you as clean as any man."

I felt a virtuous glow as Mr Swinton left my surgery with his head held high and his back straight. I had rectified a wrong of my own making, yet still retained the benefits of my earlier trickery in the palm of my hand. I could not help but congratulate myself. Charles told me once that a Highlander's triumph was victory in a battle that the enemy was unaware he has fought. I felt that smug warmth as my future father-in-law returned to his wife and my conscience eased a little more.

When it came, the marriage day was everything that Evelyn could have desired. She was the centre of attention within a circle of her family and friends, she had a handsome man at her side, and there was not a word of dissent. St George's Church is in the centre of Charlotte Square, perhaps the most imposing part of the New Town and, although the interior of the church is rather plain, the ceremony more than made up for any shortcomings. Charles was there to support me, for I had entirely dismissed my foolish suspicions, and I had Sandy Tait and a few new friends and acquaintances among the guests, including some up from Roxburghshire. Evelyn's sister Elaine was also present, a dark-haired beauty with a slightly diffident air and, as convention demanded, she and Charles danced together throughout the afternoon.

I was not involved in choosing Evelyn's wedding dress, which was of figured satin with a border of a festoon of roses, interwoven to form a continuous band of red-blossomed foliage which Evelyn assured me was the latest fashion. Feathers nearly obscured her miniature hat while for some incomprehensible reason she carried a small fan. Despite my lack of knowledge of fashion, I could see the result was spectacular as we stood in front of the altar and pledged our love.

"Well," I said when I carried my new bride over the threshold to our George Street house. "That's that then."

"Yes," Evelyn said. "We're man and wife."

I placed her down gently. The servants had lined up to welcome us back, each dressed in his or her best and all smiling. I had four servants now, a cook, two maids, and George the manservant who did the manual work and answered the door to my patients.

Evelyn and I already knew each other, so we settled down quickly and established a routine within a few weeks. She proved an excellent wife, as I had expected, and added that last touch of respectability I had lacked.

In the evenings, we talked, or played cards, visited one of our friends or sat reading in the living room by candlelight and the warm glow of the fire. In short, we were the very epitome of domestic bliss, one of those favoured couples who are perfectly satisfied with their lot and one another's company. On one occasion, when the wind roared in the chimney and sleety rain hurled at the window as if wild to break its way into the house, Evelyn told me about her travels. My wife had seen the world, from her time in India when she was young, to her more recent trip to Orkney to visit an elderly relative.

"You'd like it there," Evelyn said. "I spent hours just walking and looking at all the strange stones."

"You find interest in all sorts of things," I said. "And in all sorts of people."

"Your friend Sandy is an interesting fellow," Evelyn said with a smile. "Have you spoken to him recently?"

I looked up from the newspaper I had been attempting to read. "Not since our wedding," I said.

"I met him today, quite by chance," Evelyn told me.

A few weeks ago, I would have been instantly jealous. Now I merely smiled and asked what had been the subject of their conversation.

"Old Edinburgh," Evelyn said frankly. "Your friend Sandy seems to be an expert on the old stories."

I smiled, for the days of being scared of nightmares and strange noises had vanished in my new domestic bliss. "He can be quite enthusiastic," I said.

"I found him fascinating." Evelyn bent her head to her sewing. "He told me a lot I had not known."

Putting her sewing aside, she lifted the book I had bought in Mother Marwick's pawn shop. "I haven't seen this before," she said.

I glanced across, for, in truth, I had nearly forgotten that I possessed the thing. "Oh, that's just nonsense," I said. "I should have thrown it out months ago."

"Oh, no." When Evelyn shook her head, her ringlets shimmered in the candlelight. "You must never throw a book away, Martin. That's discarding knowledge."

Smiling, Evelyn flicked through the pages, stopping whenever an image caught her attention. "These animal pictures are beautiful," she said. "Look at this bull! It could nearly walk out of the page."

"Not into our house, I hope," I said, and we both laughed at the idea.

"And this picture of Pictish warriors," Evelyn pointed to a battle scene taken from a stone at Dunnichen, near Dundee. "I should not like to be involved in anything so bloody."

I smiled indulgently, happy that Evelyn was interested in the book. She frowned, turning her head sideways as she studied one of the pictures, an abstract design of whorls and interlocking lines. "I've seen this before," Evelyn said.

"Have you?" I looked over her shoulder. "Maybe it was in another book."

Evelyn shook her head. "Maybe," she said, "but I have never seen a book of this nature before."

"It will come to you," I said, returning to my newspaper and dismissing the conversation from my mind.

"What's the time?" Evelyn adjusted the little wooden cross she had brought from her Queen Street home. She seemed determined to disturb my reading that night.

I looked at my watch. "It's a quarter short of eleven," I said.

"I think I'll get to bed," Evelyn said. "And you should do the same. You need your sleep." She smiled. "You should think of getting some clocks in this house, Martin."

"I had some bad experiences with clocks," I reminded her. "And got rid of the damned things."

"That was months ago," Evelyn pointed out. "And I do wish you would moderate your language. We'll buy a clock tomorrow," she decided.

Rather than descend to an unpleasant disagreement, I agreed, and we scoured the city for clocks, installing two in the house and one in the surgery. As I had retained the Grassmarket surgery, not to make money, but as an act of charity to the less fortunate among us, I bought an old long-case clock for that establishment and placed it on one corner.

For the first few days, the relentless ticking of the clocks unnerved me, and I found myself checking the time every quarter-hour. When I realised their mechanisms worked with perfect efficiency, I gradually relaxed and trusted the time that the hands showed. Not once did they stop at six minutes past six. All it needed now was a son and heir, and I would have reached the peak of what a doctor could be.

I went to bed on the night of the fifth day of March without a care in the world. Life was successful, and the future stretched before us like a pathway to heaven, filled with good intentions.

CHAPTER 18

"Martin! Evelyn hissed my name as we lay in bed. "Martin!"

I half awoke, stirring uneasily to free myself from the bonds of sleep. "Evelyn? What's wrong?"

"I heard a sound," Evelyn whispered. "Down in the basement."

"It was probably one of the servants," I said, drowsily. Yet I remained awake as the old fears returned.

"Martin," Evelyn insisted, half rising.

"I'm listening," I said. I remained still for a moment, trying to work out what had happened. I heard the scraping, nothing like the night-time noises that had been so usual in this house. I wondered if I should investigate, decided that it was probably the wind acting on a loose shutter and rolled over. "It's nothing, Evelyn." However, I could not sleep. The sound, and the memories of other sounds, played on my nerves. Sighing, I sat up, swung my legs over the edge of the bed, got up and lit a candle with the dull red embers of the fire.

"Be careful, Martin," Evelyn said as I staggered to the chest-of-drawers and took out the double-barrelled pistol that I still kept loaded. My hand fitted comfortably around the stock. In a moment of near-panic, I glanced at the clock that ticked quietly in the corner and felt quick relief when I saw the hands indicated ten minutes short of three o'clock.

The scraping sound had ended, but I heard others that I could not identify. Throwing on a coat, I descended the stairs, shielding the candle so I would not alert an intruder, if intruder there were. I moved one slow step at a time, feeling the heavy beat of my heart, hearing my harsh, nervous breathing and with the stone steps cold under my bare feet.

I reached the basement and lifted the candle high, so the yellow light dissipated along the dark corridor. What I saw made me swear, while nausea rose in my throat as all the terror of earlier days returned. Somebody had broken into the house and removed the Bible from the cellar door. Not only that, but he had also picked the lock of the padlock, no doubt thinking the cellar contained something precious. Now the cellar door gaped wide open.

Hearing a slight scuffle, I saw two small figures sliding away at the periphery of the circle of candlelight. One, notable for a shock of dirty red hair, was crouched over a heavy bundle, undoubtedly my stolen Bible.

"You little blackguards!" I yelled. "Give me that Bible!"

The boys ran, jinking like hares as they fled along the corridor and into the empty front room of the basement. Dropping my candle, I chased them, only to see the one with the Bible swarm through the open window and disappear out of a circular hole in the shutters. The second boy was only a fraction later, and my despairing lunge failed to catch him.

"Come back!" I yelled, aware I was wasting my breath. Swearing, I ran to the basement door, but by the time I drew back the bolts and turned the key, the thieves were gone. I pointed my pistol down the empty street, swore again and returned to the house.

"Oh, dear God in heaven," I said as all my fears about this house flooded back. Without the Bible to seal the horror inside that cellar, all sorts of evil could escape, and I had brought Evelyn to this house of sin. "Oh, dear God," I said again, as I lifted the still-burning candle and stared at the open door. Unable to help myself, I entered the cellar, so the light from my candle flickered onto the dark ash in the mortar. A chill ran through me, damp and cold as I stood there, scarcely able to move for the petrifying fear that gripped me.

By that time, all the servants were awake and clustered outside their rooms, staring at me in wonder.

"Go back to bed," I said, thrusting the pistol inside my coat pocket. "We've been burgled, but they've gone now."

I withdrew in something like a swoon, closing the door and returning up the stairs with my mind numb with shock.

"Martin?" Evelyn was sitting up in bed, holding a candle in a brass candlestick. "Are you all right?"

"We've been robbed," I said. "Somebody has stolen the Bible and opened the cellar door."

"Is that all they stole?" Evelyn sounded relieved. "We'll buy another one tomorrow."

My wife's pragmatic solution pacified me for the moment until I glanced at the clock in the corner. It read six minutes past six.

I could not restrain the shiver that ran down my spine. "It's too late," I said. "The evil is already loose."

I did what I could. Next morning, Evelyn and I installed another Bible in the cellar door. We locked and bolted the cellar and hoped that would entrap the evil, the thing, the entity, once again. I contacted the police and showed a hard-faced constable with a Hebridean accent the circular hole in the shutters.

"That's how your thief got in," Constable MacDonald said, knowledgeably. "Open the shutters, slide open the window and the house is his to rob." He looked at me through unsettlingly pale Gaelic eyes. "You were lucky he only stole a book,"

I did not tell him what that book had been guarding. How could I? Who would believe me? Eventually, the constable left and I found workmen to repair the shutters and fit new padlocks and bolts on the cellar door although I knew, inside my heart, that the damage had been done. A criminal invading the house had allowed the evil to escape from the cellar and whatever I did would be futile.

I changed the times on all the clocks in the house, wound them up myself and patrolled the house half that night, candle in hand, until Evelyn called me to bed.

"You won't be any use to anybody unless you get some sleep," she told me severely.

In the morning, even my watch indicated six minutes past six.

"Evelyn." I could feel the change in atmosphere, with new darkness descending. "I think it best if you live with your parents for a while."

"No." Evelyn, that most loyal of women, shook her head. "We married for better or worse. Besides, what would I tell them?"

"Tell them we have fallen out," I said.

"If I did," Evelyn said, "my mother would be knocking on your door within five minutes, full of sage advice about marital quarrels and how to patch them. No, husband, dear. I stay, and we will face this together."

I was not happy with her decision and told her so, quite

bluntly, hoping to force her to safety. I might as well have tried to call down the moon.

Evelyn shook her head. "I'm staying," she said, folding her arms with a show of determination that undoubtedly deserved more than a simple kiss.

The next couple of days passed quietly and even the nights were without incident, except for the now-expected alteration of the clocks. Evelyn smiled at that. "It's only a couple of clocks," she said. "That won't kill us. Perhaps the new Bible has done its work."

I accepted Evelyn's practical attitude. "I might be exaggerating events," I said, for in truth after the golden months that had passed, it was difficult to recall the blackness through which I had lived.

"Good." Evelyn's smile always managed to instil optimism.

I stepped into the surgery with a slightly lighter heart, saw my first half dozen patients without difficulty and started when the next walked in.

"Good morning, Martin." Swinton was smiling as he walked in, sat opposite me and crossed his legs. "I believe I have something of yours."

"Good morning," I said, wondering what on earth he was talking about.

"Your old black staff," Swinton said. "I know how much it used to mean to you."

"Oh, I lost that weeks ago," I said. "I dropped it in the Water of Leith."

"That's exactly where it was found," Swinton said. "It was the strangest of coincidences! I was walking down the Canongate on my way to Arthur's Seat when I saw your staff in a pawn shop window. Why I said to myself, that's Martin's old stick, I swear to it."

"I hope you left it where it was." I could feel the icy chill gripping my heart, for only evil could come from that staff.

"Good heavens, no," Swinton sounded surprised. "After all the good deeds you did for me, I would not dream of depriving you of your favourite walking stick." He gave the slightly smug smile of a man conferring a great favour. "The old lady, Mother Marwick, she called herself, was delighted to sell it to me. She had it advertised at two shillings, but I managed to beat her price down to one-and-sixpence."

"A bargain at twice the price," I said, with nausea rising in my throat and my head spinning. "Where is it now, Mr Swinton?" I hoped he had not brought that thing into the house.

Swinton's smile broadened. "Why, Martin, I left it on your hallstand. Are you all right, Martin? You look uncommonly pale."

I fought the sensations that threatened to overcome me. I prayed, God, how I prayed, that I could negate the evil that Swinton's good deed had returned to my house. "Thank you," I said. "I am very well, thank you."

"I do hope you have not been overworking," Swinton said. "Your man told me your patients have increased of late."

"They have," I said, hoping Swinton would leave soon so I could simply open the front door and throw the staff outside. Surely, if I did that, some unfortunate fellow would make off with it, thinking he had found a prize.

"Well," Swinton rose, reaching for his hat. "I am glad I was able to help *you* for once, Martin." He stepped outside the surgery. "You are indeed busy today. I won't delay you any longer."

I could only nod weakly as Swinton left. I cannot recall much of the remainder of that day. I must have attended a round score of patients, with ailments that were uncommonly plain, for I recollect none of them, merely a procession of grey, worried faces and flabby, overfed bodies demanding my attention. At last, the flood of patients flowed to a trickle, and then the final droplet and I was alone with my fears.

"You may go," I said to George, who had never seen me so agitated. Striding past him, I entered the broad inner hall, from where stairs ascended to the living rooms above and the servants' quarters below. The hallstand stood in the outer hall, under a broad arched doorway and opposite a coloured print of Robert Burns. Even as I strode forward, I saw that staff, black and ornate, with the blank-faced skull on top and the human figures writhing up the shaft. When I looked again, I could see that the designs between the humans were circular, like carved golden guineas.

The very sight of the staff made me shiver. Opening the door, I lifted the staff and threw it outside, where it clattered on the paving stones. I slammed the door quickly, trying to still the beating of my heart.

"Martin?" Evelyn was staring at me. "Whatever is the matter?"

"Nothing now," I said, trying to summon a smile, which must have appeared like a death's head grin.

"You threw something into the street," Evelyn said. "What was it?"

"My carved black staff," I said, still shaking. "Your father brought it back. He meant it kindly."

Evelyn paled. She put one hand to her mouth. "Martin!"

"It's outside now," I said. "I hope some tramp will take it and we'll never see it again."

Evelyn nodded. "I hope so too, Martin." Walking into the front room, she peered out of the window. "It's still there."

We spent a miserable evening, checking for the staff every few moments, to see it lying just where I had thrown it. A steady downfall of rain formed a puddle around the stick.

"If that thing is still there tomorrow," I said, "I'll throw it in the river again."

"Yes, Martin," Evelyn said. "That would be best."

I no longer wound up the clocks, although I resisted the temptation to get rid of them. That night, I dozed rather than slept and, every time I woke, Evelyn was also awake, with her face worried and her hands screwed into tight balls. On at least three occasions, she left our bed to peer out of the window, each time returning wordless, but with a quick shake of her head.

"It will be all right," I assured her.

"Yes." She gave me a tired smile, with her eyes dark shadows sunk in bruised pits.

I must have slept for, as soon as it was light enough to see, I checked outside the house. The staff was gone, and the pavement was empty. I cannot describe my intense relief. I could have danced and sung at the top of my voice. Instead, I awoke Evelyn and told her.

"Oh, thank God," Evelyn said. "Thank God for all His mercies."

I slept then, to awake refreshed and enjoy a relaxed breakfast. Evelyn and I both joked with the servants, and only when I was dressed and ready for work did I see the black staff back in the hall stand.

"Oh, sir," the youngest maid told me happily, "I saw your favourite stick outside this morning. You must have dropped it." She continued with her duties, quite unaware of the harm she had done.

"Martin," Evelyn whispered, holding onto my sleeve. "Throw it into the river."

I nodded. Grabbing the staff, I nearly ran from the house and into the broad stretch of Hanover Street.

"Halloa, Doctor! I have not seen you for some time."

I spun in shock at the well-remembered voice.

CHAPTER 19

Of all the people I wished to avoid, the Honourable Peter was high on the list. Looking back now, I believe that some malignant force, some supernatural power, planted him there specifically to trap me. Unable to find adequate words, I could only stare at him as he stood in the centre of Hanover Street, leaning on an elegant gold-topped cane and smiling at me.

"Are you not talking to your old friend, Doctor?" The Honourable Peter stepped across and patted my shoulder. "Surely you have seen enough of your charming new wife by now."

I cannot explain the transformation, except to say that it was sudden and must have flowed from the staff. The memories returned – the absolute elation when I won a hand at cards, the breathless excitement of the tables, the companionship of like-minded men, the easy friendships with the women, without responsibility or doubt.

"By God, Peter." I shook him by the hand. "It's been a long time. Too long."

"Come, old boy, I just happened to be passing, on my way

home, don't ye know, and there you were, large as life and twice as ugly. Well, now, I said to myself, the old doctor is looking very respectable."

"That's me," I said, tapping my staff on the ground. "Respectability is my middle name."

We walked along George Street as the city awoke, two companions discussing the ways of the world.

It was queer that my old friends seemed to appear that morning, men and women I had not seen for months greeted me with a lifted hat or a curtsey as they emerged from shops and houses. I felt the old devil-may-care attitude return as I adopted a swagger, swinging my staff.

"Care for a good morning, Peter?"

"I've been up all night, old chap!"

"All the more reason, then. Something to wake you up for the day."

By that time, I was entirely my old self as we climbed up the Earthen Mound and strolled down the Lawnmarket to a close we both knew.

"Why, Doctor Elliot!" The lady proprietor looked genuinely pleased to see me, although it was the gold in my pocketbook that attracted her rather than anything else. "Where have you been all these months?"

I settled myself in my old spot in the corner, from where I could watch all the comings and goings. "Oh, the usual things, Peggy, my dear," I gave her rump an affectionate slap. "Getting married, becoming respectable, attending the church. That sort of thing."

Peggy screeched with laughter. "Attend church? You! Why there would be thunder and lightning if that happened, and all the angels in heaven would weep blood!"

I laughed. "Two glasses of your kill-me-deadly, Peggy," I

said, and no putting your finger in the glass, either." I watched her bottom as she walked away, smiling.

"Are you back with us, Doctor?" Peter asked. "Or just visiting?"

"I'm back," I said. "I can't think why I ever left to join these sanctimonious prigs and their infernal, stuffy lives."

"We can try the cards if you have a mind for it," Peter said. "Unless you have lost your skill."

"There won't be any tables open at this time," I said.

"I know a place," Peter said.

We tossed back Peggy's kill-me-deadly, which lived up to its name, being some foul rot-gut concoction from a hidden hope in the Moorfoot Hills. Still choking on the peat-reek fumes, I followed Peter down the Walk to Leith, where sailors filled mildly dangerous taverns, and dollymops flaunted themselves as they tried to catch my attention.

I found the cards interesting at first, but after winning a few hands and adding some weight to my purse, it grew tame, and I sought more active pursuits. Leaving Peter to the pleasures of the green baize tables, I wandered down to the docks where the rougher areas were, and dropped into a seaman's tavern. One had to be careful in such places for it was not unknown for unscrupulous innkeepers to doctor a drink so you could doze off in Leith and wake up on board some blood-boat outward bound for hell or Hindustan, whichever was the worst.

As it happened, I kept my wits about me and found my way to a dog pit, where men gambled on their dog to fight another. It was a fascinating, bloody business and I put my money on a ragged-eared mastiff fighting some hirsute creature with a foreign name. The composition of the crowd was equally interesting, for around a third were women, and many had the appearance of respectability. Their excitement increased as the fight progressed, and some leaned right over the pit for a better view as the blood and fur flew harder. I watched one attractive young woman in a costly coat who was so close to the fighting that blood spattered her face. Behind her, looking slightly bored, was Lady Clarinda.

My dog won, of course. I would have been astounded at any other outcome, and I pocketed my winnings, handed a guinea to the bookmaker, so he remembered me next time, and sauntered away, tapping my staff on the ground.

"You there! I said, you, sir!"

I felt the tap on my shoulder and turned around with my staff raised ready to defend myself, for some players take defeat hard. "Who the devil are you, sir?"

The man was erect, with a hard jaw but servility rather than arrogance in his stance. "My lady wishes to speak to you," he said.

"Does she indeed?" I asked. "And who might your lady be?" As if I could not guess.

I knew it was Lady Clarinda, who stood beside a dark coach-and-four with an imperious tilt to her face, tapping a riding crop against her very expensive boots. Disdaining to hurry, I sauntered towards her with the man, who I took to be her servant, at my side.

"Good afternoon, your Ladyship." I tipped my hat, eyeing her up.

"Where the deuce have you been all this time, Doctor?" Lady Clarinda asked, with her breeding evident in every line of her stance and wealth oozing from her clothes and coach.

"You may call me Martin," I said, noting she did not smile. "And you, I presume, have been pining for my company."

When Lady Clarinda's arm twitched, I thought she was going to strike me with her whip, which she would have enjoyed immensely, I knew. I eyed her coolly, ready to retaliate because, by God, I was not a man to take an insult from anybody. "I saw you at the dog-pit." I took the initiative. "Excuse me, my Lady." Licking the palm of my hand, I wiped a spatter of blood from her cheek as she stood, unflinching.

"You used to be known as the lucky doctor," Lady Clarinda said. "Do you still deserve that title?"

"I have heard that name applied to me," I agreed, "and I am always willing to try my fortune."

"Step inside." Lady Clarinda entered her coach, leaving the door open for me to follow. I did, of course, for I was curious to find out what she wished from me. The interior was luxurious, padded with red leather and with velvet curtains across the windows. Lady Clarinda sat opposite me, examining me minutely as I remained silent, holding my staff in both hands.

"Doctor Martin Elliot of George Street, recently married to Evelyn Swinton, whose father you helped out of financial embarrassment," Lady Clarinda said as the coach rolled through Leith with surprising smoothness.

"That's correct," I said. "I am glad you remember."

Lady Clarinda gave a smile of such sweet innocence that I knew instinctively that all the rumours about her were true. "The dog pit is not a place for a respectable married man."

"Nor for a respectable lady," I returned.

"Perhaps," Lady Clarinda conceded, "but it suits me."

"And me." I held her gaze, fully aware of what she was contemplating was not respectable in the slightest.

Lady Clarinda proved my suspicions correct when she ordered her man to drive to her house on the southern outskirts of the city.

"We'll have privacy there," Lady Clarinda told me, "although I don't give a twopenny damn what people think."

I laughed, tapping my staff on the floor of her coach. "A woman after my own heart, by God!"

Lady Clarinda lived in style, with a host of servants to look after her and a house where mere luxury would be an insult. The décor was like nothing I had seen before, with statues of classical nudes in every niche, and paintings that would shock a sergeant of marines.

"Do you like it?" Lady Clarinda asked.

"It is splendid," I said, appreciating the display that spread before me.

"The family has always collected art," Clarinda said. "Art and curios." She led me through the house, pointing out various objects. "That's a shrunken head that my father picked up in the East. And that's the headsman's axe from some German town. One of my ancestors purloined that particular object when he was on the Grand Tour."

I laughed, wondering if all her line had possessed her singular tastes.

Lady Clarinda paused at a curious metal contraption. "These are thumbscrews that the Inquisition used. I was thinking of trying them out when my tenants don't pay the rent."

"Damned good idea," I said, not quite sure if she was joking or not but rather hoping for the latter.

"And this skull," Lady Clarinda stopped at a skull that sat on a shelf, missing its jaw-bone. "I picked that up myself from the field of Waterloo." She gave me a slow smile. "We were at the ball in Brussels before the battle, you see, and afterwards, when all the fire and fury finished, visited the field for souvenirs."

"I know it is impolite to ask," I said, "but you must have been very young."

"I was 14 years old," Lady Clarinda said, "and the Duke was very attentive. Very." She smiled at some memory. "After the battle, all the ladies were collecting souvenirs. Skulls from the dead soldiers, letters, finger rings, boots or whatever we could find." She stroked the skull as if it were some sort of pet. "I don't know to which army this fellow belonged but he is rather a favourite of mine."

"I have a rival then," I said.

"A rival?" Lady Clarinda smiled. "Oh, Doctor, you do make me smile. What makes you think I have any affection towards you? We are two of a kind, you and I. We both want the same things."

I laughed at that, for I was very much in tune with Her Ladyship. Cupping one of her breasts, I squeezed lightly.

"That's the spirit," Lady Clarinda said and responded by taking a generous handful of my left buttock. We broke apart a few moments later, reluctantly putting our eagerness aside.

"You are married, then," Lady Clarinda said.

"I am," I said.

"So am I," Lady Clarinda said. "Damned inconvenient sometimes, but there it is."

"It doesn't have to be." I traced my finger over the breast on the sculpture of Diana next to me. "One can always live as one wishes, with or without one's spouse."

"My feelings exactly." Lady Clarinda cupped her hand around an essential piece of David's anatomy.

"Where?" I asked.

"Come." Taking hold of the lapel of my coat, she led me through her house to the topmost room in the western wing.

CHAPTER 20

"MARTIN?" Evelyn was at the front door when I arrived home. "Where have you been? Are you all right?"

I could see she had been up all night.

"Don't be a goose, woman," I said, tapping my staff on the floor. "I met an old friend."

"You still have that stick, I see," Evelyn said, her voice icy. "I thought you were going to throw it away."

"I decided otherwise." I pushed past her.

Although it was no business of Evelyn's how I spent my time, she seemed determined to control my life, if not by black looks and a cold attitude, then by other methods. I found the marital bed an unwelcoming environment and noticed various little signs of her displeasure over the next few days as I resumed my old life.

One sign was a few verses in her hand that turned up one morning when I arrived, bleary-eyed and hungover, at my desk in the surgery.

Clubs

Turned up by a female hand
Of all the modern schemes of Man
That time has brought to bear,
A plague upon the wicked plan
That parts the wedded pair!
My female friends they all agree
They hardly know their hubs;
And heart and voice unite with me
We hate the name of Clubs!

I read the epistle, shook my head, screwed up the paper and threw it on the floor for a servant to remove. Whether it was Evelyn's own creation or she had cribbed it from some more talented hand, I neither knew nor care. The fact that she had the effrontery to try to shame me was reason enough for anger.

I felt my mouth tighten. Who the devil did that woman think she was? She was my wife, not my mother, for God's sake. I owned her, as surely as I owned my new black horse or the carpet under my feet. As my anger mounted, I contemplated slapping Evelyn to the ground or laying my whip across her shoulders. No, I told myself. I needed to preserve my image as a happily married man, despite her provocations. I would wait and see what opportunities presented themselves for dealing with her.

My first target, I thought, would be her books. Evelyn was an inveterate reader. She devoured the damned things, sitting for hours consuming the words of Walter Scott, Hogg and God alone knew who else.

I had little time for books now that I was back to my old ways, so resolved to throw the damned things on to the fire. I started with the *Waverley Novels*, Evelyn's favourites, smiling as the flames curled around the pages, and slowly worked my way through her entire library.

When I lifted the battered old volume of designs, it fell open, revealing the whorls and interlaced design that Evelyn had claimed to recognise.

"What the devil?" I frowned. I remembered Evelyn's surprise when she saw that picture, and now that the veil of love was removed from my eyes, I could recall where I had also seen it before. "Good God!" It was the same design that the whaling men had tattooed on Charles's hip. "You blackguard, Charles! And you utter little bitch!"

I felt the anger mount within me as suspicion altered to certainty.

If Evelyn had seen that design, she must have seen Charles without his trousers. By God! She was indeed cuckolding me with my oldest companion! There was no other possible explanation, and I had been correct all along.

My first instinct was to rush upstairs to the bedroom and thrash the blasted woman to within an inch of her life. I grabbed my staff and rose, picturing her cowering before me as I laid into her, but then I shook my head. That would bring instant satisfaction but would hardly cure the situation. Indeed it would possibly drive the ungrateful bitch closer to MacNeil. No. No, I had to think of something more suitable for the situation, something more long-lasting that I could savour in the months and years to come. I wanted a Highland victory, one that Mrs Evelyn bloody Elliot did not even know she had lost.

Striding out of the house, I ignored the salutation of a bemused servant, slammed the door shut to show my fury and stormed along George Street, unsure where I was heading and aware only of the anger that burned through my veins.

"By God, I'll show her!" I said, again and again as I heard the echo of my feet on the hard paving stones. "Cuckold me, will she? And with that freckled Hebridean of all people! That back-stabbing, Highland rogue!"

Shouldering people aside in my rage, I found myself back in the Old Town among the lower orders of humanity, the impoverished wretches who infested these foul closes and filthy wynds. The very idea of rubbing shoulders with them disgusted me, yet the woman I sought was here. Tapping my staff on the ground, I negotiated the intricate network of closes to arrive at Mother Marwick's pawn shop. She looked up when I entered, with her eyes darker than ever and her brow creased into an inverted horseshoe.

"Doctor Elliot," she recognised me immediately. "Have you come for another book?"

"I have not," I laid my staff on her counter. "You sold this stick to my father-in-law."

Mother Marwick glanced at the staff. "I sold that staff to somebody," she said. "I cannot say if it was your father-in-law or not."

"Where did it come from?"

"Hell or Hindustan, for all I care," Mother Marwick said carelessly.

I leaned across the counter until my face was close to hers. "Don't play games with me, woman. From where did you get it?"

For the first time, I saw a flicker of respect – or was it fear? – on Mother Marwick's face. "A young lad brought it to me," she said.

"Who?" I did not relent.

"You're not Doctor Elliot," Mother Marwick said. "Who are you?"

"Who do you think I am?" I took hold of her throat and began to squeeze, enjoying the fear in her eyes.

"You're him!"

"Who?" I squeezed harder, watching the colour drain from her face.

"You're him!" Mother Marwick repeated.

"Where did you get the staff?" I repeated. "Who brought it to you?"

"John Menzies." Mother Marwick had to gasp the word.

I released her with a gesture of contempt. "Where does John Menzies live?"

"Wherever he can," Mother Marwick said, rubbing her throat. I revelled in her fear.

"Where?" I pressed the end of my staff against her belly and pushed, gently at first but with increasing force.

"With me!" Mother Marwick said at last. "He's one of my boys!"

"Where?" I had no idea that Mother Marwick had boys, so I did not relent until, in between gasps of pain, she told me how she organised her business.

I learned that Mother Marwick ran a thieves' kitchen off Fleshmarket Close, a place where orphans and the unwanted gathered for shelter and food, and where they learned the gentle arts of pickpocketing, theft and casual violence. From her kitchen, Mother Marwick sent her unwashed protégés all across the Old Town, occasionally even venturing across the bridges to the New. They stole anything that could be sold without being traced, and some valuables that could.

"When will little Johnny be home?" I relaxed the staff slightly.

"Tonight." I enjoyed the terror in Mother Marwick's eyes.

"He'd better be," I said, keeping my voice soft with menace as I withdrew from the shop. "He'd better be."

I spent the remainder of that day in Whisky Row, the long stretch of cellars and laigh-houses where kill-me-deadly whisky was on sale at the lowest possible prices to the paupers and broken men and women of the town. Recognising my need for sudden violence, not one of the gutter-dwellers came close to me, yet I was as sober as a kirk elder on Sunday noon when I left. Mere alcohol had no power over me that day.

Fully aware that Marwick's tatterdemalion minions were watching me, I entered her domain without warning and rapped my staff on her filthy floor. She lived in a warren of rooms that had once been the servant's quarters of one of Scotland's elite before the upper classes left the Old Town for the New. Marwick sat in an old armchair, with a horsewhip at one side and a tumbler of whisky at the other. In her home, she looked different, red-faced, with red hair and a bulbous nose and she was as ugly a woman as any I had met as she glared at me. "Well, Doctor Elliot or whoever you are. I'm here with my lads."

"I want John Menzies," I said, hearing the whisky grate in my throat.

"Find him." Mother Marwick lifted her glass, full of venom and bluster with her boys around her.

"Give me him." I noticed the bulge under Mother Marwick's rags and suspected there was a weapon there.

"What are you going to do with him?" Mother Marwick's dark eyes were nearly invisible behind folds of filthy flesh.

"I am going to thank him," I said, with what I hoped was a pleasant smile.

"For what?" Mother Marwick asked.

From the corner of my eye, I saw Marwick's brood gathering. Boys and girls from the age of about four up to 12, they were ragged and filthy, with vicious eyes and hands like claws.

"Ah, John, there you are," I turned to face the group, with a smile on my face. The tallest of the boys jumped, as I had hoped he would, with his dirty red hair blazing like a fire. I lifted my staff. "Thank you for finding my walking stick." Removing a guinea from my pocket, I flicked it across to him. "Here. Spend that on something sensible."

I saw the surprise, nearly amounting to shock, on John's thin face.

"Where did you find it?" I asked casually.

"I never stole it," John said.

"Where did you find it?" I put an edge into my voice.

"It came to me," John said. "I was looking at the river in case anybody had dropped anything and the stick was there."

I could understand that. "Thank you, John." The stick had refused to float away. It had found its way back to Edinburgh through the medium of this boy.

When I turned around, Mother Marwick was pulling a pistol from under her rags, as I suspected. Sidestepping, I swung my staff, catching the barrel of the gun, so it fell from the old woman's grasp.

"You should not play with guns," I said. Although I was tempted to beat the old witch to a pulp, I knew her boys respected her, and I needed their help. "I'm not your enemy, Mother," I said, lifted the gun and returned it.

"Oh, and John," I kept my voice casual. "If I ever find you stealing a Bible from me again, I will place you on my surgeon's table and anatomise you while you are still alive." Leaning closer, I pressed my staff against his groin. "I am a good friend, John, but an ill man to cross. Do you understand?"

"Yes," John said with his eyes wide.

"Yes, what?" I twisted the staff hard.

"Yes, sir," John nearly squealed.

"Don't forget." I tossed him another guinea to sweeten the pill. "I'll be back," I said, as I left Mother Marwick's thieves' kitchen. I had laid the groundwork of punishment and reward. Now I had to weave a web to catch my prey.

Charles MacNeil. The name thrummed through my head like the beating of a drum. That bastard had cuckolded me with Evelyn. There was no other explanation for what happened;

there was no other way that Evelyn could have seen his tattoo. But what could I do about it?

I walked the streets, fuming with rage, glowering at everybody I passed as I tapped my stick on the ground and thumped down my feet. I would confront MacNeil, that's what I would do. I would confront him and have it out. As I mused over the details of the impending meeting, I found myself smiling with grim anticipation. By God, nobody would cuckold me and get away with it!

Where and when?

I would meet him somewhere he was off his guard and nobody else there. I grinned, swinging my staff as the ideas crammed into my head. Yes, I would get my own back on Doctor Charles precious bloody MacNeil, and then I had something suitable in mind for my oh-so-respectable wife as well, with her pious church-attending and innocent smiles. Whisky Row welcomed my money once more as I sat among the broken people, ignoring their pleas for whisky while I formulated my plans. Eventually, with my mind made up, I returned to Mother Marwick's kitchen again, peering through the door and entering in with my stick over my shoulder.

"Where's young Johnny-boy?" I asked.

"Here I am, sir!" As I expected, my present of two golden guineas on my last visit had bought the lad, body and soul. We all have a price, you see, and the lower the class, the less one had to pay to purchase them. Even the unco guid can be bought, in my experience – just offer them something that shows them in an even more pious light and they will fall over themselves to do as you want. It's all a matter of applying the right pressure on the correct spot.

"Do you know who I am, Johnny-boy?" I asked, tapping at the ground with my staff.

"Yes, sir," Johnny looked up at me from his narrow, cynical eyes. "You're the man what gave me two guineas."

"Do you know my name?"

John shook his head, which was just as well for him. If he said too much, nobody would notice if a little street urchin disappeared, and nobody would care if his body was found in some pile of night soil.

"Some people call me Mr Black," I said, "others call me Lucifer." I tried to frighten this red-haired child who had the eyes of a middle-aged man. "Do you want to earn another guinea?" I held up the gold coin, then jerked it away when John reached for it.

John nodded vigorously.

"Then I want you to follow a man for me. Tell me everything he does and everywhere he goes. Follow him for a week. Can you write?"

John shook his head.

"Can any of your friends write?"

One boy held up his hand. He might have been eight years old, but from his diminutive size and scrawny frame, he appeared half that age.

"Then write down everything this man does. I will pay five shillings a day for seven days' work, which is 35 shillings. That's one guinea for you, Johnny-boy, and 14 shillings for your scribe, the writer."

"Who is the man?" John asked.

"Come with me, and I'll show you." When Mother Marwick objected, I tapped my staff, hard, on her knee, looked into her eyes and warned her to back away.

Having set my filthy watchdogs on to Charles, I left them to their work and returned to my old ways. I barely returned home, attended surgery once a week and only saw the most important clients, treated my faithless wife with cold disdain and sacked one of the servants for insolence.

While not wasting my time in George Street, I attended my clubs, with my winnings mounting day by day and night by night. It was expected that Lady Clarinda began to accompany me regularly, and we got along famously, often forming partnerships that cleaned the table. Indeed Lady Clarinda was the only female allowed in some of the clubs.

"How do you get in?" I asked her once.

"I own this establishment," she told me, smiling, which answered all my questions.

At the end of the week, I returned to Mother Marwick's with my staff in my hand and my purse weighty with gold.

"Well, my lad?" I addressed John directly, ignoring the crowd of ragged tykes that waited hopefully for crumbs from my luxurious table. They could not help me, so they were less than the dirt beneath my feet.

"He just goes from his house to his work and back," John said. "He leaves his house in Thistle Street at seven in the morning and goes back at eight at night, except Sunday when he goes to church."

"Anything else?"

"Aye," John said. "On Wednesday he went to a house in Abercrombie Street and saw a woman there. And twice on his way back from work he called in at a house in Queen Street."

"Did it have a green door?"

"Aye. A woman met him there."

That would be Evelyn, betraying me and with her parents' consent, by the sound of it. Aye, well, I dealt with Swinton once, and I could do it again, by Christ, or not by Christ, as occasion demanded.

I tossed a guinea to Johnny, added another to the scribe and, as the others watched hungrily, added a third to Mother

Marwick. I leaned over the old witch and whispered in her ear. “If anybody ever hears of this, Mother, I’ll burn you alive.”

When she looked at me, I saw the fear in her eyes. “I know you will,” she said.

Tapping my staff on the ground, I sauntered away, hatching plans.

CHAPTER 21

WAS it Robert Burns who said that the best-laid plans of mice and men aft gang agley? Or was it some other homespun poet with an inflated conceit of himself? I neither knew nor cared as I followed through the plans I had made. I had intended to serve Charles as I had served Swinton. I wished to destroy him, to humiliate him utterly and have him come crawling to me on his hands and knees to beg my forgiveness. He had dared to seduce my wife, my property, the woman I had gained with so much effort. I planned to destroy his professional reputation and impoverish him, so he lived with the most debased of society, or returned to his barren island to exist with the knowledge of his failure for the remainder of his whisky-sodden life. I would ask about his patients, take them from him and leave him with none, then spread stories about his incompetence, for a start.

With that in mind, I sought Charles's company, catching him in the darkest part of the town where there were no witnesses.

"Charles!" I lifted my staff in greeting, smiling as tradition demands when meeting an old friend.

"Martin." Charles looked wary, as well he might, the cuckolding bastard.

"I have not seen you around," I said, extending my right hand in greeting. We shook hands as I stared into Charles' eyes, searching for any signs of guilt. I saw plenty there, shifting shadows in his pupils. Aye, my lad, I thought, I have you now, and I'm going to keep you. Since regaining possession of my stick, my perception had increased, so that I could sense fear and guilt better than ever before. The only person I could not work out was Evelyn, who seemed immune. I only ever found love, concern and confusion within her. Doubtless, marriage created a barrier to my comprehension.

"Let's go for a stroll," I suggested, "unless you'd prefer a dram or two?"

I sensed Charles's nervousness. "A stroll would be good," he agreed.

Moving to his right side, I linked my arm with his, so neutralising his strongest arm and putting him at an immediate disadvantage.

"I have not seen you for some time." I took control, guiding him downhill, towards the Water of Leith. Wind, earth, fire and water – each was dangerous and each could be harnessed for one's own ends if the conditions were favourable.

I knew Canonmills well, even in the gloaming, and wandered, seemingly aimlessly, along the bank of the river, with the water churning brown on my right, the mills working slowly and the trees dipping to the music of the wind.

"I hear you have found a sweetheart?" I asked as we approached a dark bend where the trees shielded us from view. The wind was rising, rubbing the branches together. I looked behind me in case somebody was watching, but there was nobody except Charles and me.

"How did you know? Did Evelyn tell you?"

The admission was so bold that it took me aback. "Why would Evelyn do that?"

"Why not?" Charles sounded surprised.

I gripped my staff tighter as the red rage mounted within me and my carefully formulated plans for interrogating Charles about his patients vanished like snow off a dyke. "Evelyn's my wife!"

"I'm well aware of that," Charles looked around him. "It's getting very dark, isn't it? I think we'd best get back to civilisation, don't you think?"

All my previous intentions vanished when Charles spoke. My anger took over as I thought of him with Evelyn, as I thought of the pair of them together in bed, their bodies intertwined as Evelyn admired his shameful tattoo. Lifting my staff with both hands, I swung at him, knocking him to the ground. Charles roared as he fell, turning a white face to me in pretended astonishment as I swung the staff again, smashing it against his head, then his ribs and then his back. I did not feel the bones break, although I knew he was unconscious, so I rolled him over and thrust his head under the swirling brown water of the river. He lay there, unmoving as I held him, counting the minutes in my head before I resorted to the watch in my weskit.

It was five minutes past six. I watched as the minute hand moved one more notch, and I knew that Charles was dead.

Dragging the body from the river, I placed it under a bramble bush and contemplated what to do next. I had not intended to kill Charles when I brought him here, but his words had condemned him, acting as witness, jury and judge. We had merely played the executioner, my staff and I.

For a moment, I stared at the body of the man I had once considered a friend. He lay there with blood smudging the freckles on his face, and mud smearing his smart clothes. I was tempted to simply throw him into the river and allow the current to take him, but if anybody found his body, the police might ask questions. No, I tapped my staff on the ground, I had a far better method of disposing of friend Charles and one he would undoubtedly have appreciated. I began to laugh, mocking the life I once had, and then I sang, with the words of *Maggie Lauder* bitter in the dark air beside the river.

Sandy looked at me from the door of his house, and then he glanced at my staff. "I don't understand, Doc. I thought you had got rid of that thing."

"It came back to me." I stepped inside Sandy's house and took a seat. "All by itself."

"Throw it away, for God's own sake," Sandy sat a good six feet away from me. "I warned you of the evil in it."

I laughed at him. "I need your help, Sandy Tait," I said.

"No," Sandy shook his head. "I'm not doing anything for you. Not until you rid yourself of that thing."

"Oh, but you are!" I pressed the skull end of my staff under Sandy's chin and lifted him from his seat. "If you don't, the police will find out all about your grave robbing and transporting dead bodies through the streets. More importantly, I'll tell the relatives of the dead as well, and lead them to your address." I laughed in his face. "Can you imagine their reaction, Sandy? I can."

I allowed the idea to sink into his mind as I stared at him. "They would storm your house, Sandy, all the angry relatives. They would drag you into the street, kicking and punching you, and out there," I went on, gesturing towards the Lawnmarket, "they would loop a rope over some handy projection, and hang you. You know that the Edinburgh mob is not amenable to sense or reason."

I knew my words were striking home. The staff gave me the gift of eloquence, or perhaps it weakened the resistance of others to argue.

"What do you want, damn you?" Sandy asked.

"That's better, old chap," I withdrew the staff, smiling. "Just the loan of a sedan chair and two hefty porters who know how to keep their mouths shut and say nothing."

"I'll come myself," Sandy said, rubbing his chin. "Who is the passenger?"

"None of your damned business," I said, tapping my staff on the ground. "Meet me at the Bridge at Canonmills at midnight."

"That's a long carry," Sandy said.

"You'll be paid." I tapped my staff on the floor. "It's strange how all you mealy-mouthed good people become much more pliable at the gleam of gold."

I was at the bridge at 10 minutes short of midnight when the wind carried biting rain, and the trees lashed each other in protest. The weather suited me, as only the hardiest or most stupid of people would be abroad on a night such as this. After a few moments, I saw Sandy and another man carrying their sedan, leaning into the wind as they negotiated the steep hill from the ancient Barony of Broughton.

"Over here." I emerged from the shelter of a tree as the porters approached. I had taken the precaution of covering Charles's face with a sack and wrapping a roll of canvas around his body so that nobody would recognise him. "Open the door."

The second man was burly, with the battered face of an ex-pug mostly hidden by his slanted blue bonnet. He obeyed my order without question, and I bundled the body inside the sedan. "Take us to the Grassmarket," I said. "My old surgery."

The pug lifted his end of the chair without demur, while Sandy gave me a look that would have cracked glass. I led the way, not too quickly, ready to divert any stray pedestrian who looked too closely at the passenger within the sedan chair. As it happened, the time and weather kept the road quiet, and we only met one man, who was too inebriated to know if it was Monday or Christmas.

I was fortunate that I had retained the Grassmarket surgery and ordered the porters to tip the body on to the floor and leave the rest to me. They did so, with the pug waiting hopefully for me to pay him, and Sandy looking very unhappy.

"No good will come of it, Doctor," he said.

"It's only another body," I said.

"Not the corpse," Sandy said. "I mean the staff. You'd best rid yourself of it."

I laughed again, tapped my staff on the ground and threw down a handful of guineas. While the pug scrabbled on the floor for them, Sandy ignored the gold completely.

"Doctor," Sandy said. "For the sake of your immortal soul, get rid of that damned staff."

"I will not." I watched in some amusement as the pug lifted the last guinea. "I'll call on you if I need you again," I said.

"You need help, Doctor," Sandy said. "You need more help than I can give you."

I closed the door without another word as I had no further use for Sandy or his muscular, brainless companion.

I had a lot of work to do. I knew that Charles would be missed, and people would organise a search for him. The police might ask me if I had seen him, but as a respectable member of society, they would not dream that I had killed the unfortunate fellow, my oldest and dearest friend. However, it would be best to dispose of the body before it could be recognised, and what better way than in full view?

Dragging the corpse through to my anatomy lab, I quickly placed it on the surgical table, stripped it, removed any valuables for my own use and carefully burned the clothes.

As Charles's face was his most recognisable part, I cured that problem by sawing off his head. The familiar features seemed to smile at me as I dissolved the soft tissue in strong acid, leaving the head submerged until only the skull remained.

"There you are, Charles," I said. "How's that then? Now you will remain with me for ever, part of my surgery." I patted the smooth white skull. "I will let you see Evelyn from time to time, so you know I am taking great care of the one you wanted."

I was smiling as I turned the decapitated body on its side and sliced off the revealing tattoo to ensure there was nothing that could be identified as Charles. Cleaning up the body, I laid it ready for dissecting. Carefully washing the skin that held the tattoo, I placed it in a drawer and left it there while I proceeded with the next stage of my plan.

I whistled *Maggie Lauder* as I strolled to the university, tapping my staff on the ground as the rain continued to fall, weeping from the slate roofs of Edinburgh's tenements and polishing the granite cobblestones so that they gleamed. Water was such an attractive element, I thought, nature's cleanser.

"It's some time since you held an anatomy class." Dr Knox was in the university as I posted notices of my forthcoming anatomy class.

"I don't have the opportunity very often," I said.

"Bodies are hard to come by," Knox agreed, nodding sagely. "One needs a regular source of supply. I presume you resort to resurrection men?"

"I like to keep my sources private," I told him.

"As do I," Knox said, nodding. Candlelight glinted on his glasses, giving him a most sinister appearance, so I wondered if I should invite him to some of my clubs. After a short debate with myself, I decided not to. He was a humourless, cold-blooded kind of fellow, quite unable to understand the joy of what the unco guid termed as sin, and without joy, what was the point of breaking the establishment's rules? Truly, I think that the absence of pleasure and fun is the essence of hell. I see it as a place shorn of hope and laughter, where normality is grey, and the future is the same as the past, with no change or variety. The essence of humanity is colour, excitement, the thrill of new experiences. Having an existence of monochrome regularity is to live without fun, and to live within rigid laws is not to live at all. I shudder to think of a regulated life, with people lacking the freedom to laugh or tease, experiment or live to excess.

"I hope you have a good turn-out," Knox said.

"I have only a small anatomical surgery," I said. "Even a dozen students make quite a crowd," I said, tapping my staff on the floor. "I won't be challenging your position, Doctor."

"I should think not, indeed," Knox said, with an insincere little laugh. That man tried to emphasise his respectability too much. Evil recognises evil like good knows good, and I could sense the cold streak of cruelty running through Knox, so different from my hot-blooded passion. Knox would encourage sin without taking part and would appear shocked at the results of actions he had instigated. He would be an excellent politician, I thought, or a disinterested man of science who could evolve a new weapon or method of torture while turning away from the results.

I reread my notice, inviting any anatomy student to express their interest in my class. 'The first dozen will be selected,' I added, hoping for a quick response.

I was highly gratified when nearly two score medical students had appended their name to the list. I drew a line after the initial twelve, added the place and date and left the university. I rather liked that building with its classical lines, its columns and courtyard, and wished I could be in some way connected to such an august establishment. However, Dr Knox was their first choice of anatomist, and short of killing him, I could see no way of replacing his cold bleakness. I tapped my staff on the ground, toying with the idea of removing Knox as I had Charles, and displaying his body for anatomy. The idea was so appealing that I laughed out loud, which earned me some reproving glares. The courtyard of Edinburgh University was evidently not a place for humour.

"I do like your stick," Knox said when we stopped at the entrance to the university, with the windy Bridges between me and the main bulk of the city.

I held it up. "I threw it away once," I said, "but it came back to me."

"May I see it?" Knox took hold of my staff to examine it. "It's heavy," he said. "And very ornate. What do these carvings mean?"

I looked at him sideways. "The lowest one is a female, then comes a man sliding up the staff of the stick, and strings of coins connect to the human head on top. I am surprised you are unable to recognise them, Doctor."

Knox looked again. "I can't see any man or any woman," he said. "I can only see geometric designs and the skull."

I looked at the staff again. To me, the coiled woman and climbing man were plain, while even the head on top had altered, gaining definite features. "Perhaps it takes a while to work out," I said, recovering my staff, for I did not like others to separate us for long.

Waving farewell to Knox, I began the walk back, savouring

the warmth of the stick in my hand. When I reached the North Bridge, with the great chasm beneath me and the wind howling as only an Edinburgh wind can, I lifted the staff to examine it once more. Yes, the naked man and woman retained their places around the staff, but for the first time, I could make out the features of the head and face on top. As I looked, smiling, I saw an undoubted human face on the head. Before, I had only seen a skull, so my perception must have increased, somehow. Even as I looked, I saw the face alter, the nose lengthen and straighten, the chin firm until Charles was looking directly at me with his mouth open in a soundless scream.

"Dear God!"

Unable to help myself, I dropped the staff. It clattered on the ground, rolled and lay still, with Charles's face staring up at me, the eyes accusing.

Dear God! What am I doing? What have I done? I looked around in sudden horror as the reality of my situation bit hard. I had murdered my dearest friend in a fit of jealousy. I stood still, with Edinburgh's notorious wind threatening to lift the hat from my head and propel it over the parapet of the bridge into the void below. I was a murderer, and I was planning to dissect Charles's body. Nausea rose in my throat, nearly choking me as my recent behaviour rushed into my head.

Evelyn? Where are you? I need your stability now, more than ever before. But you cuckolded me with Charles!

"Are you all right, sir?" The elderly gentleman was full of concern as he rushed over and held my arm. "You look very unwell."

I stared at the man, seeing his gentle eyes as he guided me to the parapet. "Hold on here, sir, while I fetch your stick."

For one brief, betraying moment I contemplated hurling myself over the side of the bridge as my despair mounted and the unsupportable guilt of my actions overcame me. How could

I live with myself, knowing what I had done? The prospect of death invited me, with its unconditional acceptance of anybody and complete emptiness. Come sweet death, where all our cares are nothing, and our guilt does not gnaw at brains that cannot cope with more pain.

"Your stick, sir." The old gentleman tried to thrust the staff into my hand. I recoiled, recognising the evil in that length of black wood.

"No, no," I said. "Throw it away, for God's own sake, throw it away."

"That's your staff." I did not notice Lady Clarinda's coach draw up until she stood beside me. "Come on, Doctor."

"Do you know this gentleman, madam?" my kindly old duffer asked.

"I do," Lady Clarinda said. "With your permission, sir, I will take him home in my coach."

"Of course, of course," the silly old duffer said, helping me on to the black coach as Lady Clarinda captured my staff.

"Thank you, sir," Lady Clarinda said. "George Street, driver, and drive with care."

Leaning back in the luxury of that coach, I watched as Clarinda shook her head at me, then examined my staff. "What a strange fellow you are, Martin, and what curious workmanship in this stick."

I was returning to myself again as my foolish thoughts of only a few minutes ago dissipated. "It is my lucky staff," I said. "People seem to see different things."

"Oh?" Clarinda turned the staff around in her hands. "I see a naked woman at the base, a naked man crawling up the shaft and a screaming face on top, with some intricate circular patterns in between."

"That's what I see," I said. "Others can see only a variety of complex designs."

"It's warm." Clarinda smiled across to me, with her mouth slightly parted to reveal her perfect white teeth. "As if it's a living thing. I'll take you home," she said. "I'd like to meet your wife. Evelyn, isn't it?"

"That's her name." When I reached across to retrieve my staff, Clarinda pulled it further away from me.

"Not so fast, Martin, not so fast. I rather like the feel of this stick." She ran her hand over the man's body, lingering and patting as her eyes sought mine. "Do you wish to part with it? I'd pay any price you wish to name."

Ten minutes ago, I would have handed the stick over without a thought. Now, as my true personality replaced the milk-and-water doctor, I shook my head. "That staff is part of me," I said.

"I wonder." I sensed the intelligence in Clarinda's eyes as she continued to hold my staff. Once again, I had that desperate desire to allow her to retain it, to shout she could take the blasted thing, to leap out of the coach and run, and run and run and run. To grab Evelyn and hustle her down to Teviotdale and never again return to this oxymoronic city that appeared one thing on the surface but was so different underneath.

Clarinda laughed. "There you are, Martin." She tossed the staff over, and I caught it. "It's not quite time yet."

"Thank you," I said, savouring the feel of my stick even as I wondered at her words. I was incomplete without that staff; we were one person with a single merged personality.

Lady Clarinda leaned closer. "You are not the right person for the wand."

"What?" I stared at her, clutching the staff close to me. "What the devil do you mean by that?"

Lady Clarinda smiled, shaking her head. "There is too much residual goodness in you," she said.

I could say nothing to that, as the coach clattered northwards through the busy New Town streets.

When we pulled up outside my house, the coachman opened the door and handed Clarinda out, with me following. Evelyn was in the outer hall when we entered, looking anxious, compared to the aristocratic calm of Clarinda.

"Mrs Elliot." Clarinda gave a formal curtsey. "I do apologise for the intrusion into your home, but I thought it best to return your husband to you."

"I did not know you had him," Evelyn retorted, with steel in her voice and eyes. "Who are you, pray?"

"I am Lady Clarinda Snodgrass," my Ladyship said calmly. "I found your husband not 20 minutes ago, standing looking dazed on the North Bridge."

"Dazed?" Evelyn repeated, with her attitude immediately changing to concern.

"I thought it best to bring him home to you." Lady Clarinda was looking about her. "What a charming house you have, Mrs Elliot."

"Thank you." Evelyn wrapped an arm around my shoulders, although whether it was an act of solicitude or ownership, I am not sure. I will be charitable and say the former. "Will you stay to tea, your Ladyship?"

"Alas, no," Lady Clarinda said. "I merely came to deliver your husband. He looked unwell."

With another flurry of curtseys, Lady Clarinda withdrew. I heard her coach clatter across the cobbles, and Evelyn led me to my chair in the parlour. "Where have you been, Martin? And why have you still got that horrible stick?"

"It is my staff," I said. "The rod and staff that comforts me."

"That is blasphemy," Evelyn said severely. "Oh, Martin, I don't want you going back as you were. I want the man I married."

I laughed, tapping my staff on the carpet. "Where do you think the money for this house came from Evelyn? Not from my medical practice. It came from gambling, Evelyn, my dear, and this staff gave me luck."

"It changes you," Evelyn said simply. "I'd prefer an honest doctor with no money to a rich gambler." When she stepped back, I saw the tears glinting in her eyes. "Please, Martin, for my sake, for the sake of our marriage, please throw that stick away."

"I will not." I leaned closer to her, feeding on her anguish. "I'd rather throw you away than my staff."

Evelyn recoiled, covering her mouth with her hand as my words bit home. Swinging my staff, I mounted the stairs to our bedroom. "Come up here, Evelyn," I ordered.

"Martin!" Evelyn spoke through her tears.

"Come here," I ordered, "or I'll drag you up!" I watched as she obeyed. The feeling of power was very satisfying, and I wondered why I did not employ it more often. If I had, Evelyn might have been too scared to stray.

In future, I told myself, I would ensure that Evelyn obeyed me without question, or I'd take it out of her hide. As I pushed her into the bedroom, I found that idea very appealing indeed – the woman had a nerve to argue with her husband and master.

CHAPTER 22

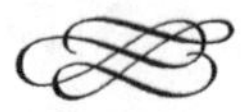

My dozen students watched as I demonstrated the gentle art of carving up a human corpse. Charles would have been proud of me as I sliced, diced, eviscerated and removed, all the while explaining what I was doing to the young men. For one crazy moment, I wished I had invited Lady Clarinda and Evelyn to view the spectacle. My Ladyship would have revelled in every second, I knew, while it would be sweet revenge for Evelyn to witness me emasculating her lover.

"What happened to his head?" One eager fellow asked.

"He lost it, I fear, Mr Edgar," I said.

"How?" This persistent man asked.

"In a mining accident, I believe." I had the story ready in case of just such a contingency. "That is why we have the body here, as a headless man isn't much use down the pit." I waited for the obligatory laugh. When a teacher makes a joke, his class must laugh, or he will mark out the dissenters.

"How about his other wound. That's new." My impudent fellow was asking far too many questions. "Did he lose his skin down the pit as well?"

"Ask him," I said. "He might tell such a clever fellow as you, Mr Edgar."

I continued with my dissection, ensuring that I asked the inquisitive Mr Edgar the most difficult of questions. There are two methods of dealing with such students; one can ignore them and hope they wither in the shadows of neglect, or one can confront them head-on and highlight their lack of knowledge until they are belittled and succumb to silence. I preferred the latter approach and fixed my troublemaker with a most steely stare as I demonstrated.

"Now you." I stepped back with Charles's blood dripping from my arms and his mutilated body lying before me. "Mr Edgar. Remove the heart, please."

Already unsettled by my pitiless questioning, Edgar was nervous and his hand was less steady than it should have been, so his incision was out of the straight when he tried to cut out Charles's heart. I stepped back, allowing him to get deeper into a mess before shaking my head in supposed irritation and showing the correct method.

When the class finally filed out, their bungling had proved a complete success. Nobody now would be able to identify Charles from the mangled remains on my table, while I had established a reason for carrying a body into my surgery. No sane man, of course, would advertise his crimes by putting his murder victim on public display, which was my next intention.

I have heard of schools of anatomy where they simply throw the dissected corpses outside so that passers-by are subjected to the illuminating sight of disembodied arms, legs and other pieces of the human anatomy. I did not do that, partly because I was in the middle of a densely populated area, and also because some inquisitive police officer might ask awkward questions. I know that many people believe the police lack intelligence, but I think the opposite. They are the worst enemy of crime and can be relentless in their pursuit of criminals.

I was fortunate in having a large fireplace and slowly burned every piece of flesh before soaking Charles's frame in acid to leave only his skeleton. To an ordinary person, such a procedure would be tedious, but to a medical man, it is fascinating to witness the effects of acid on human flesh and tissue. We are such fragile creatures to have achieved so much.

Finally, I again utilised Sandy's sedan to transport the skeleton to my house in George Street.

"What is it this time?" Sandy was in a public when I sat opposite him.

"Your sedan chair." I pushed a guinea across the table to him.

"Another body?" He pocketed the gold without comment.

"Only the frame of one," I said.

Sandy glowered at me from under his fringe of auburn hair. "For the love of God, Elliot, throw away that damned stick!"

I laughed and stepped to the door. "My Grassmarket surgery," I said. "Seven o'clock tonight."

"You're losing your wife as well," Sandy warned.

Ignoring his ramblings, I strolled away.

With Charles's remains safely in George Street, I reassembled his skeleton in my surgery, placed the skull back where it belonged and had the entire structure hanging in full view opposite my desk.

"There you are, Charles," I said, leaning back in my chair and sipping from a glass of claret. "That's what happens when you try to steal my wife."

I found it highly amusing to have Evelyn enter the surgery and stand next to the skeleton of her lover. In fact, I made a point of ordering her in so we could talk together like an amiable husband and wife, while Charles grinned inanely in the background, with every little draught setting his bones to rattle.

Only a day after I placed the skeleton, Evelyn knocked and entered my surgery in what I can only describe as a mild panic.

"Evelyn?" I looked up from my desk.

"Have you heard the news? Charles MacNeil has vanished," Evelyn said without any preamble.

"I had not heard that," I said. "What do you mean by vanished?"

"He has not turned up at his surgery," Evelyn said, "and nobody has seen hair nor hide of him for some days."

"Not hair nor hide?" I repeated. "How about blood or bone?" I thought that amusing as Evelyn stood 12 inches from Charles's skeleton.

"What?" Evelyn shook her head, "this is no time for humour, Martin. Your friend, our friend, is missing. He could be lying hurt somewhere."

"Aye, your friend Charles," I said, putting an edge to my voice. "You will miss him."

"So will you, I hope," Evelyn said.

"He is with me always," I said solemnly.

Evelyn glared at me. "Are you not even a little bit concerned?"

"I am sure he is in some surgery just now, watching all that is happening," I said, smiling.

"Elaine is distraught," Evelyn said.

"Oh? Why is your sister upset?"

"Surely, you know!" Evelyn gave me her coldest of stares. "Elaine and Charles have been walking out together for some months. Why, Charles has been confiding his feelings for her to me and visiting my parents to discuss arrangements."

I raised my eyebrows as Evelyn stormed out of the room. So the dark-haired woman in Abercrombie Street had been Elaine.

Perhaps Charles had not cuckolded me, and I had killed him for nothing. I found that highly amusing and laughed uproariously, lifting a glass to the skeleton. "A toast to you, Charles, and the women in your death." Then I remembered the tattoo and the picture in the book. "Aye, Evelyn, you are not innocent."

It was later that same day that a policeman called at the house. I had been expecting such a visit as I had been Charles's friend, so had my answers prepared when a sergeant clumped into the house in his heavy boots with his swallow-tail coat looking old-fashioned and his rabbit-skin top hat held under his arm.

"Good evening, Officer," I said, as politely as I could as the servant showed the fellow into my surgery. "Please take a seat and tell me what I can do for you."

"I am Sergeant Edward Fitzpatrick, number 39," the man said awkwardly. "I have come to ask what you know about Dr Charles MacNeil."

I gave him chapter and verse on Charles's life and career, waiting patiently as he carefully and laboriously wrote everything in his notebook. I kept him in my surgery for over an hour, all the time with Charles's skull grinning behind his shoulder and Charles's bones rattling with every slight breeze in the room.

"When did you last see him, sir?" Fitzpatrick asked.

I could not remember but threw him a few dates for good measure. "I'm recently married," I said, "so as you imagine, other things have occupied my attention."

"Of course, sir." The good sergeant closed his notebook with a slight snap.

When Sergeant Fitzpatrick left, I again toasted Charles with claret, put a glass in his bony hand and stifled my laughter.

"Nobody will ever know, old chap, except you and me."

I leaned back in my chair, stuffed tobacco in the bowl of my long-stemmed pipe, applied the candle-flame to the tobacco and smiled. I had money in the bank and not a single debt to my name, I was respected by the respectable and admired or even feared by the less reputable and had removed the man who had possibly cuckolded me. In short, I was successful in all the fields that matter.

There was one minor concern, and again Evelyn was at the centre. Twice in the last week, I had seen Sandy Tait in George Street, each time hurrying away from the corner where my house was. The image remained in my mind for some time, so I strode around town, wondering, and when I returned, I asked Evelyn if she knew anything about it. Her reply infuriated me.

"Yes," Evelyn said calmly, although she fingered Ruth Anderson's silver cross on her gown as if seeking help. "Sandy Tait was here, and he'll be back shortly."

"Will he indeed?" I felt my heartbeat increase. "Oh? Why?"

We were in the outer hall, and I had handed my coat and hat to George, although I retained my staff. I did not allow anybody to hold my staff now. It accompanied me wherever I was, and I laid it beside the bed when I went to sleep.

"We are worried about you," Evelyn said simply. She stood very erect, as always, and her gaze met mine, unflinching despite my rising anger. Her eyes were puffy and red from crying, but her expression remained as determined as I had ever seen.

"You don't need to worry," I said.

"I think we do," I said. "You have changed again, and for the worse. You are not yourself, Martin, and we were so happy."

"I am still happy now," I turned around as George opened the door in response to a knock.

"Mr Alexander Tait, sir," George said.

I fought my rising anger. "Come to see Mrs Elliot, no doubt!" I said, pushing past George to deal with this next irritation.

"You're in trouble," Sandy stood in my outer hall with his head on one side and his eyes accusing.

"Why are you in my house?" I leaned on my staff with my anger threatening to take control.

"I invited him." Evelyn spoke with the calmness of near hysteria.

"We'll discuss this later, Evelyn," I said, putting a threat into my tone. "Go to the drawing-room and leave us in peace."

"I will not," Evelyn denied me.

"I am here as a friend," Sandy said. "A friend of Mrs Elliot and a friend of yours."

"A friend?" I laughed at the idea. "You're not a friend! You're one of the dregs of the foulest closes of the city, a broken man not worth my attention. Now get out, or I'll have the servants throw you out."

"They won't put a finger on Mr Tait." When Evelyn spoke, I heard the fear in her voice.

"They'll do as they're damned well told," I said, "or they'll feel the toe of my boot up their backside when they lose their position."

"They won't," Evelyn said quietly. "I employed them, not you, and I have the last word in who stays and who goes."

I damned her for her impertinence and raised my staff, ready to teach her a lesson in manners, until Sandy blocked my threat with his walking stick.

"No, Doctor," he said, shaking his head. "There will be none of that."

"Damn you," I said, preparing to fight until I realised that his strength more than matched mine, while my life of dissipation had sapped my stamina.

"If you were yourself," Sandy said, "you would realise that Mrs Elliot is in danger here."

I sneered at the man, waiting for him to relax his guard so I could crack my staff across his head.

"Martin," Evelyn said. "Please throw away your stick. It is affecting you badly. I cannot continue to live with you as long as you possess it. I will leave you, Martin, and return to Mother unless you do as I wish."

I stared at her, unbelieving before I burst into laughter. "You're my wife."

Evelyn nodded. "I want my husband, my real husband, to come back again."

"Damn you for a snivelling bitch!" I shouted. "And you!" I pointed my staff at Sandy. "Damn you for a grave-robbing scoundrel."

"You'd better leave, Sandy," Evelyn stepped between us. "Thank you for trying."

I glared at Sandy as he left, stormed into the drawing-room and threw Evelyn's wooden cross into the fire. "And that can burn too, damn it!"

I knew Evelyn would retrieve the thing the instant I left the room, but stormed out nevertheless, with my anger as powerful as it had ever been. "I'll kill you next, you faithless bitch," I vowed. "I'll kill you next!"

CHAPTER 23

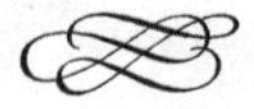

THE NEXT MORNING, after a frosty night with Evelyn, somebody knocked at the door. "It's too damned early for the surgery," I grumbled as George stepped through the hall. Evelyn followed, wiping her mouth with a napkin.

"It's Lady Clarinda Snodgrass." Evelyn came to my side and spoke in a whisper, with the silver cross glinting in a stray beam of sunlight through the window. "She wants to speak to you."

I stood, trying to regain command in my house. "I usually visit my distinguished patients in their own homes. Bring her in."

As soon as Lady Clarinda entered, I ushered her into the surgery. She swept in as if she owned the place, sat in front of me and smiled. "Good morning, Doctor."

"Good morning, Lady Clarinda," I said.

"We both know you are a gambling man, Doctor." Clarinda faced me across the desk.

"I have been known to visit the tables," I temporised, "as has your Ladyship." It felt strange to talk formally to a woman with whom I had spent many wild nights. I tried not to smile at my memory of her running naked around her apartment with me chasing her and her lapdog yapping at our heels.

"So then," Lady Clarinda said. "I have a proposal to put to you."

"What sort of proposal?" I asked, instantly intrigued.

"The sort you would do well to listen to." Lady Clarinda's servant pushed into the surgery. He stood with his back to the door and his face set like flint.

I glared at the servant. "Who the devil are you?" I demanded, for I was not accustomed to people entering my surgery without so much as a by-your-leave.

"I am the devil who knows more about you than you would wish," the servant said, with a distinct Hebridean lilt to his voice. I looked at him for the first time for, until then, he had been only a footman and who notices such people? Servants are there to work, and if they are not efficient, one gets rid of them, and that is that. One does not recall their names and faces.

The servant looked like a fighting man, an ex-prizefighter, I guessed, although cleaned up and dressed in all the finery of a titled lady's servant. I blinked, for I had seen him before.

For the first time, I felt a shadow of doubt fall upon me as if somebody had walked across my grave. "Get out of my surgery," I said to the servant. "This is a place for respectable people."

I may as well have tried to rake moonshine from St Mary's Loch. The servant stared at me as impassively as any poker player.

"My man stays," Lady Clarinda said sweetly as she leaned across the table. "Now, Martin," she said. "We both know that Charles MacNeil has disappeared of late."

"He's probably gone back to the Island of Barra," I said.

Lady Clarinda laughed. "Not he. I don't think he's left Edinburgh. Indeed, I don't think he is very far from where we are sitting at this very moment."

That servant! I remembered where I had seen him before. He was the porter who had helped Sandy carry the sedan. He had helped pick up Charles's body from the Water of Leith and the skeleton from the Grassmarket surgery.

"I can't see him," I said.

"I think you can," Lady Clarinda said. Standing up, she stepped to the side of the skeleton. "I think this is the very man. I think you murdered him, Doctor, perhaps over a gambling debt or some such trifle. I know you carried a body from Canonmills to the Grassmarket, and later performed an anatomical lesson. You advertised the latter at the university."

I said nothing, while I began to plan how to get rid of that damned servant. Those blasted Donalds were too clever sometimes, hiding their astuteness behind a mask of Gaelic ignorance while all the time they were scheming how to overcome their betters.

"I also know you had a skeleton carried from the Grassmarket to this house," Lady Clarinda said, smiling. "My man helped then as well." She shook her head. "I wonder what that nice Sergeant Fitzpatrick would say if I told him all this?"

"He would not believe the word of a servant against that of a gentleman," I said.

"Are you sure?" Lady Clarinda's voice was soft as silk. "It would make fascinating reading in the newspapers, Doctor. Your trial would cause a sensation, and whatever the verdict, you would be ruined. Grave robbing, gambling, consorting with prostitutes, and whatever happened to poor Outerston?"

"Outerston?" I started at this abrupt change of direction. "How the devil should I know?"

"He fell off Arthur's Seat," Lady Clarinda said. "Or was he pushed? You should know, Martin. After all, you were there."

"I was not!" I denied hotly.

"You were followed," Lady Clarinda said, "and you knew it."

I glanced at the servant, who gave the slightest of nods, and no more.

"Damn you!" I said. "Damn you to hell! You can't prove any of this."

"Probably not," Lady Clarinda said. "But it is true, nevertheless."

"Then there is the case of Swinton's ruination," Lady Clarinda said. "Need I go on?"

"No, damn you."

Lady Clarinda had been walking around the room, poking into drawers, looking at my books. "Oh!" she said, opening a drawer and pulling out Charles's tattoo. "How quaint. I've seen this before, on a stone carving at Orkney, and the hip of Charles MacNeil."

A stone carving in Orkney? Had Evelyn not visited Orkney? I had not experienced such a sudden twist of guilt for years.

"What do you want?" I asked.

"That's better," Lady Clarinda sat, holding Charles's decorated skin in her lap. "As I said at the beginning, Martin, you are a gambling man, and I have a little proposition for you. If you win, then nothing changes. Nothing."

I nodded. "And if I lose?"

"I want your staff." Clarinda had an edge to her voice.

"Is that all?" I asked, knowing that, accompanied by my staff, we would not lose. We had never lost more than a trifle when working together, and I did not doubt that our partnership would continue.

"That's all," Clarinda said. "Are you willing to take the

chance?" Her eyes seemed to be penetrating my soul. I had seen eyes like that before when I had dreamed of that man with the long nose.

I laughed as my confidence returned. "You cannot beat me at the tables," I said, with the echoes of my laugh resounding around the surgery, so the very skeleton seemed to be entertained. I had a vision of Charles releasing himself from his perch and dancing around the room, with his jaw wide open in amusement and those bony arms waving in the air in death, as they had been wont to do in life.

"In that case," Clarinda said, without the flicker of a smile on her face, "you have nothing to worry about."

I reached for my hat. "Come on then, my Ladyship. Let's go to the New Wig."

Lady Clarinda smiled. "Don't forget your staff," she said softly. "I will want it when you lose."

I lifted my staff, smoothing my hand across the carvings, with the naked man warm under my palm and my fingers fitting around Charles's features with neither difficulty nor guilt.

Evelyn stood in the inner hall, her face worried as we passed. I saw her speak briefly to Lady Clarinda, and they exchanged a smile, which intrigued me. What the devil did they have to smile about? Was Evelyn also plotting against me? I resolved to speak to my wife when I returned and demand to know why she was conversing with a woman who had threatened me. I disregarded her mention of leaving me as just empty talk, a wife trying to coerce her husband into doing her will.

"Not the New Wig," Lady Clarinda said, as the servant held the door of her carriage open. "The Benison."

"As you wish." I did not care in which club I took Lady Clarinda's money, for I fully intended not only to retain my staff but to reduce her to destitution. By God, I told myself, no blasted woman would threaten me in my own house, and I cared not that she was a titled lady.

Lady Clarinda smiled to me across the width of the coach. "This could be interesting," she said.

"You're damned right it could." I tried to control my temper, although I dearly wished to lift my staff and crack her across her privileged face. I had other things in mind as well, images I am not inclined to share even here, where I have admitted murder.

Lady Clarinda laughed. "Don't you think gambling for something that matters to you puts an edge to things?" She tapped my staff with her foot. "I've always wanted that stick, and I am sure you wish to retain your present condition. A hempen necklace is very uncomfortable, so I am told."

"A hempen necklace?"

"If you did not agree to this competition," Lady Clarinda said, "you might have hanged for murder." She laughed again, light and pleasant.

I was silent as the coach lurched along George Street and across St Andrew's Square to the Benison. I could hear the horses' hooves clopping on the ground and the grumble of the wheels, and then we stopped.

"Here we are," Lady Clarinda said.

We entered the familiar surroundings together, with me frowning and my head down like an angry bull, while Lady Clarinda smiled to her admirers and paused to talk to half a dozen people. A bright fire sparked one corner of the room, and for a terrible moment, I relived that old memory of the flames coiling around me as the smoke choked my lungs. I shook away the image. I had work to do and a position to regain. By God, no blasted aristocrat was going to take my staff, however statuesque her body and welcoming her smile.

As I wished to finish this foolish competition quickly, I

selected the vingt-et-un table, which required the minimum of skill and each hand passed within minutes.

"Here," I said, signalling to one of the Donalds to drag over a chair. He obeyed at once, then brought another for her Ladyship.

"An excellent choice." Lady Clarinda joined me a few moments later, sliding on to her chair with the grace expected of an aristocrat. "We will gamble as normal, Doctor, while only you and I are aware of the real stakes."

"Play, damn you," I growled, noticing that the hard-faced servant stood in a corner, talking to the Donalds in their barbaric Gaelic. They were discussing me, damn them, as the servant told them his mistress would beat me today.

"Have patience, my little man," Lady Clarinda said, smiling. "Cards are here to be enjoyed. Experience the thrill of tension, the triumph of victory, the sinking dismay of defeat and the knowledge that you might return tonight with all well in your world." She sipped at a glass of brandy that miraculously appeared at her elbow. "After all, all you have to lose is money and a little carved stick."

I put all my anger into my glare, leaned my staff against my leg and called for the deal. I will not describe the fall of every card, for that is utterly tedious unless one is actively involved in the game, but I will say that for the opening period my usual run of luck held. I could feel the staff throbbing against my leg as I won the first three hands and the little pile of gold in front of me grew into a large pile of gold.

"You are doing well," Clarinda said, with her eyes glistening and the brandy evident in her husky voice. "Perhaps you will leave this table with a heavy purse and a stick in your hand."

"There is no perhaps about it," I said. The run of victories had restored my confidence, so I began to relax, lounging in my chair as I watched the cards flick on to the green baize. Lady Clarinda was not so arrogant now, drinking deeply at her glass and signalling for more brandy.

I glanced at my hand – king of spades and 10 of clubs. "I want to end this early," I said. "I have something to discuss with my wife. Let's raise the stakes."

The other players were a nondescript lot, mere chessboard pawns who would follow the lead of the king and queen.

"Not yet," Lady Clarinda said.

I felt a surge of power from my staff and decided to prolong her torture. "As you wish," I agreed magnanimously and took 10 guineas from her in that hand.

I won the next hand as well, with two of the flats at the table throwing down their cards in disgust and one on the verge of tears. "I must win," the tearful one said. "I have creditors to pay."

Laughing at his whining, I rooked him of all he had, suggested he gamble with the clothes on his back and watched as the Donalds bundled him into the street.

"You have not lost your touch," Lady Clarinda said.

"I have not," I agreed, signalling for a glass of claret.

I won the next hand and had the pleasure of seeing Lady Clarinda empty her purse of gold on to the table. I added her sovereigns to mine and began the pleasurable process of stripping her of everything she owned. I won her jewellery, piece by piece, and wondered how an exquisite diamond brooch would look pinned to Evelyn's dress in place of that bloody silver cross.

"I have nothing left," Lady Clarinda said at last, with brandy slurring her voice. "You have taken it all, Doctor."

"Nonsense," I said. "You have a coach outside and an impudent servant." I no longer needed to force my smile. "And clothes on your back."

I saw her face pale. "I will put my coach on the table," she agreed, "but my servant is not available."

"Ah," I said, "you wish to keep your lover, then." I knew by her expression that I had hit the mark. "Bring something of your coach to the table."

I did not like the light that appeared in Clarinda's eyes as I said that. Beckoning to her servant, she did as I ordered, and deposited a single lamp from the coach. I grinned, enjoying her humiliation.

"Let's play," I said softly. "I always wanted a coach."

My luck took a turn for the worse with that hand, and I had to return the diamond brooch that I had pictured on Evelyn's breast. The next game was equally unsuccessful, and then I began to sweat as the pile in front of me gradually diminished until I was staring at a handful of golden sovereigns scattered across the cruel green of the baize. The clock in the corner seemed unusually loud as it ticked away the minutes.

Lady Clarinda raised her eyebrows as she smiled across to me. "You have a staff," she said, "and the clothes on your back." I heard the cruelty in her laughter and knew she had been teasing me all night.

"You witch," I said.

"Something like that," Lady Clarinda said. "You are the architect of your own downfall, Doctor. Your greed brought you here, for if you had cried hold when you were ahead, I would have left the table. But you must drive in your victory, and now you will pay the price."

Although the room was crowded, and a dozen people were around our table, I knew that we were alone. The audience seemed frozen somehow as if they existed in a different plane of existence and only Lady Clarinda and I mattered; only we could hear our conversation and understand the implications of our actions.

"Who are you?" I asked.

"I am your sister, or have been," Clarinda said.

"I don't understand."

"Then let me explain," Clarinda said, and suddenly she looked older, far, far older, yet so familiar that I knew we had once been close. "Your staff and my coach are from the same place."

"Which place?" I heard the tremor in my voice, for I already knew the answer.

"The other place, Doctor." Lady Clarinda's face was back to itself again. "As soon as I brought in the devil's lamp, it neutralised the power of your staff, and normal luck and skill took its place." She smiled. "And I have as much luck as you do, while I am a far better player. Shall we deal again?"

"Why?" I asked. "Why are you doing this to me?" I felt the waves of despair crash into my heart.

"You are too weak," Clarinda said. "You should be stronger, rather than having moments of softness. Why," she threw back her head and laughed, "you threw away the gift."

"The gift?"

"The staff from which you drew all the power," Clarinda said. "You threw it away more than once. You were the Guardian of the Staff but proved unworthy of our trust."

"Our?"

Lady Clarinda's face altered again until Mother Marwick scowled at me from under the horseshoe of her brow, then she became that haggard old lady once more, and finally herself.

I stared at Lady Clarinda as the people around us returned to consciousness, and the conversation resumed with its old noise and confusion.

"Play," Clarinda said.

The cards flipped on to the table, one by one, as if in slow motion. Although each landed face down, I could read the numbers without effort, as though the pasteboard were transparent. I lifted my hand, knowing I had lost, knowing that whatever power was in my staff, Clarinda's lamp trumped it.

I lost that hand and, with it, my few remaining sovereigns. I stared at the naked green baize with a feeling more of numbness than despair, for where is the destination when the devil drives the coach?

The room was hushed, with the audience watching, wordless, as the Lucky Doctor, the perennial winner, was down to a bare table and Lady Clarinda gloated in triumph.

"All right, Doctor," Clarinda said, with her eyes like brimstone and sulphur in her voice. "We'll have one last hand."

I nodded, aware of what was coming next.

"We'll play for your staff, your house and your dignity."

"My dignity?"

Clarinda laughed. "The clothes on your back," she said. "Put your staff on the table." She pushed forward all of her winnings. "There; an unfair gamble, I think, a pot of some thousands of guineas, plus my jewellery against your black staff and clothes."

I looked around for support but found none in that circle of pitiless faces. The Honourable Peter was there, gloating at my discomfort, and a dozen men I had caroused with, plus women I had known in every sense of the word. They were laughing at me, joying in my downfall, wishing to see me discomfited and humiliated.

"I won't do it," I said, rising from the table.

"Oh, you will," Clarinda said. "I wonder what Doctor MacNeil would say?"

I closed my eyes, knowing I was playing a losing hand. "Deal," I said.

The cards flicked across the table, each one a menace. Fully aware of the expectant audience, I placed my staff on the table.

It lay there, dark against the green, the carvings mocking my turmoil. In my mind, I saw the naked man turn to me, and he had Outerston's face, the eyes glinting with malice. Then he lifted a hand and pointed, while Charles mouthed the word, "Why?" again and again as he writhed under my assault. Ruth Anderson lay coiled around the base, my victim, for I had employed her in that damned house while joining all three together was a golden circuit of guineas. And all the time the clock ticked in the corner and the fire sparked in readiness.

"Your play, Doctor."

Only the crackle of the flames disturbed the silence and the harsh breathing of the audience. Once more, I could feel the flames licking around me, taste the acrid smoke in my throat; I gasped, choking as the audience gave a silent cheer. Lady Clarinda smiled from under raised eyebrows, with her face altering minute by minute. I saw in her the maids I had removed from my service, each one expelled on to the streets without a thought for the misery they faced in an unfriendly world. I saw in her face the women I had used, abused and discarded, and then I saw the old, wrinkled woman I had seen before. My sister Grizel winked as she removed her clothes in the shadow of the hangman's noose.

A twist of betraying decency convulsed me as I thought of Evelyn, and then I touched my staff and shrugged. Evelyn would be all right, and my staff had never let me down before. It was merely teasing me.

"All right then," I put my faith in the power of that staff. "My house and my clothes it shall be." I glanced at my cards. The queen of hearts and the ace of clubs. Twenty-one.

The audience cheered now, laughing, enjoying the tension of a man daring his all.

"As you have nothing else to gamble," Lady Clarinda said. "Show your cards."

The cheering stopped. I could taste the tension as I turned over my cards, one by one and sat back, wishing I could hold my staff.

"Twenty-one!" The audience roared. Only the Honourable Peter looked disappointed. The others turned their fickle glee on to Lady Clarinda, now hoping to see her destroyed. They did not care who was hurt, as long as they could enjoy the suffering of another.

"Oh." Lady Clarinda's expression altered. For one moment, I read dismay there, as if she knew she had lost the game, and I experienced a feeling of exultation. However, my Ladyship was a consummate actress, a princess of the power of deception, for when she turned over the cards, the King and Ace of Spades sat on the table.

The audience let out a roar as I stared in horror at the cards.

Lady Clarinda lifted the staff, taunting me with her smile. "Your clothes, Doctor. Put them on the table."

"You must leave me some dignity," I gasped, hardly able to enunciate as the full horror of my position hit.

"Your clothes, Doctor," Lady Clarinda repeated. "Put them on the table, or I will have the porters remove them forcibly."

There is little more humiliating than undressing in front of an audience of taunting, mocking people, especially when some were once one's friends. Their eyes watched me, joying in my humiliation, with Lady Clarinda especially enjoying herself.

"All of them," Clarinda said. "Every last stitch."

I did so, face down as the audience watched. Trying to pretend I was alone, I looked at the dark staff on the table, and as I watched, it altered. The carvings were distinct at first, showing the evil I had done in my life, from Ruth Anderson's death to the death of Outerston to the murder of Charles and the humiliation of Swinton, all joined by a string of golden guineas. The staff was a record of my progress from a well-meaning young doctor to the creature I had become. These figures faced away as the staff left my ownership. For one second, I saw it as a smooth rod of dark wood, waiting for the evil of its next owner, or its next guardian. Understanding crushed me, for that staff was merely a representation of the deeds of the bearer's life. He or she was its guardian, no more.

As I removed my clothes, one article at a time, to expose myself to the world as what I was, without covering or pretence, Clarinda grasped the staff. I saw the geometric designs reappear, one after the other, the shapes that would form into the evil she did when in possession of that singular length of wood. Only when I removed the last scrap of my clothes did I see the dark wood alter and a new image appeared, a naked man most remarkably like me, coiling around the base of the staff.

Only then did I fully understand. I had not been strong enough to withstand the evil of the staff, not sufficiently evil to embrace it fully. In common with all humanity, I was a mixture, and the staff had encouraged my evil while suppressing the good.

As I stood in a state of nature, Clarinda turned to the audience. "Get back to the tables," she ordered them, eyeing me up and down as if I were an animal on display at the market or a piece of meat on the flesher's slab. "There is nothing much to see here."

The laugher hurt even more than the physical pain as the two Donalds grabbed me by the arms. The audience jeered as the Donalds rushed me to the door and threw me out of the building, landing hefty kicks on my backside by way of farewell. I rolled on the ground, scraping the skin off my left hip and shoulder, and lay still, with the rain bouncing from my naked person. My head was in a puddle of cold water, with the street lights of the New Town reflecting on the wet ground, a combination of light and dark. I knew again that my position only highlighted the dual nature of humanity and the duplicity of this city of Janus. I saw clearly the two faces of Edinburgh, the New Town with its mask of respectability that hid cold-blooded cruelty as people scrabbled for position, and the terrible poverty of the Old that pressed people into crime. Yet I had met more genuine kindness with the poor than with the respectable. I remembered the small acts of help I had received, given without hope of reward, as compared to the outwardly magnanimous gestures of approval once I had established myself and could return one favour with another.

I pushed myself upright and saw Lady Clarinda's dark coach with the bundled-up figure of the coachman sitting on his perch and the six-horse team in the traces. Each horse was black as coal, each with a dark plume above its head as they pawed the ground, waiting for the command to move.

"Cheer up, my man." Lady Clarinda appeared behind me. "You are the creator of your own fortune, remember?" She smiled at me and began to sing.

"Wha wadna be in love
Wi' bonnie Maggie Lauder?
A piper met her guan to Fife,
And speir'd what was't they ca'd her;
Right scornfully she answer'd him,
Begone you hallanshaker,
Jog on your gate,
ye bladderscate,
My name is Maggie Lauder."

Her laugh was honey-sweet yet bitter as gall, a duality that had haunted me ever since I entered this accursed dark city. I saw other women there, with Mother Marwick at her side, shaking her old head. The two stood side by side, the attractive and the repulsive, the young and the old, pressing closer until they became one person, with the repulsive beauty of pure evil and an ancient face I had seen before. Grizel Weir shook her head and blew me a kiss. Sobbing, I stumbled away, broken in body, purse and soul.

I cannot say how I returned home that night. I have only a hazy recollection of staggering, with the hot tears burning my eyes, the tune of *Maggie Lauder* in my head and the ground hard under my feet. I must have hugged the shadows to avoid the few people who frequent the New Town after dark, and when I came to the George Street house the door gaped open and the rooms were deserted of all human life.

I had hoped for words of comfort from Evelyn, perhaps some shred of hope. Instead, there was nobody. I was alone in a house I no longer owned, with only bitterness and the ghosts of memories to accompany me.

"Evelyn?" I shouted, and the echoes mocked me. "Evelyn?" I yelled again and moved from room to room, increasingly alarmed as I found each as empty as the last.

There was no doubt. I was alone in the house; the servants had gone, and Evelyn was not there. Her note was short and bitter.

"*My dear Martin,*" it read,

> *"I do not wish to leave you, but fear I have no choice. I hope you can discard that terrible staff and return to your usual self. For some time, I had been working with Dr MacNeil and Alexander Tait to try to alleviate your condition. Dr MacNeil, as you know, is engaged to my sister in Abercrombie Street. However, as Dr MacNeil has vanished, your condition has worsened and will continue to worsen until you lose that staff.*

When you do that, please come back to me at the Queen Street address.

Your loving and concerned Wife,

Evelyn"

I stared at that letter, trying to work out the details. Charles was not betraying me with Evelyn. That staff, that terrible, devious staff, had taken me astray, it had lost me my wife, my friend and my home.

It was then that I heard the clocks begin to tick.

What did they signify? I had only one answer. My time was ending. Life had allowed me the opportunity to do good with my medical practice or to embrace evil, with the staff, and I had failed at both. The staff had not made me an abomination. Rather, it had amplified a side of me that already existed.

The ticking seemed louder now, echoing around that empty house that I could no longer call my own. I staggered to the surgery and slumped on my familiar chair, with the fire lighting itself in the grate and Charles's skeleton grinning at me.

I saw the dark ash blow in under the door, strangely distinct against the night's darkness, with a glow that must have emanated from the fire. As I sat, unable to move, the ash formed into the figure of a man, tall, with a gaunt face and a prominent nose. I felt the fear overcome me and opened my eyes to scream, but no sound came as Major Weir, the Wizard itself, strode toward me. The brown eyes stared into mine as the thing came closer, then it entered my body and consumed what remained of my soul.

I have nearly completed this account, this confession if you will, and the ticking of the clocks surround me, penetrating my mind. Each tick stabs into me as if to deepen the message that each mortal soul has only a limited time on this earth, and we have freedom of choice how we spend it. We each have decisions to make.

Tick, tock, tick-tock.

Life grants each of us paths to follow and people with whom we can associate. We can choose to be selfish and grab for ourselves what could be shared. We can choose to help or to hinder.

Tick, tock, tick-tock, tick.

We can spend our days and nights in good deeds or vicious pleasures. Even the least favoured of us can help others. Oh, dear God, I can smell the smoke now. I can see the grey-white smoke easing through the crack under the door as it slides into my surgery.

Tick tock, tick, tock.

The images I experienced with the fire were not of the past. I had fancied them to be the staff showing me how it had writhed in the flames that consumed Major Thomas Weir. I was wrong. I was so wrong. The staff was warning me of my destiny unless I altered my path.

Tick, tock, tick.

The smoke fills my surgery now, biting acrid in my throat, stinging my eyes, filling my nostrils. Through the smoke, I see the skeleton of Charles, with that hideous skull on top and his features gradually reforming as though he was approaching me, alive again, or I was approaching him in death. I can see that well-remembered face. "Oh, Charles, can you forgive me for my ill-founded suspicions and for murdering you?"

Tick, tock.

The body was intact, Charles as ever was, laughing as he swam to Cramond Island, his freckles merging as he smiled. My friend, my trusted old friend, waiting for me on the other side of the fiery divide. Should there not be a river here? The

Styx? With a dark boatman? Or was that only for the classical heroes of old?

Tick.

One last tick. I do not want to die. I am not yet ready to cross that dark river, although the waters could help quench this fire that raged around me. It is hot. "Mama, it is hot today; can somebody open a window? Please open a window to allow in the cooling breeze. I cannot stand this heat."

The flames are rising now, closing on me, curling around me as I sit here at my desk. The pain is acute. I will put my quill down shortly, nice and tidy on my desk so I can go to my maker. I see Charles there, and somebody else. Who is that at Charles's side? Who is that dark figure?

The feathers of my quill are smouldering. I can write no more. I can hear the rumble of a coach and the clatter of hooves. Oh, forgive me, whoever reads this. It could have been you. Forgive me.

Martin Weir Elliot.

EPILOGUE

CALEDONIAN MERCURY, 15th *April 1826*

It is our unpleasant duty to relate that Doctor Martin Elliot died in the late house fire in George Street. Dr Elliot has been unwell for some time, suffering from a disease of the brain that occasioned hallucinations. A large crowd gathered to witness the conflagration, with many cheering, doubtless unaware that Dr Elliot was within the building. Some of the spectators claimed to hear a man singing Maggie Lauder, an old tune that many of the crowd also sang. When the fire was eventually extinguished, it was discovered that every surviving clock in the house had stopped at six minutes past six, which was the exact time of the doctor's death. Another intriguing factor was the strange survival of a manuscript on which the unfortunate doctor had been working. A wooden cross also survived the fire, by some miracle.

Dr Elliot is survived by his wife, Mrs Evelyn Elliot or Swinton, the daughter of Mr Swinton, the well-known solicitor of Queen Street.

Caledonian Mercury 18th March 1827

Marriages. Mrs Evelyn Elliot or Swinton, the relict of the late Dr Martin Elliot, to Mr Alexander Tait. It may be remembered that Dr Elliot was killed in an unfortunate house fire last year. Mr Tait was once a distinguished architect but of late has become an acknowledged expert in the history of old Edinburgh. Mr Tait was a friend of Mrs Elliot's late husband.

HISTORICAL NOTE

Major Thomas Weir was a real person. A dedicated Presbyterian, he was said to be a Lanarkshire man and a soldier during the religious and civil wars of the 1640s. He was sent with the Scottish Army to Ireland in 1641 to help suppress the rising there, so would doubtless have seen his share in the horrors of that campaign.

When he was major of the Edinburgh City Guard, Weir wore a dark cloak and strode along the streets looking down to the ground, while his big nose made him look even more formidable. Weir was one of the guards when the Royalist Marquis of Montrose was carried to his execution and tormented the prisoner as much as he was able. He was famed for his piety and power of prayer, never married and lived with his sister, first in a house in the Cowgate and later in a small courtyard off the West Bow. However, people also commented that Weir was never seen without his black staff. In time, stories became current that the staff could run errands to shops, answer the door and moved before him as he strode up the West Bow and down the Lawnmarket.

However, Weir lived a double life. While, outwardly, he was the epitome of Christianity, when he was older he became sick and confessed to an entire catalogue of crimes, sins and horrors. He confessed to incest with his sister, and crimes that included bestiality and witchcraft. On 14 April 1670, he was strangled and burned on the Gallow Lee, between Edinburgh and Leith. His last words were said to be "I have lived as a beast and must die as a beast." He burned for a long time, as did his staff, which was thrown into the fire after him. It was said to twist and turn in the flames.

Weir's sister was hanged for witchcraft in the Grassmarket, after confessing to travelling with the devil in a fiery coach. Her mother was also said to be a witch, and Grizel claimed that the devil had given her brother his blackthorn staff with its strange carvings topped by the likeness of a human skull. Before she died, Grizel Weir, otherwise known as Jean, tried to throw off all her clothes.

Weir's house in the West Bow soon gained a reputation for being haunted, with music-making and laughter. Sometimes the Major himself would call in his flaming dark carriage drawn by six horses, and occasionally the staff would appear, searching for its owner.

The house no longer stands, having been demolished along with much of the West Bow when Victoria Street was built.

The hill where Weir was burned no longer exists as it was used to make mortar for the houses of Edinburgh's New Town, but the spot where Grizel was hanged can still be seen, opposite the public house called, with typical Edinburgh black humour, The Last Drop.

Dr Knox was also a real person. He was the anatomist to whom Burke and Hare, Edinburgh's most notorious mass murderers, sold the bodies of their victims.

Helen Susan Swift.
Scotland, 2020.

Dear reader,

We hope you enjoyed reading *Dark Capital* Please take a moment to leave a review, even if it's a short one. Your opinion is important to us.

Discover more books by Helen Susan Swift at

https://www.nextchapter.pub/authors/helen-susan-swift

Want to know when one of our books is free or discounted? Join the newsletter at

http://eepurl.com/bqqB3H

Best regards,

Helen Susan Swift and the Next Chapter Team

Dark Capital
ISBN: 978-4-86745-904-1

Published by
Next Chapter
1-60-20 Minami-Otsuka
170-0005 Toshima-Ku, Tokyo
+818035793528

18th April 2021

CPSIA information can be obtained
at www.ICGtesting.com
Printed in the USA
BVHW071837030521
606337BV00006B/978